THE RINGLEADER
LEGEND OF FURY

Thanks, David.
Enjoy more of the
adventure!
Bonnie Lanthorpe

ISBN: 978-1-68313-060-4

First Edition

Printed and bound in the USA

Cover art by Davis Lanthripe
Interior design by Kelsey Rice

THE RINGLEADER
LEGEND OF FURY

BY BONNIE LANTHRIPE

P

Pen-L Publishing
Fayetteville, Arkansas
Pen-L.com

OTHER BOOKS BY BONNIE LANTHRIPE:

The Ringleader

To my sons, Jim and Davis

CHAPTER ONE

Summer got off to a slow start, but I had no idea how fast it would fly by, some of the crazy things that would happen, the mystery I would become obsessed with, and how my mom's special plans would end up fitting right into all of it. Mowing jobs, hanging out with the guys, and a couple of weeks at camp would take up some of my time, but there wasn't much else to get excited over.

To top it off, there were no plans for a family summer vacation because, according to my mom, "something special" was in the works for later on, like . . . *maybe*. That could mean fall break, Thanksgiving, maybe even Christmas for all I knew. All I had to say was it better be *big* to make up for not going *anywhere* all summer long.

One bright spot in my life was studying for my driver's permit. I sat at my desk and, for maybe the hundredth time, looked at the application I'd picked up at the Texas Department of Public Safety. There were lots of boxes to check and blanks to fill out. No problem: I had this.

Patrick Michael Morrison I wrote in the first blank. In the next, age: 15. I left off my height and weight; I figured I would be taller than five feet nine and weigh more than a hundred and thirty pounds when it was time for the real thing. But the black hair and blue eyes would stay the same so I filled in those spaces.

It would be months before I could actually take the test, but I wanted to be ready.

It didn't take long after school was out for major boredom to set in. But no way was I going to mention that around my folks. They hear you say something like you're bored and they'll find something for you to do in a hurry. Which, in my case, would probably involve the garage. Honestly, sometimes I think people have garages built as part of their house just so their kids can clean it. I was sure ours had been.

My friends and I kept trying to plan something, but Brendan was either practicing soccer or playing it. The sports-jock of our bunch, he was always involved with something that either rolled or bounced or both. Then Jeremy went off to spend some time at his uncle's ranch and didn't know when he'd be back. I mean, what was up with that? And Max and his family took off on vacation for two weeks. Oh well, at least *somebody* got to go on vacation.

My best friend, James, didn't have any plans in the works either and we decided we couldn't just sit around and wait until *maybe* everyone would be in town at the same time to do *something*. So we came up with an idea.

Parts of a really rocking video we'd made were filmed in the open field on the other side of Mr. Nelson's pasture. But, we'd never actually gone *into* the woods out there. Mr. Nelson had finally convinced my dad to lift the restriction he'd put on our going across the pasture as a short cut after we'd tried to tip one of Mr. Nelson's cows. So one morning before a mowing job, James and I cut across the pasture headed toward the woods. We were on the other side and far into the open field in half the time it would have taken if we'd had to go around. When we got close to the tree line, we took a break and sat on a log and I dug bottles of water and a couple packages of mini-Oreos out of my backpack.

After a few cookies, I put them away and stowed the water and we scanned the area for what we thought would be the best way to enter the woods.

"That looks like a pretty good place over there," James said, pointing to where the trees weren't as dense as the rest, and we chose that way to go. Only a few yards into the thick growth, we realized things were not what we had expected. The ground changed and the underbrush and trees got thicker. Something just felt *different*. We'd have to investigate things, which was right up our alley. But exploring didn't feel the same without the other guys. We decided we'd wait until we could all search the woods together, and turned back.

We left and made our way back through the trees into the clearing and headed home. While we were climbing through the fence to cut across Mr. Nelson's pasture, I looked back at the woods and saw something I hadn't noticed before. "Hey, James, wait up."

"Yeah?" James scanned the field, trying to see what I pointed out. "What are we looking at?"

"James, I think the woods . . . I guess I always thought it looked the way it does because the trees are all different sizes. But I'm not so sure. I think the trees are pretty much the same, it's like they're growing on a kind of a hill or something. Maybe that's why it felt different."

He scrunched his eyebrows and really checked out the trees in the distance. In a minute, his face relaxed. "You could be right, Patrick. We will definitely have to check it out. But another time, though. Don't you have a mowing job?"

He was right. I barely had time to get back, get the mower out and down the street to Mrs. Gorley's house. "You're right. Another time." I bumped the fist he held out for me and we picked up the pace for home.

On the walk back, we talked about making another video and James told me about a special effect he'd come up with that we might use. Filming was a hobby of his.

"So, tomorrow? Your garage?" he asked when we got to my house. James lives down the street from our house so it's real handy for him to come over. And our garage was clean. I should know, I clean it a lot.

Next morning, I mowed the Woodson's yard two houses down. James came after lunch, and I told Grammy we would be in the garage working on a project.

My dad's mom lives with us. Just before my brother, Brett, left for the Air Force, Grammy moved in with us so she wouldn't be all alone. She's really sweet, and makes great treats. My favorite is those marshmallow and crispy rice things.

"Well, you boys be careful," she told us and started down the hall to her room. I figured it must be close to time for her favorite TV game show.

"Hey, Grammy, can you help me with something?" I asked before she made it to the hallway.

"Why, of course, Patrick."

"Well, you see, this project James and I are working on, we need some thread. I think. Do you know where Mom's sewing box is?"

"Oh, I think it's right in here." She stood next to the coat closet and opened the door. She took a minute looking inside then reached up on a shelf and brought out what looked like a big woven basket. She carried it to the hall table and opened it up. Inside was a tray with lots of spools of different sizes and all kinds of colors of thread.

"Now what kind of thread do you boys need?"

Did it really matter? How confusing.

"No bright colors, Patrick," James whispered at my shoulder.

"Uh, maybe black?" I told Grammy.

She touched several of the spools until she found a black one. "Will this do?"

James poked me in the back and told her, "That looks like just what we need, Mrs. Morrison."

Grammy handed the spool to me.

"Thanks, Grammy." James and I headed back to the garage.

"You boys have fun," she said and turned quickly down the hall to her room. She must have been missing some of her TV show.

We went into the garage and I pulled a box from one of the shelves and carried it to my dad's workbench. I took a dart board and seven steel-tipped darts out of the box, then we mounted the board on one wall of the garage. After tying the thread around the shaft of one of the darts, close to the feathers, we stuck the dart into the board. We rolled out the spool and strung the thread out several feet. We worked without saying anything while we did the same with the rest of the darts until all seven stuck out of the board in a cluster, with the strings trailing across the floor of the garage.

"Okay," James said, looking at our handiwork, "now let's tie all the ends of the strings together." We bunched the ends together, made sure the threads were all the same length, and looped them into a knot.

"Ready?" James asked with a huge grin.

"Whenever you are."

He handed the threads to me and got his camera ready. James gave me a thumbs-up and aimed at the board. "Pull!"

I yanked the threads and we watched as the darts flew out of the board and clattered to the floor. Not exactly the way we'd planned. About half the darts came out a few seconds before the rest did. We wanted them to all come out of the board at the same time and not fall so quick.

We replaced the darts again and gave it another try. One of the threads broke so we had to untangle it from the rest and tie another length to the dart.

It wasn't as easy as we'd thought it would be, but, after a few more tries, I finally figured out that when I pulled, the motion had to be quick, in one smooth movement.

After several takes, everything went perfectly. All the darts flew from the dart board. And it was the exact effect James had been looking for. When we ran the video in reverse, it looked like the darts had all been thrown at the same time, hitting the target together. It all went so fast you couldn't even see the threads. Pretty cool. The guys were going to like this. Now we just had to think of some way to use it.

CHAPTER TWO

I stayed busy the next few days mowing lawns. Seemed like everyone on my street suddenly wanted to hire me. Okay by me—it just meant I'd have more money saved up to buy a car someday.

Jeremy's family decided to come back from his uncle's ranch sooner than they'd originally planned and I was surprised when I got a text message from him a few days after James and I had been over in the woods.

Jeremy: Got idea for new project. Interested?"

Me: Me too. Get together?"

Jeremy usually has family stuff to do after dinner, so it surprised me when he said he'd be at my house after he'd eaten. I called James to let him know what was going on and he made it over by the time Jeremy rode up on his bike.

We went into my room and sat on the floor before I asked, "So? What's the project?"

"You first," Jeremy said.

I could tell he was only being polite, that he was excited and really wanted to tell us about whatever was going on. After a couple more rounds of 'you first—no, you first', I insisted he tell us before we told him about what we'd discovered in the woods. It didn't take much insisting.

"Rockets." Just one word. He looked at us, eyebrows raised, head bobbing up and down, like we were supposed to know what he was talking about.

James and I looked at each other then turned back to look at Jeremy. "Rockets?"

"Yeah!" Jeremy's eyes were popping, a big grin on his face revealed a lot of metal. *Hmm,* I wondered, *when's he going to get his braces off?* Anyway, I was supposed to be paying attention to what he was saying because he was off like . . . heh, heh . . . like a rocket.

"Yeah, rockets. A little while after we got to my uncle's, he took me to a shed near his barn and . . . Guys! I'm telling you." Jeremy waved his arms around like crazy. "He had all these *rockets*!"

"Like space stuff kind of rockets?" Whoa, now that would mean one very large shed.

"No, dummy!" Jeremy looked at me liked I grown another head. "Model rockets. Like the kind you make from a kit and stuff." He actually snorted, like I really was some kind of doofus. "Uncle Denver used to really be into rockets. I mean, he had a *serious* hobby. When he lost interest—well, actually, I think Aunt Barbara decided he lost interest—anyway, he just locked the stuff up in the shed and it's been there ever since."

Old Jeremy was so excited he couldn't sit still. His face lit up like a . . . well, a rocket. I just couldn't help it. Heh-heh, I chuckled to myself.

"I'm telling you guys," Jeremy said, pacing excitedly around the room. "It was a blast!" He suddenly stopped and bent over laughing, slapping his leg—just like something Max would have done. "Hahaha? Get it? Rockets? A blast?"

Yep, just like Max.

And yes, we got it. I wasn't the only one unable to resist the rocket jokes. But I had some questions anyway. "You mean like shooting off some bottle rockets or Roman candles, fireworks kind of stuff?"

"Isn't that illegal?" James asked. He was right, there *were* restrictions about any kind of fireworks within city limits.

"Not *that* kind of rocket, James." Jeremy said. "C'mon, guys, be serious."

Yeah, James. Don't rain on our parade so soon. "Hey, buddy, this sounds like something all of us can do together. If all of us ever get back together, that is."

James and Jeremy nodded in agreement. I could tell that James had gotten over the legal thing real quick, and was thinking about the possibilities of this rocket project. And I was pretty sure the guys would like Jeremy's idea over what James and I had to share. I mean, really, what's not fun about blowing something up?

Okay, so one of the things I learned later was that you don't *want* the rocket to blow up.

And I learned I had a lot to learn about rockets.

We talked it over and decided to wait until Max and Brendan could be in on this new project. Then Jeremy said, "Okay, Patrick, if we're going to wait on the others to launch rockets, we'll need something to do until they get back. You said you had an idea for a new project. Out with it."

"Oh, well, it's not all that exciting really." When I started explaining about going into the woods, it actually didn't sound so great compared to the rocket idea.

But Jeremy actually thought it was a good idea. "Hey, what's not to like about it? It's a chance to scout out new territory."

True. My friends and I were always up for adventure, exploring was at the top of our list of things to do. So we decided we wouldn't decide about anything until everyone could make the decision. In other words, we were going to wait until the other guys got back before we did either project.

By the middle of the week Max and his family were back in town and Brendan didn't have any practice or game on Saturday. After lunch, we met at my house, as usual. It was just the place we always seemed to end up. We still avoided going to Jeremy's house. Like I've said before, his mom is a nice lady and all, but she could take up a whole morning either asking a lot of questions or trying to feed you. We didn't go to Max's either . . . *Why is that?* I wondered, as if it had never crossed my mind. I don't think I ever knew. We just never did. Besides, my house was closest to Mr. Nelson's pasture and we could walk over to the field.

We waited to talk until we went into the cul-de-sac and sat on the curb. I said, "Okay, so we've got a couple of choices for a project."

I looked at Jeremy. He nodded. I went first.

"So, while the rest of you guys were gone, James and I thought we'd check out the woods—"

"Hey!" Max jumped up. "What're you guys doing checking things out without the rest of us?"

I swear, that guy's snout can go to pout in a nano-second.

"Sit down, Max," Jeremy said, tugging on Max's pant leg.

"But we're all supposed to explore together!"

"You weren't even in town, Max."

Max jerked his pant leg out of Jeremy's grasp and turned on him, accusingly. "Did you go too!"

"No, Max. I didn't. Patrick said we were _all_ gone. Remember?"

"Oh, yeah . . . right. Uh, okay then." Max plopped back down and tugged at some grass.

"Go on, Patrick," Jeremy said, and looked at Max as if to say 'just listen.'

I gave them a rundown on our going into the woods. "But we stopped before we went very far because we discovered something we thought we'd all want to explore together."

"As long as it doesn't involve any drainage culverts or ponds or elephants or crazy people or mad cows, I guess I'm ready," Max grumbled, still sulking.

"None of those things, I promise." So what if all that stuff had happened before with one of our adventures? I felt pretty safe in promising it wouldn't happen again. I mean, what were the odds? Right?

They looked around nodding, urging me to go on.

"First, Jeremy has an idea you might like better."

Heads swiveled toward Jeremy. The minute the word 'rocket' came out of his mouth, he had their undivided attention.

"But you were at your uncle's ranch, with lots of room for shooting off rockets," Max said. "The only thing close to a ranch around here is Mr. Nelson's pasture. We just got out of trouble with him so I don't think he's going to like the idea of us blowing things up around his cows." He looked like a pout might be on its way. "Where are we going to find a place like a ranch?"

Does Max ever see the positive side of anything first? I had no idea where we were going to go, but I was sure we could find a place. This was just too good to pass up.

Jeremy must have been thinking about this and had it figured out. "Actually, over by the woods where we filmed part of the video should give us plenty of space."

"But we'll have to get a rocket first," Max said, looking around at us. "How are we going to go get a rocket? Do we even have a way to go get a rocket? We don't have enough time, do we?

Nope, never the positive first. And now he was pouting.

"Where do you even get a rocket anyway?" Max continued, like a dog gnawing a bone. "How much does a rocket cost anyway?"

We were all groaning about that time.

"Well, Uncle Denver just happened to give me a few to bring home with me." Jeremy grinned and patted his backpack. He knew how to get Max back on track. "Not a problem. He gave me everything we need to set one off."

"You've got a rocket in there!" Brendan spoke up for the first time, pointing at Jeremy's pack.

James and I were in on the rocket being in the backpack. We'd figured the guys would go for rockets over exploring the woods and agreed Jeremy should come prepared.

"Yep," he said. "And ready to launch."

Brendan was on his feet in a second. "What are we waiting for?"

"But . . . but," Max sputtered. He had to run to catch up to us, we were so far ahead of him.

Jeremy talked all the way across Mr. Nelson's pasture and over to the big open field filling us in on what his uncle had told him about flying rockets. I couldn't decide whether it sounded complicated or not, but either way, I was pumped. We stopped when he found a spot he thought would make a good launch site.

We sat on the ground and watched him take what he explained was a launch pad, a reel of fuse, an igniter and a twelve-inch rocket from the backpack. This was definitely not going to be like sticking a Roman candle in the ground and lighting it then watch it go up and explode. When he got it all set, we got up and followed him several feet away from the rocket.

We sort of hunkered down on the ground around Jeremy as he held the ignition device. He looked around at each of us. Real dramatic like. "Ready?"

We nodded and he flipped a switch. We began a count-down just like we could have been at a regular space launch or something.

"Ten, nine, eight, seven, six, five, four, three, two, one, BLASTOFF!"

Whoosh! The rocket rose into the sky almost quicker than my eyes could track it. It went so fast! Rising upward with a thin trail of smoke following behind. I shielded my eyes with my hand and watched as the vapor suddenly stopped coming from the end and the rocket seemed to hang in the air. Then it began to sink. As it picked up speed we jumped up and raced toward where it looked like it was going to come down—right by the fence next to Mr. Nelson's pasture.

"Did you see that!" I screamed, everyone yelling excitedly back and forth as we ran.

Brendan, the jock and fastest runner of us all, beat us to the spot where the rocket lay in some tall grass and weeds. But he stood back, watching it, and waited for Jeremy to get there. After all, Jeremy was the rocket man.

"Is it safe?" Max asked when Jeremy reached down to pick up the rocket.

"Sure." Jeremy took it up then passed it around so each of us could check it out. It was a little warm at the bottom, and sooty.

I turned it over in my hands, careful how I handled it. "What do we do with it now?"

"Use it again." Jeremy took it from me and brushed some grass from it.

"Serious?"

"Sure. It'll take a new engine—you always have to have a new engine—and some other stuff, but yeah, the fuselage," he said, patting the long tube part of the rocket, "this baby can be used again. As long as it isn't damaged." He checked out both ends of the *fuselage* and looked up at us with a smile. "Everything looks good."

We passed the fuselage around again, talking about how quickly the rocket went up, and came down. I was thinking how quick the whole thing was over.

"I don't suppose you have another one or a way to rig this up again?" Brendan held the cylinder up, a smirky grin on his face.

"Naw. Sorry." Brendan's face fell a little when Jeremy took it from him and turned it over in his hands. "This is all that I put in the pack today. I wasn't sure you guys would go for it."

"Are you crazy?" James said. "That was awesome! Of course, we'd want to fire, uh . . . *launch* a rocket." Any thoughts he'd had before about legal stuff were long forgotten.

"You said your uncle gave you more?" Max said.

"Yeah."

"Well, can we do this again?" Max asked, shifting from one foot to the other.

Jeremy looked around at the rest of us. We nodded, smiling like a bunch of apes. "Sure."

"When?" Max asked.

"I don't know." Jeremy shrugged.

"Well, when do you *think* we can do it again?" Max pressed further.

"Gee, Max, I really don't *know*." Jeremy was clearly frustrated with Max at this point.

Max's shoulders slumped. "Well, what are we going to do now?" He looked at us for an answer.

"Patrick had an idea," Jeremy said. "Tell them, Patrick."

"See those trees over there?" I said, pointing to the woods. "I always thought they were just all different sizes and stuff, but I'm not sure about that now. When James and I came over here, we noticed something we hadn't when we were filming our video. When we started looking around, it was sort of like we were walking uphill—not like steep or anything, more like going up a ramp, or a slope for sure. We thought it could be interesting if we all took a look together. Actually, we didn't want to go without you guys."

"Sounds good to me," Brendan said. "Let's go."

James and I fell in beside him and Jeremy and Max joined us as we moved back toward the woods. "I don't know if it's a hill or what," I said as we walked, "but I want to see what's up there."

Once we entered the tree line, the incline wasn't all that steep. We weren't even breathing hard when the ground leveled off and we found we were standing in a small clearing. I figured we must be at the top of where we were going.

In the middle of the open space, some tree stumps circled a bunch of stones that looked like it might have been used as a fire pit. It all looked as if it had been placed like that on purpose. I didn't know what I'd thought we'd find, but it was beginning to weird me out, the hairs on the back of my neck stood up.

James came and stood next to me. He said quietly, "What do you make of this?"

Brendan stood nearby and looked at me. He nodded, one eyebrow raised, like he was wondering what all this meant.

"What?" Max yelled. He'd seen our look. His eyes narrowed as he looked from Brendan to James and me. "Are you guys up to something?"

"No."

Jeremy had made his way around the circle and stood next to us. "What are you talking about?" He hadn't noticed the looks between me and James and Brendan. "Patrick? What's going on?

"No way!" Max fumed, pointing a finger at me. "You promised, Patrick. Nothing screwy."

"Well, I didn't plan on finding *this*." I spread my arms and motioned around the circle at the tree trunks.

"Oh, brother. Here we go again," Max grumbled and plopped down on the stump farthest from us.

Each of us took a seat too. No one said a word for a while. Max looked like he was going to bust a gut if he didn't say something.

"Okay. Will someone clue me in? What is the big mystery?" He swept his arms in wide circles mimicking my movements. "What's so special about *this*?"

Brendan's head dropped to his chest and he huffed out a big breath of air. Brendan's patience usually ran pretty thin with Max. He could never understand why Max was so slow to catch on to things. I didn't know what was going on here but it was obvious to me, and it seemed to everyone but Max, that there was *something* going on. I mean, those big stumps didn't get there all by themselves. And the rocks had to have been placed the way they were. I got another shiver up my spine. "Look around, Max."

"I'm looking!" As usual, Max was way over the top in his reaction. His eyes were getting bigger by the second and his voice was getting higher with every word. "All I see is a bunch of old logs–which are not very comfortable by the way." He squirmed on his seat, trying to get more comfortable. He pointed an accusing finger at the stones and said, "And, in case any of you haven't noticed, it looks like somebody's been up here burning a fire. Which, I might also add, is *totally* illegal. There's a fire ban around here, you know. Whoever did it is *so* breaking the law."

"Hey, Max." I said it in a normal speaking voice so I could check out something I'd noticed. He looked over at me when he heard his name. Weird. Or maybe just good acoustics. While he was talking, his voice had carried across the circle like we were sitting right next to each other having a regular conversation in a normal voice. "Look, buddy," I said, "somebody had to put these logs here like this. By the looks of them, they could have been here a long time. See how the wood is dark and worn? Don't you want to know how they got here? Like this?"

He looked around, his eyebrows scrunched together like he was trying to grasp it all and figure things out.

"And . . . I think those stones have been here just as long."

"How long?" His head snapped around to look back at me.

"The trees the logs came from could easily be well over fifty years old, I think." I had no idea if what I was saying could be true, I was just messing with Max's head. "Maybe a hundred or more."

"And you think someone put them here on purpose?"

"Looks that way to me." I glanced at the others who were nodding like they could believe it was possible.

"Who? Why? What would anybody do that for?

"I don't know, Max," I said, shaking my head. "I don't know."

I didn't say anything else, but I had the same kind of feeling I'd had when we came out of the culvert in the spring. We'd just been exploring then too, checking things out. I wasn't sure what I'd seen in that drainage pipe back then, and I didn't know what was going on here now, but just like before, it felt just plain spooky. I also knew I wasn't going to let it rest until I'd figured it out. And just like before, I had no idea where my search would lead me.

CHAPTER THREE

We sat on the logs and bounced ideas around, but didn't come up with any solid reason why they were there like that. Some of our ideas were pretty far out there. At least Max didn't recite his famous theory for most anything he couldn't understand or explain: the ghost of a crazy giant renegade Indian named Fury was behind it all.

"Why don't we spread out and look around?" I stood up. "We aren't going to figure anything out just sitting here." I started walking away from the center of the area.

We all fanned out away from the circle, like the spokes of a bicycle wheel.

"Hey, guys," Brendan called from one direction after he'd gone several yards. "The trees are really thick and I can't see far through them but it definitely goes down over here."

"Same here," Jeremy yelled.

"Yeah. Over here too." Max sounded off to let us know that he saw the same thing.

I angled over to where James was coming back toward the circle. "So now we know we're at the top of somewhere," he said.

"Right. And what I'd like to know is where did the tree stumps come from?" I told my friend what had been going through my mind. "Those look like they came from trees much bigger than any of the trees growing up here, James. It looks like someone had to have put them up here."

When James and I joined the others at the circle, all of a sudden I got that weird feeling again. Each one of us had taken a position behind one of the stumps facing each other across the space. I saw Jeremy and Brendan shiver and look around, as if they'd gotten the same spooky feeling.

Not Max. He'd plopped down on the stump in front of him, wiping at his forehead. "Okay, guys. We've seen what there is to see. Are we ready to go back now? It's hot. I'm tired, and I'm getting hungry."

Max was always hungry. I itched to go down a different side of the hill from where we'd come up. What was down another direction? Were there any clues to what we'd found here in the clearing? I didn't know why it was so important to me to know. It just was. I could tell James and Brendan were as curious as I was, but it was getting late and we wouldn't have much time to explore any more anyway. Besides, Max would complain every step of the way.

"Yeah, sure. It's probably time we headed home," I said. We all had things to do later. James had some meeting to go to, Brendan had some kind of ball to kick or chase, and

Jeremy, as always, had some family thing. Me, I was sure the garage would need my attention.

Max was already on the way down the slope before I picked up the backpack and started walking with the other guys.

"Well, I don't know about you guys," Jeremy said as he fell into step along beside me. "But I don't think we've seen everything there is to see here. I say we take a better look. When can we get back?"

Good old Jeremy. Never ceased to surprise me, always up for another adventure, even if it might be a little spooky.

"As soon as we can, if that's okay with everyone?" I said as I looked around at my friends. My teeth rattled when Brendan slapped me on the back, his way of letting me know he was behind my idea all the way. James grinned from ear to ear. Oh, yeah, no doubt about it, we'd be back here real soon.

On the walk back to my house, Jeremy talked a mile a minute about the rockets his uncle had given him. Sounded like he had all types and sizes, with engines and everything we'd need to launch them. Brendan had practice the following Saturday, but the one after that looked to be clear for the rest of us. We had a plan and a date.

"See ya later, guys," Max said as soon as we were in my front yard then jumped on his bike and headed for home. Guess he really was hungry.

I grabbed a basketball from the garage and the rest of us shot some hoops in the cul-de-sac. After a while, my mom came out on the front porch.

"Jeremy, your mother called for you to come home." She stopped before she went back into the house. "Patrick, don't you have some things to do?"

That was code that something in the garage was waiting for me.

Brendan passed the ball to me. "See you tomorrow, buddy," he said as he and James started down the side walk. Jeremy pushed off on his skateboard alongside them.

"Yeah, tomorrow." I waved goodbye, knowing I'd see them in the morning at church. I put the ball away and closed the garage door. I looked around, but the garage looked just fine to me. My stomach was grumbling and I could smell spaghetti cooking before I even got in the house.

CHAPTER FOUR

After church and Sunday lunch next day, I checked out sites about rockets. I discovered there is a *lot* of information on rockets on the internet. .I was really excited about talking to the guys about one in particular that caught my eye. That would have to wait, though, because tonight was video chat time with my sister, Taylor.

After graduation, Taylor went to spend the summer with our brother, Brett and his family in England where he was stationed with the Air Force. Which meant *she* got a vacation. But I couldn't hold that against her, it was a great opportunity for her to travel and do some sightseeing before she started college. It also meant she was out of my hair for the whole summer too, but, I had to admit, I missed her. Besides, I didn't have anyone to give me a ride whenever my parents were at work, or busy, or Grammy was doing something when I needed one. Getting my learner's permit was still months away.

We all took turns talking to Taylor, Brett and Pam, and the kids before it was their bedtime. They were planning a trip to Scotland and Wales the following week. I couldn't help being a little envious of Taylor. I could only hope my mom, dad, and I would get to travel to England for a visit with them before they rotated back to the states. Although they didn't expect to still be there in two years when I would be graduating from high school. And if we weren't going to take a vacation this summer, I sure couldn't expect a trip to England any time before that . . . if then. I could only dream of something special in my future.

I had to get up early the next morning because I had a yard to mow, but I kept tossing and turning, unable to go to sleep because I kept thinking about the stuff I'd read about rockets that afternoon. One in particular.

When the alarm went off in the morning, I pushed the snooze three times before I finally rolled out of bed, then had to rush to get dressed and take the mower down the street to old Mrs. Bursen's house. I was busting with news of what I'd found on the internet and all the ideas I had, but I didn't have time to call James until that afternoon.

"Can you come over?

"In an hour?"

"Sure. See you then."

After a ham and cheese sandwich, some chips and a big glass of milk, I took a shower and had just finished dressing when James got there. We went back to my room and I shut the door.

"Dude," I said, sitting down on the side of my bed. "Guess what I found out on the internet."

Up to then, I hadn't let myself get overly excited about what I'd found, but as soon as I started telling James about it, and I could see the expression on his face, the ideas started pinging around my brain like a metal ball in a pinball machine.

"Have you talked to Jeremy yet?" James asked.

"Not yet. I just ran across this stuff late yesterday, and you know how Sundays are around here. But it's all I could think about while I was pushing that mower back and forth this morning."

"Well, call him. Right now. See if he can come over."

I picked up my cell and brought Jeremy up on speed dial. He didn't answer. I went straight to voice mail and I told him to call as soon as he got my message. Next I texted him with the same message. Then we waited. After a few minutes and he hadn't called or answered my text, I couldn't stand it any longer. I said, "Come on, James, I'll show you what I found."

We went into what was originally meant to be the formal living room. There is a family room at the other end of the house next to the kitchen, but my mom and dad had set up our living room more like a game room; Foosball, an air hockey table, a TV for playing games and videos, and a couple sofas and chairs filled the space. It worked great with three kids and having their friends around when we first moved into the house, and it had been kept that way.

It's also where the desktop computer is. My parents take the parental control issue seriously, with all kinds of blocks on our system. I guess it's a good thing I don't mind having rules. I knew they did it because they love me and wanted to shield me from things they felt weren't appropriate. Takes the pressure off me. James and the other guys were used to the rules and were okay with it too. Their parents were pretty much like mine–they just didn't have the living room/game room arrangement.

I clicked the screen on and scrolled down to the site I'd seen earlier. I got up and let James take my place then waited a minute to give him a chance to read over the material.

"Holy cow!" He looked at me then went back to the screen. "We have *got* to do this," he said, almost in a whisper, his eyes riveted to the information he was reading.

"I know . . . Right?"

Just then the door bell rang. I was surprised that Jeremy stood on the porch when I opened the door. He usually has something to do at home and has to clear it with his mom first.

"I figured I'd just come on over." Obviously, he had gotten the voice mail and text. He stepped inside. "What's up?"

I motioned him over to the computer and James got up and gave him his seat in front of the screen. He asked Jeremy, "Did you know about this?"

Jeremy took a second to scan the information on the screen, swiveled around to face us then leaned back, his elbows resting on the arm of the chair, his fingers linked together in front of him. There was a small smirk on his mouth, and I could see it coming. "Oh, sure." He shrugged smugly.

I couldn't believe it. I stared at him then at the screen; there was a complete description, with details and drawings, of a rocket that carried a *camera*. The camera activated at a certain elevation and took pictures below. So what he was saying was we could take pictures from a rocket!

"I just happen to have a setup pretty much like this."

"You're serious?" James asked.

"Well," Jeremy said with a sly grin. "I didn't want to show you all my tricks at one time."

I punched him on the shoulder as James grabbed the front of his shirt and pulled him from the chair. Jeremy swatted at us like he was defending himself from our pretend blows. Then we were scuffling him to the floor, poking and jabbing him in the ribs, all of us laughing like a bunch of hyenas.

"Hey, guys," Jeremy said once we were out of breath, sprawled on the carpet. "I just wanted to spread out the fun, you know."

I propped up on my elbow, my hand under my head. "Yeah, I can see that, I guess. But, hey, buddy, I think we need to get on with it."

"Right," James agreed. "Have some fun."

It seemed like Jeremy had just been waiting for us to do some research and a chance to talk to us. We sat cross-legged facing each other while he told us about how a camera could be mounted on a rocket, and how it worked. I got more excited by the minute and couldn't wait until we could tell Brendan. And Max.

CHAPTER FIVE

I should have known to be careful and ease Max into the news of taking pictures from a rocket. Max is always going way overboard one way or the other, either mumbling or grumbling, all for it or totally against it. This time, he was all for it and ready to go to the field and set up the rocket and fire it up. Right then.

"Max. Buddy. We have to wait until next weekend." I explained, again, Brendan's practice schedule.

"But what about now? Today?"

"I've got things to do. We all have things to do."

"I don't."

"Well, we do. If you want, I guess you can go launch the rocket by yourself."

"But I don't . . . Oh. Right. Guess not."

It took a few more minutes to talk him down, but I knew he'd bug us until the time came to get that rocket in the air. And, he'd be the first one at my house when the time came.

I have to admit, the time seemed to drag by. I mowed lawns, went to Youth Group at church, shot some hoops with the guys, ate, slept and dreamed of shooting off that rocket.

The day finally came and I asked my mom if the guys could sleep over the night before. She knew something was up; whenever I ask if the guys can sleep over, there is usually something up. I told her that we were experimenting with a rocket Jeremy's uncle had given him. My dad thought it was cool, and after I assured her that Jeremy had done this before, she said it was okay.

I managed to leave out the little detail that we'd already sent one up.

We turned the lights off around midnight but kept chattering about the next day. When Pinto, our wire-haired dachshund, came in and started licking my face in the morning, I was ready to get up. It was only six thirty, but I was awake and started shaking the guys. My dad was already in the kitchen making pancakes–a Saturday morning tradition around our house. He had a stack ready for us when we gathered around the table. After we'd cleaned the plate, and downed about a gallon of milk, we headed to the garage where Jeremy had stowed the backpack and rocket.

Dad followed us out. Jeremy slung the pack over his shoulder, and I opened the garage door. I turned and waved at my dad as we walked down the driveway.

He waved and called, "You boys be careful." He was still watching us from the drive when we turned the corner.

We talked all the way across Mr. Nelson's pasture and started into the open field. Except Jeremy was really quiet, looking around with his head to the ground, a serious look on his face. I heard him sort of mumble, "Lucky there's no dew."

I didn't get his point, and pulled up next to him and nudged his arm. "What's that, buddy?"

"No dew. I can't believe I didn't think about it before, but if there'd been dew . . ."

Brendan fell into step with us. "What about the dew, dude?"

"I was just so pumped we were finally going to get this rocket up," he said, his eyes on the ground, "it just didn't cross my mind, that's all."

Jeremy is one smart dude, maybe a genius, but sometimes he acts like we can read his mind—like we were supposed to know exactly what he was talking about. The fact there was no dew was clear to him, so it should be clear to us, and the reason why that would be of any special interest. Uh . . . nuh-uh.

"Hey, you gotta help us out, buddy." Brendan put his hand at the back of Jeremy's neck and gave him a light shake. "Okay, so what are we missing here?"

Jeremy looked from Brendan to me, smiled and ducked his head. We go through this all the time. It's just Jeremy.

"Right. Okay. The fuse," he said. "If there's dew, the fuse will get wet from the grass and can't reach the rocket. No ignition."

Oh, was that all? Of course it made sense now. Hooray for no dew.

We stopped to set up in the same spot where we'd launched before. Max was looking at the woods in the distance.

"I told my grandpa about what we found in the woods," Max said, jerking his head in that direction. "You know what he told me?"

I had no idea, but I was sure we were going to find out. Max's grandpa was full of stories, mostly old legends and ghost stories, things like that. It was hard to believe that Max took them serious, but he believed what his grandpa told him. And Max loved to share them. I was ready to tune him out like we usually did, but what he said next caught my attention.

"Granpa says it might be a mound like—"

"That's it! A *mound*. Not a hill exactly, but a mound. I like the sound of that, Max. A good description, really."

Then he had to go and say, "An *Indian* burial mound. They're all over the place, Granpa said. Tribes buried their dead sort of like a mass grave, I guess. He said that would probably explain the tree stumps and fire ring in the clearing at the top."

Arrgh. Here we go again. Max and his grandpa's tales.

"He said we probably shouldn't have gone up there, you know, where the fire pit and tree stumps were. Probably it was some special place for rituals and stuff." Max was as serious as tattoos.

Well, we already had been up there, so what were we supposed to do about it now? Next thing he was going to tell me was we were under some spell or curse or something? Before I could go off on him, Jeremy unzipped his backpack, and Max and his grandpa's wild stories zipped right out of my brain.

We clustered around him and he pulled the rocket out. It looked pretty much like the others, only a little bigger and the nose cone wasn't the same. It felt different too. We each took turns holding it, turning it over in our hands, testing the weight and balance, while Jeremy got out the launch pad and other gear.

We helped him get everything set up then bunched up close together and began the countdown. At 'ONE,' Jeremy flipped the switch and smoke began to stream from the tail. But it didn't go anywhere. We looked around, at Jeremy, back at the rocket.

At that moment, the rocket made a loud noise and took off. But not up like we expected. It fell over on its side and swooshed through the grass like some kind of crazy-wild hyper snake. We were on our feet but didn't follow after it this time because we couldn't tell where it was going to end up.

I couldn't believe my eyes when the rocket spun around, made a U-turn and headed straight for us! At first we just stood there, unable to move. Then we scattered. All except Jeremy. I stopped in my tracks and watched him. Oh my gosh! I was going to lose one of my best friends. The rocket was headed straight for him.

I screamed, "Jeremy, get out of the way!"

The guys all stopped running when they heard me and turned to see what I was making such a fuss about. Then they were yelling too.

Jeremy didn't budge an inch. He stood his ground, eyes glued on the long white cylinder streaking closer to him. We watched the rocket as it got closer and closer then all of a sudden stop within a foot in front of him. Unbelievable!

"Are you crazy!" I yelled, running to him and keeping my eye on the rocket laying at his feet. "Are you out of your mind!"

"Oh, my gosh! Oh my gosh!" Max gasped with each step, trying to keep up with the others as they ran up.

Jeremy, calm as anything, leaned down and picked up the rocket then looked up at me like he'd just realized we were standing there around him.

"Dude!" Brendan said, his hand on Jeremy's shoulder. "You gave us a scare. What were you thinking?"

We all waited to hear what he had to say, but he looked at us like he didn't understand the question.

"The rocket?" Max said.

"Yeah?"

"You know the one headed straight for you?" Max shouted inches from Jeremy's face. "You could have been killed!"

Jeremy frowned and stepped back from Max. "I wasn't in any danger."

He looked around at the rest of us, slowly realizing that we'd been worried about him too. His eyes met mine and I gave him my best *Care to explain yourself?* look.

"Oh. I get it." He looked down at the rocket in his hands. "But, guys, I really wasn't in any danger." It only took one look at our faces for him to see we weren't exactly buying it so he went on. "See, the rocket only has X amount of fuel. That, together with the engine, determines how far up it will go, how long it will stay in the air. It's pretty standard." He turned the rocket over in his hands. "That smoke before it took off?"

We nodded, waiting for the rest of his explanation.

"Well, the fuel had already started burning and I knew it wasn't going to go as high as it was supposed to. I just didn't know it wasn't going up at all. But when it took off, I calculated the amount of time that was left, how long it would burn and how far it would go. When it turned, I could see when the nose cone and camera disconnected. It was all pretty much over by then, like when the rocket goes up, runs out of fuel and comes back down. I knew there was no more thrust left." He shrugged and smiled. "So, no danger."

Like I said–genius.

"Well, you still scared the squat out of us." Max fumed, his face bright red.

"Come on, Max. It was on the ground, not aimed at any body parts. I could see where it was going and that it was slowing down. I could have jumped over it if it hadn't stopped when it did."

"I still think you're nuts."

Jeremy eyed Max for a second. "Well, Max, old buddy," he finally said, crouching by his backpack and digging around inside. He straightened, coming face to face with Max again. "All I can tell you is . . . Get over it."

Okay, now this was *big*. A few months ago, Jeremy never would have looked Max in the eye and said something like that. He mostly just followed whatever Max said, putting up with his wild crazy ideas, his whining and complaining all the time, and his being negative about everything. We all put up with it too, but we never said anything. It was just the way Max was. He was our friend and even if he did irritate us we overlooked it or around it. I guess Jeremy had had enough.

Max was the first to look away. He looked down at his feet and nudged some grass with his toe, mumbling, "That was still scary."

"So, I'll try and not scare you again, buddy. But you just gotta learn to trust me. Okay?"

"Okay."

Something had definitely shifted in their relationship.

It was then I noticed something else. Jeremy was a tad bit taller than Max. Always the smallest of all of us, he now stood almost eye to eye with me and James. He'd shot up over the past couple months. He'd filled out some too and his voice was deeper. *Huh. How about that?*

Something like this had never happened before and Brendan, James and I sort of shuffled around waiting to see how this was going to play out.

"So, you guys want to try that again?" Jeremy pulled another rocket out of his pack. I was so stunned that it didn't register at the moment that the rocket he was holding seemed bigger than the dud we'd just watched crash and burn. Well, it didn't exactly crash, and it didn't burn, but . . . You know what I mean.

My throat was dry. "Are you serious?" I croaked. We moved a step closer to take a look.

"Yeah, I calculated something like this could happen and I didn't want to waste the morning in case it did so I brought spare parts." He looked around to see our reaction. "It'll take a few minutes to put it all together again. What do you think?"

Was he kidding? Of course we wanted to do it again. Jeremy sat on a big log and held the fuselage out to Max. "Hold this for me will you, while I get the camera rigged?"

They sat side by side on the log; Jeremy's dark curly head almost touching Max's spikey hair as they worked together getting the rocket ready for another launch while the rest of us watched and waited.

CHAPTER SIX

Things were back to normal with Jeremy and Max working together on the rocket. It was barely middle of the morning, but it seemed like as good a time as any to break out some Oreos and water. I handed them around as we recounted almost every move of the crazy way the rocket sped out of control. Of course none of us admitted to being scared.

Jeremy had everything ready to go again before we knew it. We hadn't even eaten all the Oreos. We still had half a pack left and I shoved them back into my pack. Jeremy walked the rocket over to the launch site, then reeled the fuse out as he walked back to where we waited by the igniter. We counted down and Jeremy flipped the switch.

The fuse connected with the rocket, there was a SWOOSH, and the rocket burst into the air. We watched it rise then begin to arc over the tree line far off to the right. It was so high up we could barely make out when the parachute and camera deployed. Then the fuselage was falling fast, headed straight into the trees, the parachute floating down behind it. We were up and running in the direction where it would most likely go.

"Hey! Guys! Guys!" Max was screaming, waving his arms frantically.

What was Max being so dramatic about now? But I slowed down to look where he was pointing and saw a thread of white smoke rising from where the rocket had taken off. Oh, my gosh! The grass was on fire! I yelled at the others and as soon as they saw the smoke, we all veered without missing a step and ran toward it. Retrieving the rocket and the camera would have to wait.

There was more smoke than flames, hardly any in fact, but it was beginning to spread. In seconds, we stomped the fire before it had time to get out of control. Breathing hard, we scuffed dirt up and over the ashes, our eyes on the ground to make sure there was not even the tiniest spark left. I hurried to get my backpack and came back with bottles of water.

Jeremy took the water from me, poured it over the black-ened grass. Then he started running, shouting, "We have to find the rocket."

"Dude. Give us a minute to catch our breath." Brendan splashed some of the water over his head and face. "It can wait."

"We can't!" Jeremy headed in the direction where we'd last seen the rocket. He yelled over his shoulder, and kept running. "What if the rocket sparked a fire where it landed?" Instantly, we were hot on his heels.

When we got to the trees, Jeremy stopped and held up his hand. "Look, guys, someone needs to walk where the trees aren't thick," he said, pointing to where they thinned out. "They'll be like a spotter; they can see better where we need to go. The rest of us will spread out about ten feet apart, deeper into the growth. But always keep the next guy in sight and everybody move at the same pace. I think that'll give us the best chance of finding it."

Man. I hoped that was a good idea, that we'd run across the rocket instead of find ourselves running from a raging forest fire. At least I didn't smell smoke. Yet.

We decided real quick that Jeremy should take the outside and sprinted away from him into the trees. We took up our usual formation: Jeremy, Max, James, me, then Brendan. We moved carefully through the underbrush and vines and stuff, doing what Jeremy said and kept each other in sight, calling out once in a while, just in case.

It was hot, with hardly any air moving among the trees, and I kept sniffing for a hint of smoke. No one mentioned taking a break, though. After about what seemed an eternity, but was more like maybe fifteen minutes, Jeremy yelled, "Guys! Guys! Over here! Over here!"

I didn't move until Brendan came crashing through the brush and we took off together to where James and Max waited for us. Jeremy was waving the fuselage in the air.

There didn't seem to be any fire anywhere, but there was no sign of the parachute and camera, either.

"Everybody fan out and look for the camera," Jeremy said. I'd taken about two steps when he added, "Be sure and watch where you step, you know. Oh, and look up in the trees. It might have got stuck up in one."

Did anyone mention a needle in a haystack? No. I waded carefully through a lot of tall grass for several minutes. I could still see the guys at a distance then my foot hit something that definitely was not a tree branch or vine. *Oh, no!* I thought at first, my heart sinking, scared to look down, afraid I'd see the camera crushed under my foot. I picked my foot up and moved backward very carefully. Whatever I'd bumped into was too big to be the camera. I was sure—almost.

I leaned over and pulled at bunches of the coarse grass, pushing it away from whatever my foot had hit then I jumped back. It took a second for my brain to register that I'd uncovered a tombstone! *No way!* A tombstone?

It was laying flat on the ground, and, as I pulled more grass away, there was no mistake. The name, dates, everything, were hard to make out, but it was definitely a tombstone. I turned to yell at the guys to come check it out and tripped over another marker that was sticking part way out of the ground. I scrambled backward and ran into another one. I was in a graveyard, for crying out loud!

Looked like Max had been right about one thing–the mound was a burial ground after all. At least a graveyard. I had the feeling that Indians wouldn't have marked some graves with head stones, though. Hadn't Max said it was more like a mass grave for everybody?

Right then I just wanted somebody to see what I was seeing. I started yelling at the top of my lungs for someone to get over there. Camera or no camera, somebody needed to come see this.

James came loping over and by the time he got there, I'd cleared the surface of the first marker to try and make out the inscription.

"Whoa, dude," he said pulling up short, gaping at the gray slab under my hand. "Is that what I think it is?"

"Yeah. And so are these," I said as I pushed grass and leaves off others.

I thought I might be sitting on another one, but I didn't want to move and find out for sure.

Brendan and Jeremy came blazing through the brush, yelling, "Did you find it? Is it okay?" They came to a screeching halt when they reached us and saw what I'd uncovered. They'd barely had time to take in what they were seeing when Max came barreling right behind them.

"Hey, guys, I found it. Right where I'd already looked. I don't know how I missed it, but I retraced my steps and there it was! Like it just appeared out of nowhere." He almost crashed into Brendan's back as he stumbled forward. He roughly shouldered between Brendan and Jeremy, the camera held out in front of him. "Here it is. See?"

Then he saw what we were all looking at. "Oh, geez," he gasped. His knees buckled and he plopped down on the ground. "Oh, my gosh," he squealed and popped up to his feet. "I think I just sat on a tombstone!"

"Yeah, Max, looks like you were right about this being a burial ground after all. Just maybe not an *Indian* burial mound."

Max was looking pretty pale right about then. His freckles and red hair really popped. I thought he was going to faint.

"Don't anybody move," I said, twisting around looking for more of the slabs. They were looking too, and no one was moving an inch. Max hadn't sat on a tombstone, but there was one a foot from him, hidden beneath some vine-like growth.

"I'm not touching that thing," he croaked out when I told him to clear it off and see if he could make out any writing on it.

"Come on, Max, it can't hurt you."

"Yeah, well, you said there wasn't going to be any screwy stuff this time either, and look where we are." He sat back down on the ground and pulled his knees up, wrapping his arms around them. He held tight to the camera which had suddenly taken back seat to our present situation.

Our movements were slow as we carefully searched the area looking for more graves. We found five headstones sort of clustered together, maybe like a family plot. They were pretty much the same size and seemed to be about the same age. Most of the lettering had worn away, but we were able to make out a date of 1800-something on a couple of them. There were only parts of some of the first names, except for

one guy named William. We could make out only a few letters of other names, nothing making a whole word. We tried
to piece something together, but came up with nothing. It
was all very frustrating and we finally gave up.

After we'd gotten a good idea of how the markers were laid
out, we fanned out and looked to see if there were others.
Max was more than eager to move out of the cluster of grave
markers. Each of us had gone about fifteen feet or so from the
first ones we found when we heard Max shrieking. Then we
watched him heading out of the woods.

"Max, hey, Max! Wait up," I yelled. "I don't think this is
what you think it is." I didn't go after him because I thought
he'd stop. He didn't. He was out of there like he was running
for his life. I looked at the others who seemed as stunned as
I was at the way Max was acting. Jeremy grabbed the rocket
and his backpack and ran after our friend.

"Oh, well," Brendan said, throwing aside a stick he'd been
using to poke around in the grass and brush. "We're not coming up with any answers anyway. Might as well go see what's
got old Maxie all stirred up this time."

We didn't catch up to him and Jeremy until we were half-
way across the clearing. We could hear Max yelling before we
reached them.

CHAPTER SEVEN

"I'm telling you I know what I saw!" Max stabbed Jeremy in the chest with a finger, his other hand still gripping the camera.

"What's going on, Max?" His eyes looked wild when I walked up to him, his face pale and sweaty. His red hair stuck out in all directions like his head was on fire. "What happened back there?"

He glared at me, snorting noises coming out his nose. "Patrick Morrison, you promised nothing crazy. I don't know why I ever believe you!" He was up on his toes, he was so upset. "You just can't stay out of stuff, can you?"

"Hey, buddy, I don't know what's got you so wound up," James said, taking a step toward Max. "But—"

"You're just as bad as *he* is!" Max screeched at James. He turned to glare at Brendan. "Both of you are. You'll do whatever he says." His eyes narrowed and he looked back at me. "And now you've got Jeremy following right along behind you. Well, I'm not. Not this time." He turned and started walking toward the fence by Mr. Nelson's pasture again.

The way he was acting, I didn't think I was going to get a straight answer from Max so I asked Jeremy, "Do you know what's got him so freaked out?"

"He's scared, Patrick."

That was not an answer I expected. I just couldn't see Max being *that* scared of a few old tombstones. He wasn't the bravest of the bunch, but this was way over the top—even for Max.

"Just come on. Back to your house. Give him time to settle down," Jeremy said, hurrying off to catch up with Max.

I was sure Max had told Jeremy what made him weird out like that, but he wasn't going to say anything unless he knew it was all right with Max. There wasn't much else Brendan, James and I could do, so we hustled to catch up with them.

Max sat under the basketball goal in the cul-de-sac in front of my house. That's where we usually went to talk over things and make plans. At least he hadn't gone home, he'd stayed and waited for us. He still clutched the camera in his hand. Jeremy sat next to him, without talking, giving Max some space.

James, Brendan and I took a spot on the curb next to them and waited.

Finally, Brendan said, "Hey, Max, thanks for spotting that smoke. If you hadn't seen it, we might have been toast." We all agreed and seconded what Brendan said, trying to get Max to open up.

But Max wasn't talking yet.

James picked up a stick and scratched at the pavement. "Yeah, what happened with the rocket? Even with the other one whizzing like crazy through the grass, nothing happened. It didn't catch anything on fire."

For a few minutes it was like we were in a daze, trying to get our heads around what had just happened. And it killed some time until Max was ready to talk about what was going on with him. What had happened back in the graveyard.

"I think I might be able to clear up what happened with the rocket," Jeremy said, standing and brushing off the back of his pants.

He frowned down at the rocket in his hands, the second one we'd launched, the one that caused the fire. "I guess I might not have taken into account that this rocket used different fuel. That made it more powerful than the others, making it go higher and farther." He was shifting from one foot to the other like he was talking his way through the process more than he was explaining to us.

Then I remembered the idea that flashed through my mind when I'd thought the rocket looked different than the others. That's what it was. It was *bigger*. Jeremy had some explaining to do.

"Well, see, I think the camera was a little big for the first rocket. Caused it to be top heavy, you know. That's the reason why it fell over and scudded around like it did. I'd wondered about it before we went to fire it, that's why I brought a . . . uh, another rocket." His eyes darted around to see what we were thinking about what he was saying.

What could we say? That he might have told us? That we didn't know anything about rockets and were just out for the adventure. Talk about not knowing what to say. I sure didn't.

When we didn't say anything, Jeremy went on. "Well, uh, I guess I was right. The second one was able to handle the camera, plus get more speed and distance." He ducked his head and rubbed the back of his neck then looked at us. "I'm sorry, guys. I miscalculated."

"So, what you're saying is you knew the first rocket might not work? And you didn't bother to tell us?"

"Uh . . . yeah."

"And it was like a test run?"

"Mmm-huh. I guess so."

"And the second one—the bigger one—was 'just in case'?"

"Uh . . . yeah, pretty much."

I looked around at the others. No one seemed to be upset. When all was said and done, it had all turned out pretty good in the end. "Well . . ." I shrugged. "Whatever." If no one else was bothered, I figured it was okay by me. "It was a great shot." Everyone nodded they thought so too. All except Max.

Was that what had Max acting all nuts? That Jeremy had miscalculated and hadn't filled us in on what could happen, and got him yelling at Jeremy—and the rest of us—in the field? Usually, he would be the first one to put up a real fuss about any little thing that went wrong, but then he'd get over it and go on. But this time he was real still and quiet. His face

49

was hidden in his arms which lay across his knees. Jeremy sat down next to Max and nudged him with his leg. "Max, look, I'm really sorry. About the rocket, the fire. Honest, I didn't mean to scare anyone."

Max didn't move or say anything.

Jeremy looked around at us, his expression clueless as to what to do next, his eyes asking for our help.

James tried. "Hey," he said, "for a minute there I was a little worried myself."

"Yeah, me too," Brendan added, which was surprising since not much ever scared him.

We waited for some reaction from Max. Nothing seemed to be working.

"No kidding," I said. "I was a *lot* worried. We could have had a major fire."

"And been in major trouble." Jeremy nodded and motioned for us to keep talking. "Remember, like Max said before, there *is* a ban on starting fires."

We had to strain to hear what Max said. "That didn't scare me. We put that out."

"That's right, buddy," Brendan said. "Because of you, we got it under control in time. You spotted the smoke."

Max turned his head slightly and looked at Jeremy. "You know," he mumbled. "The tombstone."

Like I said, I never figured a few old graves would shake Max up. Looked like I figured wrong. I mean Max can be hugely dramatic about things, getting all excited and everything, but then he calms down and moves on. I'd never seen him act like this before.

"They were just a bunch of old graves, Max. Kind of spooked me there too, for a little while." Then a thought came to me. I looked around and said, 'But, what are they doing there? How'd they get there?' I wondered if they might have anything to do with the tree stumps and fire pit, but I'd wait to say anything about that.

"You know what? I think we've uncovered a mystery here, and I'd like to find out more about what's going on. How about it, guys?"

"Yeah!" James jumped on the idea, then backed off. "But, wait up, Patrick. Those graves have been there a long time. Where would we even start?"

"Maybe the library?" Jeremy offered, ready to be doing something.

Brendan thought maybe we could check some public records of some sort.

Our focus had immediately shifted. We had a mystery to investigate, and everybody had an idea—except Max.

I didn't realize it then, but, without even thinking about it, we had pretty much brushed off what was going on with Max altogether. I should have paid attention. It wasn't until much later that I realized what he'd said. Tombstone. As in *one*. There was no *s*.

After a few ideas, we decided we'd head over to the library and start our investigation there. Before we could grab our bikes, Max held up the camera and asked Jeremy, "What do you want me to do with this?"

"Oh, yeah," Jeremy said, taking the camera housing from Max. "Thanks, Max. I'd forgotten about that."

"So? What happens with it now?"

"Well, we gotta see what kind of pictures it took. But it'll take a few days to get it developed." Jeremy placed the camera in his backpack and zipped it up. "I'll take care of that. Okay?"

Max shrugged and got on his bike, heading for the library which was only a few blocks from my house. Only thing, we'd forgotten that it closed at one o'clock on Saturdays. We missed it by only a few minutes. But it reminded us that we were hungry, really hungry, and we all decided it was a good time to call it a day and for everybody to head home.

CHAPTER EIGHT

Next day was the usual: see the guys at church, home and Sunday lunch, then cruising around the internet for a while. Sometimes my dad will shoot a few hoops with me, but he had some project he was working on that afternoon and none of the guys could come over. I shot a few baskets and lost interest real quick. Gaahh. Major boredom.

We didn't chat with Taylor that night, they were all on their mini-vacation in Wales. At least *someone* was having a vacation. I tried to get into a movie my parents were watching, but I had a hard time staying awake. No action, no car chases, nothing got blown up, no one died, got shot or maimed. No monsters or aliens. Just a lot of talking and violin music, and sighing from my mom. I decided to go to bed early.

I got up and said goodnight to my parents, but my mom reached for my hand. "Just a few more minutes, Patrick." She pulled me down beside her, her eyes never leaving the TV. "It's almost over . . ." Another sigh. I choked on a groan and sat back.

When the credits *finally* rolled, my mom smiled and gave my dad one of those *looks* they have sometimes. Then she settled back into the couch and turned her attention to me.

"Okay, now honey, I want to talk to you about something."

"Uh-huh?" I wasn't sure I liked the sound of this.

"Well, you know how you were supposed to go to camp next week?"

"Yeah?" *Supposed to go? Don't tell me I'm not even going to get to go to camp.*

"Well . . . it looks like there isn't going to be camp this year."

"Mom!"

"Just hear her out, Patrick." Now my dad was in on the plot to keep me from having a summer vacation–of any kind.

"There just weren't enough kids signed up to go–only you and the other boys." I knew when she said 'the other boys' she was talking about *the guys,* James, Brendan, Jeremy and Max. That was a given.

"C'mon, Mom. No vacation and now no camp?"

"Mr. Meeker talked to me and your dad this morning about something he thought you might be interested in, instead of camp."

Mr. Meeker, was a really cool guy who taught the Youth Group at church. He was also one of the leaders at camp, and I always looked forward to going because he made it so much fun.

"Mr. Meeker knows about some underprivileged kids who live in an apartment complex in a poor part of town," Mom told me. "They don't get to go to camp or have any kind of activities all summer.

"About the only fun they have is running through the water sprinklers when it gets really hot."

"So what does that have to do with not going to camp?"

"Mr. Meeker is trying to put a group together who can spend time with the children at the complex. Like have a day camp for them: games, activities, projects for them to do. Sing some songs, things like that. Maybe you and James can do your puppet show like you do for the little kids at church."

It sounded to me like we'd already been recruited.

What a downer. I really wanted to go somewhere, even if just for a week.

Then my mom said, "Mr. Meeker has spoken to the other boys' parents. Apparently, they're trying to decide what to do."

"Patrick, I think the boys are just waiting to see what you're going to do." My dad thinks I have a lot of influence over our bunch, like I'm their leader or something. I don't know where he came up with an idea like that. They just seem to like my ideas for stuff to do.

"You boys could do a lot of good, son, giving those kids a bright spot in their summer, maybe something that would have an impact on them for a long time."

My mom and dad were totally on board with this whole idea and the more I thought about it, the more I thought it might not be too bad. The guys and I had been going to church camp together since we were in fifth grade and it was pretty much the same every year. It was lots of fun, a great learning experience, and probably the reason we were all so tight. But maybe it was time we started thinking about helping others.

"Let me check with the guys," I told my parents, and began texting with them. Within a few minutes, we had all agreed. This day camp thing—we'd still be all together, every day for a week. We might even have some fun with those kids. It turned out to be better than I thought.

We got together with Mr. Meeker the next day.

"You boys have a special opportunity with this project," Mr. Meeker told us. "Some of these kids have never been to school. Some don't speak English, and if they do, not very well. They need some help to get them ready to enter school."

There were kids who had never been to school? I had a hard time with that one until Mr. Meeker explained that their entire village had been relocated from their country to ours and they had to learn a whole new culture they hardly knew anything about.

"There will be teachers, adult volunteers from the church, leading the educational part of the camp. For adults as well as the children. You boys will help them out and interact with the kids there, let them hear you speak English, stuff like that."

This is going to be a big responsibility. But I liked Mr. Meeker and if he thought we were up to it, then I was willing to help out. The guys and I spent the week making our plans with the help of our teacher, getting things ready for the next week. The following Monday, Mr. Meeker picked us up that morning in the church van and took us to the apartment complex where we set up the activities and puppet shows for the kids. Someone brought lunch for us and the kids, and in the afternoon we played games with them.

There was this one little guy who latched onto us the minute we got out of the van. His name was hard to pronounce so we just called him the closest thing we could get to it—Jimjoe. He was seven years old, but so small he looked like a four-year-old. He caught on to English really well and was a terror playing soccer. He loved the puppet shows and asked us every day if we would be back the next day.

When our last day came, he didn't cry but he did have big tears in his eyes. I'd heard people say they didn't know who got more out of something, but I never knew what they meant until I spent time with those kids. Especially Jimjoe. We really did have a great time.

Our focus was on the day camp, but now and then I thought about the rockets, the mound and the graves. I had to find some time to get back to investigating the graves.

CHAPTER NINE

Our summer was flying by much too fast for me. We had less than a month before school registration, and we still hadn't seen the pictures from the rocket. As it turned out, because it was so old, the film had to be taken to a special shop to be developed. It still wasn't ready by the end of day camp.

We didn't have that much time left to shoot more rockets and we were getting antsy to shoot at least one more as soon as possible. Max was up for it, he just didn't want to go back over to the mound. Boy, talk about things hanging on. He wasn't getting over it, and he wasn't talking about it. Not to me anyway. I got the idea that he might be talking some to Jeremy, but Jeremy wasn't saying anything either. Max was beginning to act like his old self and, since he kept steering us away from going anywhere near the mound, we had to come up with another idea for where we could launch the next rocket.

We met at my house, as usual, when we had something to plan. We sat out on the curb and Max told us what he had in mind. "There's that field up the street from here where they're getting ready to build."

I knew exactly where he was talking about.

"Everything has been bulldozed and cleared off and there's no building going on yet. Nothing," Max told us. He added, "And, hardly any grass or anything that could catch fire,"

We all thought that would work great and wanted to know when we could start.

"But listen, guys." Max had more to say. "Jeremy was telling me about something else we could do, like put other stuff with a parachute attached *inside* the rocket before we launch it. It'll release and the parachute and whatever else is inside will come down."

"But isn't that what we did with the camera?" *What was different?*

"Not exactly," Jeremy said. "The camera and housing were on the outside of the rocket.

Max was grinning really big now. He was up to something. He nudged Jeremy. "Tell them Jeremy."

"Yes, do tell us," I said. "You two look like you're up to something. C'mon, tell us what's going on."

"Nothing, really." Jeremy said, looking at Max. He got a really goofy grin on his face, too, as he and Max snorted at some secret.

"You gotta tell them," Max urged. "They have to hear this."

"Okay. Okay." He hitched forward on the curb. "Well, see, my Uncle Denver, the one who gave me the rockets, told me about this time when he was a kid and he and some friends

shot off this rocket. They were really into playing war and soldier and stuff. They had some old fatigues that had belonged
to their dads or uncles, somebody. Anyway, they'd put them
on, take their BB guns and air rifles, and go out in the fields
behind my uncle's house and play war up in the hills."

"Sort of like when we made up like zombies for our video,"
Max pitched in.

"Right. So anyway, they had a neighbor down the road, a
Mr. Pogue, who was sort of paranoid. He thought everyone
was out to overthrow the government, didn't trust anyone,
thought everybody was out to get him. He was something like
a survivalist too, and had 'No Trespassing' signs all over his
property. A real whacko. And, he was nearsighted.

"So, my uncle and his friends were out playing one day,
wearing their fatigues and army gear and stuff, and they put
this toy soldier–parachute and everything–*inside* a rocket
and set it off. It goes up, the nose cone pops off and it was like
the soldier ejected and came floating down. The guys started
running across the field, pretending they were going to capture an invader when they heard a shotgun and some pellets
whizzing near them."

We all gasped.

"Mr. Pogue had been in his yard and saw the rocket, but,
without his glasses on, couldn't see clear enough to tell that it
or the parachute and soldier were toys. By the time he ran in
his house and got his glasses and binoculars, and his shotgun,
the rocket and soldier had landed. But what Mr. Pogue did
see, or what he *thought* he saw, when he looked through the

glasses was a bunch of guys in camouflage, carrying weapons. He thought the country was being invaded!"

"Oh, my gosh!" I looked at James and Brendan. Their eyes bugged, mouths gaping.

Jeremy and Max doubled over laughing.

"Wait a minute," James said at that point. "You're kidding. You're pulling our leg, right?"

"Nope."

"This guy really shot at your uncle?" I couldn't believe it. "Was anyone hurt?"

"Oh, he shot at them all right. He missed, but Uncle Denver said he couldn't sit down for a week after that. Neither could his friends."

"Huh? I thought you said the guy didn't shoot anyone, that no one was hurt."

"He didn't. Their folks 'tanned their hides,' as he put it."

"Whoa. That's rough." Brendan let out a big breath.

"It's the way they did things back then, Brendan," Jeremy said. "There was no being sent to their rooms, or put on restriction, stuff like they do today. Uncle Denver figured they got off easy. He admitted he and his friends got in trouble a couple of times with Mr. Pogue before, raiding his watermelon patch and apple trees."

"So then what happened to Mr. Pogue?"

"After the guys apologized—"

"Whoa! Hold on just a minute. *They* had to apologize?"

"Yep. That's another thing they did back then, Patrick. And I seem to remember us having to do some apologizing ourselves not so long ago."

I knew exactly what Jeremy was talking about, but I didn't remember anyone being with me when my dad made me apologize to Mr. Nelson for us messing with his cow. I chose to let it pass, I was more interested in hearing the rest of the story. "Okay, so then what happened?"

"Everyone agreed to keep their distance from each other. The boys would stay clear of Mr. Pogue's property and, after the dads had a private talk with him, he agreed he'd try and be less suspicious and more tolerant—and keep his shotgun locked up."

Jeremy and Max were still looking at each and sniggering. Even James and Brendan had goofy grins. *For crying out loud!* I decided they had all gone nuts.

"So this is your idea?" I said, flabbergasted. "You want us to find some psychopathic, nearsighted, crazy old geezer, and get ourselves shot at! I guess you want us to get our hides tanned too?"

That brought on more spasms of laughter from all four of them.

When they calmed down a little I said, "Will someone tell me what's so funny? And what has all this got to do with us shooting another rocket? With something inside?"

"Oh, not a whole lot, I guess," Max answered. "I just thought it was a really cool story. Jeremy said he hadn't told you guys yet and I wanted him to tell you before we talked about my idea."

There was more? Might as well sit back and find out what they'd come up with this time.

It might have been the craziest thing they'd thought of yet.

"Well, remember Sweet Beulah . . ." It hit me then why we didn't go to Max's house. The rest of us couldn't stand snakes. Sweet Beulah, a really ugly albino boa, was Max's pet and he was always getting her out of her cage and wanting us to hold it and stuff. Bleckalala. I shuddered just thinking about it. I had to concentrate and clear my head to follow what else he was saying.

". . . and I just got some mice for Sweet Beulah."

Yuk. I'd seen Max feed that snake once and never wanted to witness that again. That's all I needed. As if snakes weren't bad enough, just throw in a couple of mice. Made my stomach heave just thinking about it. Why were we talking about this anyway? Could we just go on to some other topic? Get back on track, and rockets.

"I figured we can rig up some kind of a harness for one of the mice, attach it to the parachute, and put it into the rocket," Max was saying. "The rocket will go up, the mouse will eject with the parachute and we can watch it come back down."

I could tell by the look on Jeremy's face that he and Max had cooked this up together.

"He's kidding, right?" James asked me, shaking his head.

"I don't think so, James," Brendan said. "Patrick?"

"I think he's dead serious."

"But what if something goes wrong?"

"Well, that mouse was dinner for Sweet Beulah, anyway."

I wasn't really sure what I thought about the idea, but when he put it that way, it did make sense. Sort of. Heartless as it sounded, that mouse was toast either way. So we agreed and began work on a design for a harness for the mouse.

When everything was ready, we met in the field of the construction site a couple of days later. Jeremy had all the rocket gear, Max brought the mouse in a pocket of his backpack. We'd put together what we thought was a pretty good harness but when it came time to test it out, the mouse was having none of it. I wasn't having anything to do with it either, satisfied to let Max do the honors.

The others were more than happy to leave it up to Max to get the mouse in the harness, too. He had to work at it. Most people think that mice don't have skeletons, but they do, they're just very, very flexible and this one kept wriggling out of the rig. Finally, Max cinched it on the best he could, attached the parachute and wound it with the cords around the mouse's tail.

The opening at the end of the long tube of the fuselage must have looked like a safe dark place to get away and hide because Max had barely relaxed his hold on the mouse when it made a break for it and darted inside.

"Well, I didn't expect that," Max said, "but now I don't have to figure out how to get it in there." He quickly placed the packing in behind the mouse before it had a chance to change its mind and come back out. He handed the rocket off to Jeremy and he sealed it. We were ready to shoot the rocket.

I wasn't sure how I felt about the whole thing. I figured the mouse had a pretty good chance of coming out of the launch alive and kicking, at least a better one than the alternative. But it was creepy to think about. One thing for sure, we'd better get the show on the road or the thing might suffocate before we ever got the rocket off the ground. Although, if it did suffocate, then at least it wouldn't end up a meal for Sweet Beulah. Snakes only eat live prey.

Everything was ready to go and we went through the launch process. With the usual 'swoosh' the rocket headed skyward. We were able to track its ascent by the contrail it left behind, and binoculars helped us spot when the mouse and parachute ejected.

We watched as air filled the parachute, and there was the mouse dangling from the harness beneath. Before they made it half way down, we could see the mouse's legs pawing at empty air.

"Hey, look at that," Max cried. "That thing is running in mid-air!"

I'd never seen anything like it. The mouse's legs were pumping like its life depended on it—well, I guess it actually did—before it ever hit the ground. It was wild, and we were laughing like crazy.

It was coming down within a few yards of where we stood and we hurried over to recover it as soon as it touched down. The mouse scurried to get away the minute it felt solid ground under its feet, running first one direction then another, like it was disoriented. After the trip it had just had, who could blame it?

Max scooped it up before it had a chance to escape. The parachute still trailed behind it so I didn't think it could have gotten very far. At least it would have been easy to track.

Max and Jeremy were together, checking everything out, then Max told us, "Everything looks like it's all still together." He hesitated a minute, just watching the mouse. Jeremy said something to him that I couldn't hear. Then Max looked at us and said, "So, what do you say, guys? Do I take it home to Beulah or do we send it up again?"

"Send it up again? How are we going to do that?" James asked. "I thought the rocket was a one shot deal." He looked at me and raised an eyebrow as if he was looking to me to make a decision. He was looking the wrong direction. I still didn't have my head around what had just happened.

"Not a problem," Jeremy announced, and pulled another rocket from his backpack. "After some of our other shots, I decided to always come prepared with a backup."

It must have been our dumbfounded silence that Max and Jeremy took as our agreement and approval, because before James, Brendan or I could get a word out, Jeremy was holding the cylinder so Max could get the mouse inside for another round.

But, if they thought it was rough getting the mouse in the harness, getting it into that tube was even trickier. The mouse took one look at where he was headed and, as if he had figured out this was no safe dark place, he began to squirm, trying to get out of Max's hand. I think at that point, if it could have figured out how to, it would have spread all four legs, latched its toes to the rim of the mouth to the opening and hung on for dear life. As it was, Max was too quick and had it inside, stuffing the packing in behind it again.

"Hey, Jeremy, we need some more wadding.

"That's all there is."

"So? What're we gonna do?"

"I think it'll be all right. Should be enough." Jeremy held the engine plate, ready to seal the end of the rocket for launch.

"Are you sure?"

"It'll just fire a little hotter . . . I think." Jeremy attached the plate, gave it a twist, hooked the fuses up, and headed toward the launch pad.

Stunned by their decision to put the mouse back up, I watched all their movements like some kind of goob.

James and Brendan were just as dazed as I was, I could tell, because they looked like goobs too. Like mindless robots, we followed Jeremy and Max to the pad where Jeremy had the fuse ready to ignite and begin the countdown.

Then it suddenly registered in my mind what Jeremy had said, and imagining fried rodent, I finally found my voice. "What do you mean it'll just fire a little hot?"

"ONE," Max cried and Jeremy pushed the ignition switch.

I didn't even have time to yell WAIT!

The rocket streaked upward, the cone popped off and the parachute and the mouse floated down. Only this time, the mouse was swinging by its tail. It had wiggled out of the harness and luckily had gotten tangled in the cords. Otherwise, it would be heading down a lot faster to a huge SPLAT.

Like before, the mouse's feet were going ninety miles a minute, trying to find traction, and only gripping empty space. It *was* pretty comical, I had to admit, and couldn't help but chuckle.

Before it hit the ground, I understood what Jeremy had meant by the rocket firing hotter. The parachute was clearly scorched. Since the mouse's feet were already moving at high speed, it started running as soon as it got footing. Max lunged after it.

"MAX! Stop!" Brendan, James and I yelled at the same time.

"Let it go," I said.

Max stopped, looking down at the tattered parachute in his hand. The mouse had managed to slither out of the harness and it had slipped off the mouse's tail. Max turned and looked at us then turned to see the mouse making a break for it. He didn't know what to do, which way to go. He looked at Jeremy, who nodded his head.

"Let it go, Max," Jeremy said.

"Yeah, Max," I said. "It's earned its freedom."

He stood up, the parachute dangling from his hand. We all watched the mouse scurry from one cluster of weeds to the next as it raced toward the underbrush and freedom. The last we saw of the mouse was its slightly sooty butt.

CHAPTER TEN

Even after it was clear we probably weren't going to see the mouse again, we watched for a while anyway. But he'd made his break and wasn't coming back. He just might have had a heart attack and died if he'd seen us again. I smiled, knowing, even after what he'd been through, at least he wasn't going to be dinner for Sweet Beulah. Now, all he had to do was avoid being swooped down on by an owl or a hawk, or serving as a snack for a coyote.

Max helped pick up the gear and Jeremy stashed it in his backpack. I had mine over my shoulder and looked around to see if everyone else was ready to head for home. No one said anything as we turned to leave. What was there to say? If they were like me, they were still trying to sort out what had just happened. We'd done what we came to do, and it was way more than I could have imagined.

Now it was time to leave. Max and Jeremy walked ahead, I was a few steps behind, with James and Brendan bringing up the rear as we walked from the field.

I was lost in my own thoughts and had just taken a big swig of water when I heard a snort from Brendan, followed by one from James. I looked around just as Brendan wiggled the fingers of one hand toward James, imitating the mouse's feet as it 'ran through the air.' James wiggled his fingers back at Brendan. Their faces were bright red from trying to keep from laughing out loud.

The image of the mouse and how it had looked swinging from the parachute flashed through my mind and, before I could stop it, water spewed out of my mouth and nose. Brendan and James took one look at me and doubled over, hee-hawing like a couple of donkeys.

Max and Jeremy looked around to see what was going on. It didn't take long until we were all on our backs on the ground, our arms and legs sawing at the air acting out the mouse's movements and laughing until we were out of breath.

We didn't have any plans to shoot off any more rockets in the near future. What we'd just experienced would be pretty hard to top.

The rest of the week got kind of crazy around our house. Taylor was coming home in ten days and you'd have thought my mom was expecting the Queen of England instead of my sister. It was like she had gotten all spacey about it. She decided to do a total makeover on Taylor's room. Knowing my sister, I wasn't sure she'd appreciate it. Her tastes and my mom's sometimes clashed. And besides, what was the sense of redoing her room when she was just going to be going off to college not long after she got home. Nuts, right?

My dad got my mom to at least wait until Taylor got home. Good move, Dad. Although, it didn't keep Mom from going to the grocery store and buying all of Taylor's favorite foods, every snack she liked, any treat she had ever asked for.

At first, all the attention my sister was getting really got to me. She wasn't even here, for crying out loud. Then I thought about all the stuff Mom kept bringing home and I figured if I played my cards right, I'd be eating pretty good for a while.

I didn't make a big deal out of it, but I was glad Taylor was coming home. No way was I going to admit I had missed her. But I had. It was going to be great having her around again. And, I'd have a ride again. I couldn't wait to tell her about the mound, and the rockets, and especially about the Flight of the Mouse. She would love that one.

Then there was a storm of house cleaning. I even had to sweep corners of the ceilings in my room in case there *might* be any cobwebs. Like, my sister was even going to notice. Did mom even remember how Taylor's room had looked before she went to England? I was sure a few months in the UK hadn't changed that about her. But when my mother got her cleaning hat on — same thing happened when company came to visit too — it was just best to take the broom and the dust pan, and hunker down, and expect half of your stuff to disappear. And keep repeating, "It will all be over soon. It will all be over soon."

Thank goodness that happened the minute Taylor un-packed her bags. She'd brought gifts for each of us, even our dog Pinto, and we opened them and 'oohed' and 'aahed' over heaping helpings of Mac and cheese and chocolate pudding, my sister's favorites.

It was days before I got to spend any time with Taylor. She and mom chattered non-stop about merry old England and Brett, Pam, the kids, and plans for school. And would you believe it . . . she wanted a total makeover of her room! Mom was downright giddy but, honestly? Taylor was going to be off at school before the paint even dried.

"Hey, Patty!" I heard my sister calling me, but I just ignored her. She knew how it irritated me when she called me that. I told her every time she did it, but she just kept right on. She'd done it since we were little kids, and thought it was cute. I did *not*.

Besides, Taylor had been too busy for me since she'd been home so I decided I didn't have time to answer her. Even when she knocked on my door.

The door opened just a little and I could see her peeking through the sliver of space. She pushed it a little farther and stuck her face through the opening. "Patrick, buddy, want to go get some yogurt?"

How could I stay sore with an offer like that on the table? We took the long way to our favorite frozen yogurt place, and

I started at the beginning of when we shot off out first rocket. Taylor laughed so hard she was gasping for breath by the time we got to the yogurt place. But I saved the part about the mouse until last. After we got our yogurt.

My sister hadn't had any of our favorite treat all the time she was at Brett's so she took the largest cup they had. The big cup was standard for me. I *always* got the big cup.

We heaped our favorite flavors of yogurt into the paper containers and piled them high with toppings . . . anything chocolate, sprinkles and our favorite . . . gummy worms. Taylor had chowed down about half way through her bowl when I got to the first mouse launch. Her jaw dropped and a yogurt coated gummy worm she was chewing on fell out of her mouth.

"Patrick! You didn't!" Red faced, she looked around to see if anyone had heard her. She grabbed some napkins and wiped her chin then started cleaning up some yogurt that had splattered on the table. I waited to finish my story.

Taylor's eyes got bigger and bigger as I told about the second rodent launch. Then . . . "OH MY GOSH!"

This time *everyone* in the place turned to look at her. That made the story even better. "Patrick Michael Morrison," she hissed across the table. "I do not believe you guys. Are you ever going to grow up?"

That burned. I thought she'd think it was funny. What had happened to my sister? She sat up straight in her chair, acting all prim and proper, like the subject of the mouse was closed. She spooned up another bite of yogurt and put it in her mouth. I leaned back, watching her, and put my hands on the top of the table to think about this unexpected turn of events.

Then, I couldn't help myself, the timing was just too good. I began to wiggle my fingers like the guys and I had done when we imitated the mouse. I skittered them across the table toward her.

I thought Taylor was going to choke on her yogurt. She pressed her lips together and grabbed for a napkin. Too late. Clown colored sprinkles shot out of her mouth and landed all over the table . . . and me. We had everyone's attention again. I couldn't help it, I was cracking up.

Taylor calmly stood up, picked up her purse and what was left of her bowl of yogurt. You'd have thought my sister was the Queen of England herself the way she walked out of that place. I thought I'd really done it. I just knew my sister would never get over this one. I didn't have another way home so I followed her to the car, knowing I was going to get chewed on all the way to the house. I opened the car door and slid into the passenger seat, daring to sneak a look at Taylor and expecting her to be madder than I'd ever seen her.

She threw her head back and laughed like crazy. Between bursts of laughter, she said, "We have got to Skype with Brett. You have got to tell him!"

Yep. My sister was really home. I could relax and fill her in on the mound and the tombstones. There was so much more to tell her. We talked for a long time after we got home.

CHAPTER ELEVEN

So what is it about females that makes them get totally air-brained about shopping? There were only a couple of weeks before school orientation and I figured Taylor would be getting ready to leave for college soon, too. I must have missed the bulletin, but I didn't take much time to really think about it because Mom and Taylor decided I needed a new school wardrobe.

"Patrick, you're going to be a Sophomore in high school now," Mom said.

"You really should have new clothes," Taylor added.

I thought it was just a good reason for them to go shopping. But did they have to include me? Unfortunately, they didn't ask my opinion.

I tried every excuse I could think of to get out of it: I didn't feel good; I had to mow lawns. I was so desperate, I even said maybe I needed to work on the garage. Nothing worked. I was stuck . . . in the back seat with Grammy. In the front, Mom and Taylor yakked away from mall to mall.

They all told me how sweet I was for carrying all the shopping bags. Gag. There was no justice in it all. The only thing that made the day bearable at all was when we ran into Jeremy and his mother at one of the stores Taylor insisted we *just had* to go to. She promised it would be our very last store.

Jeremy took one look at me and rolled his eyes. Then he winked and nodded toward a table piled high with T-Shirts. We headed for it and each picked up one. Exactly alike.

"Ooh, love it," Jeremy fake gushed. "Don't you, Patrick?"

"Love it, love it, love it," I agreed, trying to sound girly, like Taylor, as best I could. I winked at Jeremy and turned to my mom. "Can I have it? Please?"

Jeremy did the same with his mom. I mean, really? How could any mom not get matching shirts for their *little boys*?

Taylor eyed me like she wasn't buying our performance, but it didn't matter. Mom and Grammy were already at check out. Mrs. Wilson was in line right behind them. Jeremy and I took our shopping bags and skipped out of the store. Once outside, we cracked up and gave each other a high five. I was so glad to be out of that mall and done with shopping.

From the conversation they were having when we got home, it sounded like Taylor was going to talk Mom into another trip to the mall for shoes. No matter how much I protested. Come on. There was a limit to the torture, after all.

Rescue came with a call from Mr. Meeker.

My mom answered when the phone rang. She talked for a minute or two then called, "Patrick?"

My youth leader wanted to know if me and the guys were up to spending a few days with the kids we'd helped in day camp. I jumped at the chance. I didn't even care if my friends weren't up for it. It was a perfect excuse to not have to go shopping any more. But the truth was, I actually looked forward to seeing some of those kids again. Especially Jimjoe.

It took only about an hour to put a schedule and material together. We were ready when Mr. Meeker came by to pick us up the next morning. When we pulled up into the parking lot at the apartment complex, a gang of faces with big grins greeted us. I spotted Jimjoe first thing. We fell into the routine quickly: lessons, lunch, games and activities. Time to go home came faster than I could imagine. We said goodbye and promised to be back the next day. They had been practicing and studying and were doing really great. Some of the kids would need an interpreter when they got to class, but for the most part, they were ready to go. Especially Jimjoe. He wasn't as upset this time when we said goodbye.

The camp only lasted three days that time, and on the last day, when we went by Jeremy's to pick up him and Max, Jeremy got in the van with a grin on his face and an envelope from the photo shop in his hand. Max didn't look quite so thrilled.

"Is that the photos from the rocket?" I said, pointing to the package in Jeremy's hand. I couldn't believe we were finally going to see the pictures. The process to get them developed had taken much longer than we thought it would.

"Finally!" James grabbed for the packet, but Jeremy held them out of his reach.

"Hey, let's wait, okay?" Jeremy glanced at Max who acted as if he didn't have any interest in the pictures. "Maybe at lunch—"

"Lunch!" Brendan squawked. "You know we'll never get a chance at lunch. The kids will be all over us. Besides, why do we have to wait?"

Jeremy glanced at Max again. He was looking out the window, pretending he was totally into something outside the car. Yeah, right. I was sure something was going on.

"You're probably right, Brendan," Jeremy said as he opened his backpack and put the envelope inside. "Maybe we should just wait until we get through today. We'll have more time to get a good look after we get home."

End of discussion? When did Jeremy get to be in charge? Then I remembered that it *was* his rocket and camera, after all. Plus, he'd been the one to have the film developed.

But there was definitely something going on here, and I was ready to get to the bottom of it as much as I was to see the pictures. I figured Jeremy had already looked at the pictures, and I'd have bet anything that Max had too by the way he was acting.

Before I could say anything, Mr. Meeker was parking the van and it was time to get started with day camp. To be honest, my mind just wasn't in it that day. It was on what was in Jeremy's backpack.

When we finished for the day and headed home, I told Mr. Meeker, "You can just drop us all at my house."

I didn't even ask the others if it was all right with them. I wasn't going to wait another minute to see those pictures, and I didn't think Brendan was in a mood to wait either. I figured James would go along with whatever we did, and Max would just have to do the same. We piled out of the van and told Mr. Meeker goodbye. As soon as he drove up the street, Brendan put his hand out. "Okay, Jer, old boy, let's see those pictures."

Jeremy looked at Max. *What the heck is going on?*

"Let's sit on the curb, okay?" Max said and walked over to the place in the cul-de-sac where we always talked about things. "But I warn you . . ."

Max has a way of being overly dramatic, we always figure that's just Max. But this was different. I couldn't put my finger on it . . . just *different*.

And my interest in what was in that envelope zoomed about a gazillion percent. Then Max said something that pushed my curiosity totally into warp speed.

"First let me tell you about the tombstone."

CHAPTER TWELVE

There it was again, Max said tomb*stone*, like in *one*. The same way he'd said it right after we'd shot up the rocket with the camera. Those weird prickly things were running up the back of my neck again, and I was trying to keep my imagination from frying my brain.

I sat on the curb with everyone and hung onto every word Max said. "So, you guys remember when we lost the rocket and the camera? And we found the grave yard?"

Heads bobbed up and down with each question, but no one said a word. Max had acted so wacko at the mound that day, and would never say a word about what happened I sure didn't want him to stop now. He was finally going to tell us what spooked him so bad. This had the makings of something good. After all, he had "warned" us.

"Okay, so," he went on, ". . . remember when we spread out to see if there were any more markers, more graves?"

More head nodding and "um-huhs" and "yeahs."

"Well, I found some away off from the first ones you found."
Max looked around at us.

I think this is called "pausing for dramatic effect." Now,
that was more like our buddy Max.

"And there was this *one*."

"And this is important because. . . ?" Brendan never had
any patience with the way Max dragged things out and got all
excited and way over the top about almost everything.

The Max we knew normally would have gotten upset and
glared at anyone interrupting him, but he surprised us by
staying calm as he went on. "A name was real clear on one."
He stopped and swallowed hard, looked at Jeremy then down
at the ground.

Hey, was he going to cry?

"Go on, Max," Jeremy said, "you gotta tell them."

"Come on, Max, out with it," I said. The suspense and drama were killing me.

He looked up at me then. "You're not going to like it."

There went the creepy-crawlers up the back of my neck
again. Goose bumps raised up around the hairs on my arms.
"Out with it."

"It was the *name* on the headstone. That's part of what got
to me."

"Okay. So?" Would he just get on with it, for crying out
loud. "What was it?"

Max picked up a stick and began to write in the sand that
had piled up in the gutter.

Man, oh man. This guy had a future in the movies or some-thing. James leaned over me and Brendan got up and stood behind us so we could see what Max was writing.

Etched in the sand was : F - E - U - R – E - Y.

When he was finished, we sounded out the word. Feurey . . . *Fury.*

A deep growl started in Brendan's throat and he spun around, kicking at the dirt and gravel. "Arrgh!"

James and I looked at each other, our mouths hanging open. Had Max honestly expected us to fall for that, again?

Back before school was out in the spring, we'd gone into a drainage culvert and discovered something we couldn't ex-plain. We finally were able to solve the mystery of what it was and how it got there, but while we were searching for an an-swer, Max told us this wild story his grandfather had passed along to him; a legend about the ghost of a giant, crazy ren-egade Indian called Fury. Max was convinced the story was real and the answer we were looking for. And he kept try-ing to sell the same old story over and over. Was he serious? Feurey?

"Come on, Max," I barked at him. "Again? Get real!"

"Told you, you weren't going to like it."

"Well, can you blame us?"

"I'm just telling you what I saw."

"And I'm telling you, I'd have to see it for myself." I couldn't believe this guy.

"Fine. That doesn't change what I saw."

"So, this is what I think," I started."You get scared around a bunch of old tombstones and take off. Then you don't want to admit you're scared so you try to think how to fix it so we won't give you a hard time." Max was watching me pace back and forth as I talked. "Then, while we're worrying about you because you won't share with us what's bugging you, you spend all the time trying to come up with a really good story. And decide to drag out that stupid old Indian ghost story?"

"That's not the way it is at all. I knew how you felt about that and I knew how you'd react, but I really just wanted you guys to see it."

I was so ticked, I wasn't even listening to him. "Well, hah, hah, Max. You got us real good. Okay? So, why aren't you laughing?"

He didn't look happy, like he was going to laugh or something. In fact, he looked pretty gloomy, but I was too upset to care. I stood up and jammed my hands into my pockets. James or Brendan hadn't said a word so far. I motioned toward Max, stammering, trying to get some help from them. "So? Are you okay with this? Aren't you going to say anything?"

James just shrugged and, in his best Texas drawl, said, "Naw. You're doing a right fine job, as I see it, pardner."

Jeremy poked Max with his elbow and said, "Go on. Tell them the rest."

Max turned white as a sheet.

"The rest of what?" I demanded to know.

"Just give him a minute, will you, Patrick?"

I stopped my pacing and looked at Max . . . and Jeremy. They were being very quiet. Unusually quiet. Wait just a minute, I thought. Jeremy had gone after Max when he ran from the graveyard that day. They'd stopped talking when we caught up to them.

"That's what you guys were talking about when we caught up to you in the field that day, isn't it?" I asked Jeremy, accusingly. "He told you about this *Feurey* stuff then, didn't he?"

"Yes."

"You've known all along?" I couldn't believe Jeremy could have kept something like that from the rest of us.

"Look, guys," Max said, finally finding his tongue. "Seeing the tombstone like that . . . yeah, it shook me up a little. It made me nervous, but I figured it had to be some crazy coincidence. Like I said, I knew how you guys felt about that Fury story Grandpa told me, but I still wanted to see what you thought about it. Even if you all got mad at me, I was just about to call you over to check it out. But before I could yell, something ran behind me." He stopped and took a deep shaky breath before going on. "I turned around to see what it was . . . and *that's* when I got scared and decided to get the heck out of Dodge."

"Will you just spit it out, Max," Brendan said. "What you're saying is that you weren't afraid because of the graves or that tombstone, but some critter running through the brush freaked you out?"

"It wasn't a critter."

"Honestly, Max . . ."

Max jumped to his feet and got right up in Brendan's face. "It looked like a man! Okay?"

Whoa, now that was a new one: First Jeremy facing up to Jeremy, now Max facing off with Brendan. I'd have to think about this later, though. Right then, Max was going on with his tale.

"He was running really fast and I only barely got a look at his back. But he would have had to have been *right there–*," Max pointed his finger, stabbing toward the ground next to his foot. "I mean, like right there, that close to me And I'm telling you, I never even saw him. He tore through the brush like it wasn't even there, and then he was gone, like he just . . . vanished."

Max had let his crazy imagination get the best of him again, but, I had to admit, for a second, I got a few goose bumps. He could come up with some really good stories. He was so good at it, there were times I wondered how we might put that little talent to use.

Brendan and James looked like they weren't buying the whole tale either. It was just another one of Max's *things*.

"All right, okay, whatever. But what does that stupid story have to do with anything?" I demanded, pointing to the envelope he held, wanting some answers. "With those?"

Max turned to Jeremy. "I told you they'd think it was stupid."

"Take a look," Jeremy said and handed the envelope to me.

James and Brendan looked over my shoulder as we scanned the pictures. They were blurry, but we were definitely seeing tree tops and what had to be the tombstones in the graveyard.

Finally seeing actual pictures from the rocket got me pretty excited then, and I forgot about Max's story and calmed down a little. "These are great, guys! We did it, got pictures from the rocket." I looked from Jeremy and Max around to James and Brendan. "But I still don't see—"

"Keep going," Jeremy said.

I looked up at him then did as he said. I flipped through a couple more pictures and there were the tombstones just like Max described, several yards from the first ones we found. I looked at Jeremy and was just about to ask, "So there's more grave markers, what's the big deal?" but stopped when I turned to the next shot. And kept flipping. There was nothing but a bright blur in the middle of all the rest of the pictures.

Aw, no. After all that work and then waiting forever for the pictures, for the most part the bunch of them were ruined. What a hack.

Jeremy and Max were watching us when I looked up. Jeremy said, "Well?"

I fanned through the pictures quickly looking at them again then looked back at Jeremy and Max. "What?"

"Don't you see it?" They stood up and Max pointed to the last four pictures I held in my hand.

"Maybe if I knew what I'm supposed to be looking for.

Looks to me like a bunch of ruined film." I checked them out again. Nothing.

"Hey, wait a minute," Brendan said, taking a couple pictures with the bright burst of light out of my hand for a closer look. He looked at them like it was his first time to see them. "Oh, my gosh," he said and grabbed the others and shuffled them like he was comparing them. After he'd done that about a dozen times he looked from Max to Jeremy and back at the pictures. "Oh, my gosh."

"I know, right?" Max nodded with a kind of sickly grin.

"What?" Now they were really messing with me.

Brendan held the pictures and looked at me like he'd just seen a . . .

I backed away from them. *Nope. No way. I am not going there. Not happening.*

If it had been anybody but Brendan I wouldn't even have taken another look at the pictures, just let it go. Plus, I knew he would never get on board with any of Max's weirdo ideas. But because it was Brendan, I took another look.

James and I scanned the pictures together, and I barely heard him go, "Ooh." When I turned to look at him, I noticed he was looking sort of greenish too. He grabbed the pictures and placed one of them in my left hand, one in my right, and pushed my hands together so the pictures were end to end. He handed a couple to Brendan and they butted them up to the ones I held so that we saw them like one long slow-motion action shot.

It was blurry, more like a shadow, and I'd missed it—we'd all missed it at first—but there was no doubt about it. *Something* was running through, or out of, the burst of light in the middle of the pictures into the next frame and so on.

Remembering what Max said about the name on the tombstone, for a fraction of a second, I imagined something big with long flowing hair and moccasins, bare chest, buckskins and Indian beads.

Talk about prickly chilly-willys.

"Max, I don't know what to say."

"Well, I'm not going to say Granpa was right. And I'm not saying there's an Indian ghost running around here. But I know what I saw on that tombstone. And you all have seen those pictures. So you tell me."

"I don't know what's going on but I'd say we have a mystery on our hands and I, for one, plan to get to the bottom of it," I said.

CHAPTER THIRTEEN

We sat on the curb passing the pictures back and forth, looking at and studying them. I was seriously trying to make sense of what was going on.

At last, I said, "Okay, so do we believe in ghosts, or not?"

"I don't," Jeremy was quick to answer.

"Nah," James put in.

"Nope," Brendan said.

"Me neither," said Max.

"What?" I didn't believe what I was hearing. "Max, a few months ago you were trying to convince us that the ghost of some deranged Indian was running around in the drainage culvert we explored."

"Okay, you're right, I guess I do."

I knew it! He hadn't changed his tune one bit.

"Come on, guys," Max continued. "Think about it. That story my grandpa told me has been around for a long time. He didn't just make it up. And there were some pretty strange things going on in that culvert, things we never did come up with an answer for. Remember? Like that noise?"

He had us there, we'd been able to come up with answers to almost everything that happened in the culvert, but there had been a noise we never did find an explanation for.

"Then, there's the tombstone with a name that *sounds* like Fury." He pointed at the pictures I held in my hand. "And now there's those.

"So, we think the woods is really a burial mound–an *Indian burial mound*. That place with the tree stumps and the fire ring? What if that is some kind of sacred place? And the spirit of Fury is angry with us 'cause we desecrated it?"

Max was turning into as good a story teller as his grandpa. But he did get our attention.

Brendan snorted. "What a load of it."

Max looked like steam might come out of his nose and ears any minute. He got right up in Brendan's face again. (He had to stand on tip-toe to do it, but there wasn't an inch between them.) "All right then, Mr. Big Sports Jock-man, what's your explanation for all the evidence?"

Brendan made that rude sound again. "Evidence? Hah! Max, it's just a bunch of coincidences you've strung together to try and prove your point."

"So what's *your* point?"

"Well, one, I don't believe in ghosts. Two, I don't believe that crazy ghost story about a crazy renegade Indian. Three, I agree with Patrick–there is a mystery here, no doubt about that. And, we need to work together to figure what's going on."

I couldn't have said it better myself.

Brendan took a step back from Max. "You going to be okay with that?" he asked Max.

Max, more in control, gave a quick nod. "For now."

When they both sat back down on the curb, I said, "So, where do we start?"

After about thirty minutes we came up with a list:

1. We decided the woods *might* be an Indian burial mound.

2. There were graves at the bottom of the mound.

3. What could we find out about the graves?

4. What about that tombstone with Feurey written on it? What did that mean?

But the biggest question of all: What exactly was it we saw in those pictures?

We had a lot of thinking to do.

But, at the moment it was time to break it up and for the guys to head home. We had a youth banquet to get ready for.

Our youth leaders at church always had a banquet to kick off the coming school year which began the middle of August. It was hard to believe we only had two weeks until we'd be back in class. Mr. Meeker decided to give special recognition to the kids who had taken part in the summer day camp, with a slide show and everything. And, he talked me into giving a speech. How did I get roped into these things?

CHAPTER FOURTEEN

The banquet wasn't so bad after all. At least I made it through my speech without losing my dinner. Actually, I had a good time. I didn't even mind wearing my new clothes until a couple of girls came up and gushed, "Oh, Patrick, how nice you look." Gack!

The highlight of the night came when Mr. Meeker surprised us by having some of the kids from the apartment complex come to the banquet. Jimjoe was with them and they sang some of the songs we'd taught them. In English. I had to admit I was proud of that little guy.

After that weekend, the guys and I had a hard time finding any way to get together. There's always a last minute rush that always seemed to happen to get everything done before school starts. Like we hadn't had any time during the summer.

When I finally got a chance to get on the computer and research burial mounds, I didn't find much. I'd have to dig deeper. But I did find out that immigrants named Feurey had come to the United States back in the 1800s. That was another thing I'd need more time to investigate. But something else was on my mind.

I'd noticed that Taylor wasn't saying much about college and, from what I could tell, it didn't look like she was doing anything to get her stuff together. I can be a little dense at times so I decided to go and talk to her about it.

Her bedroom door was open but I knocked anyway. We have a rule about that. Entry by invitation only. She was sitting on her bed with her laptop. She looked up from the screen and tilted her head to one side, letting me know it was okay to come in, then went back to whatever was on the screen.

"Hey, I was just wondering," I said, waiting by the door. "You haven't said anything about school since you've been home. No packing, nothing. So, what's the deal?"

"Plans have changed." Just like that. She didn't even look up from the laptop.

That was it? Plans have changed? Well, excuse me . . . she could *not* think I would settle for that. "Since when? What's up, Taylor?"

My sister is super smart and I knew she had been accepted to a couple schools she'd applied to. So what was going on?

"I've just decided to wait," she said, looking up at me and shrugging. "That's all."

"Wait on what?"

Oh, my gosh! A wild thought rushed into my brain. Had my dad lost his job? My mom? Were we broke? Couldn't they afford to send Taylor to college? But, hold on, wait just a minute . . . didn't she get a scholarship to one school? A tuition waiver for her first semester at another?

"Wait on what, Taylor?" I asked again.

"Patrick, just drop it, okay?" She looked back at the computer like she was totally engrossed in what was on the screen. And acting like she was Miss Queen of Something-or-Other and dismissing me from her presence.

I wasn't buying it and I was not going to leave her room until I had an answer. This was too big. You just didn't turn your back on free money for college. Not Taylor, for sure. She'd been planning for college since she started kindergarten. I closed the door then sat on the end of her bed. I stared at her until she looked up at me.

She watched me for a minute like she was trying to make up her mind about something. Then she said, "Swear you won't say a word."

Aha! I knew something was up. "Out with it."

"Well, you know how, from the time we were little, Abby and I talked about going to college together someday?"

"Yeah, I remember. But did you forget that our cousin doesn't want to come to Texas for school and you're not in favor of moving to California? As I recall you two could never agree which college, though."

"Right."

"I also remember that you have already graduated and she won't finish high school until next year."

"Right. Well, maybe."

Was it just Taylor, I wondered, or were all big sisters huge drama queens and had to drag things out forever?

"Taylor, for crying out loud, would you just tell me what's up and quit dragging this out?"

"And you are *not* going to let Mom know I told you *anything*?"

I wanted to strangle her. But, I zipped my lips, crossed my heart, and raised my hand.

"Well, you know how you guys," she said, sitting up taller, "the family, didn't go on vacation this summer?"

"Don't remind me. But what's that got to do with you and going to school?

"Will you let me finish?"

I zipped my lip again and nodded.

"So, I know Mom has told you the family might do something *special* at a later time?"

I didn't know how Disney World or white-water rafting could have anything to do with Taylor's plans for college, but I was cheering for my dream for one of those to be connected in some way and was willing to stay quiet until the Grand Plan was revealed. I was about to find out my dreams would not be coming true.

"Well, instead of everyone going to Grandmother and Papa's for Christmas this year like we usually do, we're all going to meet in Arkansas at Grandmother's old home over Fall Break!"

The 'everyone' she was talking about was my mom's family: her sister, Aunt Liz, Uncle Nathan, and our cousin Abby;

her brother, Uncle Clint, Aunt Judith, and the little darlings, Kate and Jillian. To be fair, they weren't the little pests they used to be any more so I figured it might be time to ditch the 'little darlings.' Grandmother and Papa live in Oklahoma City and the whole gang went to their house for Christmas every year. Now they'd decided to change things up? Did that mean nobody was going to Oklahoma for Christmas? My head was beginning to hurt.

Taylor had this happy face like she was expecting me to jump up and down and yell "Whoopee!" or something. Well, she had another think coming. Seriously? Grandmother's unbelievably small, out-in-the-sticks-in-the-middle-of-no-where-nothing-ever-happens home town? I'd been there a couple of times, and, believe me, it was nothing to jump up and down about. For sure it didn't deserve the kind of face Taylor was wearing.

"I don't believe it." I slapped my forehead and flopped back on her bed. "I've spent the whole summer with nothing happening but mowing lawns and cleaning the garage, thinking about all the cool places Mom and Dad might be planning to go. Hoping that eventually something special was going to happen like Mom said. Now this?"

"Patrick Michael Morrison, how can you say that?" Taylor gave me a look like I had something hanging from my nose.

I rubbed my finger under there, checked it, just in case. Then I glared at my sister while she kept talking.

"From what you've told me, you have spent *hours* of free time with your friends. You've shot off several rockets–even a real live mouse, for heaven's sake—and taken pictures from one." She paused a second to scowl at me then went on. "Which, by the way, you haven't told me how the pictures came out."

And I wasn't going to tell her now.

Let's see," she kept going, "you've explored what you think might be an Indian burial mound. Then you and your friends spent a week volunteering at a day camp for some little kids who *really* didn't have anything to do all summer. You probably made a big difference in their lives. I wouldn't call all that *nothing*, Patrick. Sounds like a pretty full summer to me."

She'd left out the tombstones, and the suspicious image in the pictures of the graveyard, and the *almost* fire. Oh, that's right . . . I never told her about that stuff.

The way Taylor put it, I suppose I'd had a busy summer. But my mother's idea and my idea of a *special* trip, or vacation, were planets—make that galaxies—apart.

"Okay, okay," I said, sitting up and facing Taylor. "I guess I have had a lot of stuff going on, but where did this whole idea of going to Arkansas and Fall Break come from? *Why* aren't you going to school now, and what has any of *this* got to do with *that*?"

"That's just it, Patrick. There's a chance Abby and I will be able to go to school together." Taylor's face was all lit up like a puppy who'd just had a double treat. "Just like we always talked about!"

"Taylor, come on . . ."

"You're right," she said, putting her hands up, palms facing me. "I'm getting ahead of myself." She took a deep breath and let it out before she went on. "Abby, Aunt Judith and Uncle Clint are coming to Arkansas so Abby can check out the university there. Well, I'm going to check it out too."

She jumped off the bed, almost dancing around the room, talking a mile a minute. "Actually, we've both checked it out, on line. So have Aunt Liz and Uncle Nathan, and Mom and Dad, so it's not like we don't know anything about the school. We do. We just want to check out some other stuff, but I'm applying, Patrick. I'm pretty sure I'll be accepted. Abby can graduate from high school early, and we can start next semester together. Only there's a couple things we have to work out first, which is part of the reason for the trip. I'll tell you about that later."

Taylor turned to look at me like she had just discovered the cure for zits, cooties and braces; all the problems of the entire universe; and that I should applaud her or something. Only for me it felt like my world was spinning out of control.

I hardly ever got mad— *really mad* —at my sister. Right then I was *really, really mad.*

"So you're saying that even though I've had a really *full* summer, and didn't get even one day of a vacation—you're telling me that this whole *special trip* over Fall Break is all about *you!*"

"It's not like that at all, Patrick."

"Sure sounds like it to me!" I was off the bed and at the door in a flash then turned back to tell my sister, "You know,

Taylor, I was glad you got to spend the summer in England with Brett, I really was. And I was glad when you came home, but, you know . . ." I had to get out of there before I started to cry like a little kid. I jerked the door open. *"This is not fair!"*

I couldn't get out of the house fast enough. I knew if I didn't leave, my sister would come after me. She'd follow me around the house, try to come in my room. I was in no mood for her explanations, no matter how good she thought they were. I did not want to be told any reasons why I should be happy.

By the time I stopped, I was on the other side of Mr. Nelson's pasture, in the open field. I found the spot where we'd launched the rockets and sat on the ground, looking at the woods. I tried concentrating on what had happened here to get my mind off Taylor and her trip.

The woods weren't just the woods anymore. It was a mound, an Indian burial mound and a graveyard. Maybe it held the answer to where the legend of Fury came from. I had lots of questions: Did it have anything to do with that tombstone with the name Feurey on it? Were the tree stumps and fire pit in the clearing at the top really a sacred meeting place? The biggest question in my mind right then was, *was it all connected in some way?*

The answers would have to come another time. I'd been gone from the house for quite a while, my parents might be wondering where I'd gone—that is, if they missed me at all. If anyone did think to look for me, they'd never imagine the field or woods. It wasn't a place I would have gone by myself before. I didn't have my cell phone with me. I was so bummed when I left the house I forgot to take it. Besides, I was getting hungry so I stood up and dusted off the seat of my pants and headed for my house.

By the time I stepped into our front yard, I'd cooled off . . . some. I was still pretty sore at my sister, and I guess at my parents, too, since they'd all been in on the Fall Break Trip. But I was going to have to figure out some way to suck it up and get through it. I still needed a way to get around, which meant I needed Taylor to drive me. When I thought about it, I decided it might just work out for me after all. I knew a secret I wasn't supposed to know, and if I played my cards right. . .

Yep, things just might be looking up.

CHAPTER FIFTEEN

All during dinner that evening, Taylor kept giving me *looks* like she was wondering if I was going to rat her out. When I asked to be excused from the table, she couldn't stand it any longer.

"Oh, Patrick," she said, smiling all sweet-like, "you want to go get some yogurt after while?"

I wasn't falling for it. I stood up and picked up my plate to take it to the kitchen. "I don't think so," I said, smiling back at her. "But thanks anyway."

My sister knows how I love frozen yogurt and will never miss a chance when someone offers to go get some. Surprise all over her face, my answer was not what she expected. "Are you sure?"

"Yeah, I'm sure." I knew she was just trying to get me out of the house and use some of her big sister logic and reasoning on me, and I wasn't ready for that. Yet. I was enjoying this way too much.

I called James and Brendan and they came over and we shot some hoops for a while. When we said goodbye, I went in the house, straight into the shower, and then to my room. And closed the door. Taylor knocked on my door, but I pretended I was asleep. She knocked again but when I didn't answer, she gave up and left me alone. I drifted off to sleep wondering how long I could keep shutting her out. Let her stew, I figured.

I slept like a baby.

The next morning, I was up early. I had three yards to mow and I wanted to get them done before it got really hot. As usual, my thoughts went to the mound, the tombstones, the pictures, and the rockets, while I followed the mower back and forth across the grass.

We'd talked about shooting up another rocket, maybe one with a digital camera. If we decided to do that, Jeremy would have to figure out how to rig one. It would take some planning. Still, it was a possibility.

No one actually said they didn't want to go back over to the mound, but no one said they did, either. The truth was, we were all still a little spooked by whatever it was we saw in the pictures, which were too closely connected with the mound and the graves and the clearing at the top.

I had to get that stuff out of my head. Then the idea hit me: Maybe what we needed was to make another video! I couldn't get Mrs. Gorley's yard mowed fast enough so I could go home, clean up and eat lunch, and call the guys.

As soon as I finished a grilled cheese sandwich and some corn chips, I took a glass of milk into the front room and sat down at the computer. I wanted to check out something before I called the guys. The information wasn't hard to find and I was on the phone in minutes.

I called James first.

"Hey, Patrick, what's up?."

"Are you up for another movie?"

"To make one? Sure. What've you got?"

"What do you think about a western? An *alien* western?"

"Sounds like it could have potential."

"So, you want to get together?"

"When?"

"Right now."

"Be right there."

"Bring your camera."

James has the camera, I have the ideas, and we all work out the details together.

I called the other guys but it would be an hour before everyone else could be at my house. But what was cool was they would *all* be able to come. When James got there I told him what I had in mind and showed him what I'd found online so far.

He looked at the site and I asked him, "You think we could do that?"

"Sure, but what for? What's your idea? Another zombie alien movie?"

The video we'd shot in the spring had been about an invasion by blood-sucking, flesh-eating zombie alien vampires. James had been behind the camera. The other guys were the aliens and I played the alien vampire hunter. I do a pretty good bush accent, like from Australia, and everyone thought it was cool and insisted I use it. I didn't know if it would work this time. I'd ask them when everyone got there.

First, I told them about the idea I'd had. "I thought we could figure out some way to use blood packs. You know, have a shoot-out of some kind and have the packs explode like we'd been shot."

I could tell from the grins on Brendan's and Jeremy's faces that they were all in, ready to start. I cut Max off before he could begin with his questions. "From what I saw online, we can get fake blood easy, and it's not expensive. We make the packs ourselves."

But Max wanted to know, "How?"

"I don't know for sure, but I have some ideas," I said, looking at the others. "I'm sure we can figure it out."

"Where are we going to make the movie this time?" Max started with the questions. No doubt he was wondering if we were going to go near the mound again. I expected the whining and complaining to come next if we didn't get ahead of him.

"We can decide where we want to shoot the scenes later, Max. But you guys have to help me come up with a good story line first."

"Are we going to do the alien zombie thing again?" Brendan asked.

"Well, remember, they *were* supposed to all be killed in the other video," I reminded him. I looked around at everyone. "But that's up to you guys."

Jeremy shrugged. "So a couple might have survived. No big deal. We can figure something out." He asked me, "You going to do your Aussie hunter character again?"

"That's what I wasn't sure about. I was thinking we could do a Western, you know, like a cowboy shoot out. But I didn't know if the accent would work."

"I like it, I think you should use it," Max said, grinning, not acting so annoying now. "Australia has cowboys too, don't they?"

"Sure, Rick," Brendan said, leaning over and punching my knee. "Do the accent."

Rick was the nickname Brendan gave me when we'd first started exploring, mostly because I wore an old floppy-brimmed hat of my dad's when we went out. I didn't mind the name, it made me feel kind of like I was Indiana Jones on an adventure or something. I ducked my head, a little embarrassed, but I was smiling inside.

"Like I said, we'll figure something out," Jeremy told us, looking around the group. "Are we the zombie aliens again?"

"What if there's another good guy?" Brendan checked in with a new idea, already plotting the story with a twist. "You know, someone else, from another place on earth, someone who had fought the aliens too. But a couple got away and he's tracking them down. They're after Rick, so the earth guys team up and work together to get rid of the aliens once and for all."

"Two good guys against two bad guys," Max said, his head bobbing up and down. "I like that."

Next was going to be the touchy part. To be honest, I figured I'd be the main character again. The guys always seemed to think since I came up with the ideas, that's the way it was. But we'd never had another good guy, another hero. I asked, "So, who's going to be the other good guy and who's going to be the aliens?"

You could have blown me off my feet with a good sneeze when Max jumped up, volunteering, "Me! Me! I want to be one of the aliens."

The others seemed as surprised as me. Then Max stopped and looked at me. "The aliens *are* the ones who get shot . . . right? They get to wear the blood packs?"

Should have known. Max wanted to wear the exploding load, to get all bloody looking.

"Yeah. I think the good guys would be the ones shooting up the aliens." I looked around. "What do you all think?"

"Maybe they could get some injuries, you know, just to make it more bloody?" James had a good point. That way there would be a real Wild West shoot-out.

"Right," Brendan chimed in. "The aliens would be dead and the heroes would be shot up, but still standing."

His idea got a thumbs-up from everyone. Now we just needed someone else to volunteer for the other characters.

Jeremy raised his hand. "I'll help Rick finish off the aliens. Brendan, is that okay with you?"

"Sure, buddy."

"So, we have a plan?" I asked.

They all nodded.

"When do we start?" James wanted to know.

"As soon as I can get the blood packs and we decide where to film. We should have the story line worked out by then."

The way things worked out, we weren't able to start filming before school started. We got our order in for the blood packs but there was a backlog; there would be a delay. That was a huge surprise. *Who else would be ordering blood packs?*

The delay gave us time to get our story lined out. Brendan and Max would be the alien zombie vampires. Brendan would be The Big Guy, the alien invader leader. After all, he was the jock of the gang. He was taller and had a lot more bulk than the rest of us.

So our story line would be that we'd taken out all of his soldiers except one . . . Max. They were out for revenge and coming after us.

The delay also gave us some time to dig around and find stuff to wear. Real grungy stuff. I'd used a bow and arrow in the last video but, since we wanted blood to explode out of the aliens' bodies, we needed guns. We made some play pistols look like old western six-shooters for me and Jeremy. We rigged up cheap plastic semi-automatic looking toys we picked up at the toy store for Brendan and Max. We were ready for a showdown.

But our showdown was going to have to wait for the fake blood to come. And for school to begin.

There was just one thing I had to do before then. I had to make peace with Taylor.

CHAPTER SIXTEEN

We wanted to start our sophomore year of high school off being cool—or at least try to be—and we'd decided we didn't want to ride our bikes like we did the year before when we were lowly freshmen. Not the first day. Fall semester began near the end of August and it was still very hot in central Texas then and we didn't want to arrive at school, brand new *sweaty* sophomores. Not cool, not cool at all.

Brendan had his license already but no car yet. He, James, and I live on the same street, only a few houses apart, and planned to ride to school together at some point. But for now, if we were going to get to school without our bikes, or walking, the three of us would have to depend on my sister to take us. That meant I had to do some major making-up with her.

I hadn't talked to her much since I'd found out the real reason behind no vacation for the summer and the plans for Fall Break. It was hard, actually, because, when it comes right down to it, Taylor is really a cool big sister and I missed hanging out with her. And it was super hard to stay mad at her. So it wasn't going to be *really hard* to get us back on good terms. All I had to do was ask her, really nice like, to go for yogurt and things were back to normal.

I couldn't believe I was actually looking forward to getting back to school. My friends and I had spent a lot of time together over the summer, but this was going to be different. Different school, different schedules, different classes, but still together every day. Maybe it had something to do with being in an air-conditioned building all day.

James and Brendan met at my house and we piled into Taylor's car. She dropped us in front of school on her way to her part time job downtown Dallas.

"Hey, Tay, thanks for the ride," I said, leaning into the open window. "It means a lot."

She smiled, reached over and tapped the back of my hand. "I know, little brother, I know. Have a great first day." She smiled and pulled away from the curb and out of the parking lot.

We shouldered our backpacks and headed for the front entrance.

"Hey, Patrick, wait up!"

I turned to see Max yelling and waving as he and Jeremy hurried to catch up with us. They lived farther from school than James, Brendan, and I but didn't ride their bikes either.

We found out as we went into the building they got one of their mothers to drop them off around the block then walked. That's what I would have done if it hadn't been for Taylor.

It felt good to be with them as we all walked through the doors together. A bunch of real cool dudes.

James and I had pretty much the same classes, as usual. Not only did we look like we could be brothers—same straight dark hair, blue eyes, and pushing six feet now—our brains worked the same. We both liked history and science and music; I was in choir, he was in band.

Brendan had always been the jock of our bunch but he did have history with us. Jeremy and Max were in the same AP math class. Max could be overly dense, (plus believe in ghosts, jeesh), but he was a whiz at math, like Jeremy, but not as smart.

The only class we all had together was science. That could turn into something very interesting. I hoped our teacher was nice. Maybe even have a sense of humor? He might need it with the five of us in one class.

He was okay. But I could tell right off there would be no slacking off in his class. He would expect a lot from us, new high school sophomores or not. My first look at the science lab and I knew we might be in trouble. There was just *so much* to experiment with! As it turned out, we didn't have time to come up with anything on our own. Mr. Barrett had really neat stuff, and he had projects already planned and a schedule to keep.

Actually, being in high school wasn't all that different than the year before. Only different location, different building. It took most of the first week to get used to everything. Our lockers were all in the same corridor, which was very cool. We had lunch at the same time and the cafeteria was awesome. By the second week, it was all routine. We started looking at our schedules to see when we all had a day when we could begin to work on our video.

The fake blood came the second week of school, and we got more than I'd expected. I figured I hadn't checked out how much came in the order. It wasn't a big problem because it didn't cost a lot. And, with extra, we'd be able to rehearse the shoot-out scene before we actually filmed it. There was a problem though. When I'd gone online and ordered the blood, another thing I'd missed was that we'd need an igniter. The blood wasn't expensive, but an igniter was.

"Guys, I am so sorry," I apologized. "I can't believe I didn't think of that."

"Hey, don't worry about it. I think I have a solution to our problem," Jeremy told us. He'd been online, too, and saw how to make blood packs and how someone had made an igniter. "I think I can do it," he told us, turning to Max. "Think we can take care of this little snag in the plan?"

"Are you thinking what I'm thinking?" Max said, grinning as Jeremy nodded. He turned to me, and said, "We got this."

Okay, then, that settled it, I figured. Since they seemed to be sure they knew how to do it, it would be their job to put together an igniter for each blood pack. Jeremy and Max were going to take the fake blood and make the packs and have everything ready for when we got together to try them out.

CHAPTER SEVENTEEN

The wait was much longer than we thought it would be. There was a pep rally on the second weekend. Brendan was on the field of course, but Max, Jeremy, James, and I were in the bleachers, cheering like crazy.

The weekend after that, James and I had a combined choir/band concert scheduled. Brendan had another thing with a ball, catching one or throwing one. It was hard to keep it straight. Max and Jeremy were in Math Club and Math Club does not have pep rallies or concerts, but they came to the concert and clapped like they were really into it. We always cheered for each other, whatever we did.

Our weeks were filled with assignments and homework.

We saw the Labor Day weekend coming up and it seemed like some kind of miracle that we were all going to be in town. There was a picnic for our youth group Saturday night, but we were free the rest of the day to get things set up and make sure we had thought of everything.

Jeremy's plan was brilliant. He and Max filled small plastic baggies and sealed them up. They taped a bag to a two by two inch piece of metal (made from a coffee can) and taped a firecracker to the bag.

Okay, so you couldn't buy firecrackers where we lived, nowhere even close. If we saw any fireworks, it had to be at a park or stadium or something. But, remember, Jeremy had visited his Uncle Denver, and wherever Uncle Denver lived it was possible to get firecrackers. And Jeremy had brought some home. Maybe not so smart for a smart guy, and I had no idea what he'd planned to do with them since he couldn't set them off. But it turned out to be great for our plan to explode fake blood packs.

The next part was pure genius. Jeremy and Max had taken a solar igniter and battery from the rocket engines and made the igniters for the blood packs. We were in business!

Usually, I'd have the guys come stay overnight when we had something planned for the next day. But, since we were going to test everything out for the effects in my back yard, they just came early the next morning. My dad did make his traditional Saturday morning pancakes for all of us though.

When we finished eating we headed for the garage and my mom came into the family room. All my friends know she is not a morning person and didn't bother to say anything to her and just filed out of the room. She would have had some coffee and ready to be friendly by the time we got dressed and created the good guys and the aliens and came back through the family room.

In the garage, Brendan stripped to the waist, ready for the blood packs to be taped to his body. He turned toward me, his chest out, a sly grin on his face.

"Oh, quit your bragging," I said, my palm making a popping sound as I slapped his bare skin. Brendan was very proud of the few chest hairs growing there. The first—and only—one of us to have any.

"So, you got any more since the last time we saw your magnificent torso?" James teased Brendan.

Brendan got a little red then and got serious about taping the baggies to his chest. He and Max had three each. The firecrackers were in place and Jeremy set the igniters. It was time to get dressed.

Jeremy had brought some of his little sister's sidewalk chalk and we ground it up and smeared the powder on Max and Brendan's faces. Brendan's brown hair was cropped short for sports and he rubbed the stuff all over his head. He looked gross. We'd have to come up with something different and really gruesome when we actually filmed the video. I found some hair wax and Max spiked his hair into a bright red greasy looking mess. They wore mostly anything we could find in the rag bag and my mom's charity donation bag.

Max had gotten a couple of old stained camouflage hunting jackets from his grandpa for me and Jeremy to wear over some old shirts and the grungiest jeans we could find. I put on the grubby shoes I wore when I mowed lawns. We got some dirt from the flower beds by the front porch and rubbed it on our faces.

Jeremy crammed a ball cap down over his dark crazy-curly hair. As soon as I put my 'Indie' hat on, I felt like Rick the Adventurer again. Ready for action. We picked up our weapons and went into the house.

Mine and Jeremy's guns looked great. We'd spray-painted them silver. Like real old-time six-shooters. No one had a good idea why we had guns like that, we just liked the idea of using them. We were lucky when we found the toy semi-automatics for Brendan and Max. They made noise and shot sparks out the end. Amazing what you can get at a dollar thrift store. We taped some PVC on the ends with duct tape and sprayed over the whole thing with gray paint.

"Whoa!" my dad said when we came around the corner into the kitchen. We stopped so he could get the full effect. "You boys resurrecting the alien vampires?"

"Yup." I grinned at my dad, and tipped my hat.

"But I thought you killed them all off in your other video." My mom was fully awake now and checking out our new threads.

"Well, you see, we have a twist this time," I explained to my parents. "It's like we didn't know there were two we missed, see. The leader and his number one. Oh, and we've got another good guy this time, too. The aliens are coming after me, he's coming after them," I explained and turned and pointed at Jeremy. "And we're all going to have a showdown."

"I see, like a shoot-out," said my dad.

"Yep."

"Oh, look at your guns," Mom said, turning attention to our weapons. "Did you boys make those?"

I explained about the guns and she told us how clever and creative we were. She always thinks we are clever and creative.

"And we've got some new special effects too."

The guys got excited and started talking all at once about how cool this new gimmick was going to be.

"Hey, wait a minute," my mom said over all the chatter. "Did I hear someone say something about blood?"

"Yeah! That's what's so cool. We made these blood packs and—"

"Hold on there, mister. Blood? Uh-uh, not so cool." Mom had her serious face on. "Explain."

My mom is usually pretty laid back about stuff so I figured it was the blood that did it. She was in full Mother Mode right then.

So I explained: From me getting the idea to use blood packs, to ordering the fake blood, to Jeremy and Max coming up with a way to ignite them. "It's all fake, Mom," I said, "just like the guns." I held up my pistol. "We just want to try it out and see if it works. You want to come watch?"

She looked at my dad.

"Sure," my dad said, wiping his hands on a dish towel. "It'll be fine, Jennifer," he assured my mom.

"All right, I want to see what this is you boys have put together." My mom got up from the couch. "Wait until I get a robe, Patrick. I'll be right out."

Dad winked at me and waved toward the door. We hustled outside as she disappeared into her bedroom.

After trying out different spots in the yard, Jeremy and I stood a few feet from the patio, Brendan and Max went to the other side of the yard, several feet away. Then we waited.

I should have known my mom would do more than just throw on a robe. When she *finally* did come out of the house, she had on jeans and a T-shirt and it looked like she'd done something with her hair . . . no more bed head. I made a noise that wasn't exactly a growl and gave her a look. My dad cleared his throat and gave *me* a look. Mom just ignored me.

Everyone got into position: Brendan and Max across the yard from me and Jeremy, with their weapons aimed at us. James was going to shoot the scene like Jeremy and I were drawing our guns and firing. He wasn't going to really film us but he looked through the lens to see how the scene would look when we actually did it.

Mom and Dad stood on the patio and James said, "Okay, on the count of three. One, two, three, Action."

Brendan and Max raised their weapons, aiming at us, fake ack-ack sounds coming from their guns and sparks spitting from the barrels.

Jeremy pointed his gun and fired. Pop! Pop!

I made a quick-draw action, bringing my cap pistol up and firing. Pop! Pop!

Brendan's chest exploded, fake blood soaking the front of his uniform. He dropped his weapon and staggered backward, holding his chest, then sank to his knees. Bright red spots burst from two places in Max's front. He fell to the ground beside Brendan.

"Oh! No! OH!"

"Cut!"

Alien zombies, adventure heroes, James and my dad, everyone turned to look at my mother. She was holding her face between her hands, shaking her head, her eyes big as Frisbees.

Really, Mom? I thought she totally understood this whole scene was fake . . . fake heroes (well, maybe just a little hero), fake aliens, fake guns, fake blood.

"Mom?"

"Oh." She barely whispered, her cheeks bright red.

My dad put his hand on her shoulder. "Jennifer, are you all right?"

"Uh . . . yes, um . . . I think. Sure." She looked at me and gave me a really crooked, silly looking smile. "I'm sorry, guys. I didn't mean to mess up your film."

"Oh, we weren't actually filming anything right now," I said. "But you knew it was all fake, I told you."

She took a deep breath and let it out. "You're right, Patrick. I knew what to expect, but, you know, I've just never seen my son *shoot* someone. The blood and all. Honey, I mean, it looked so real." She shivered. "Too real."

"Then I guess we've got ourselves some really cool special effects for our video," I bragged.

"Patrick." My dad gave me one of his *looks* that meant I should check my attitude, and twitched his head toward my mom.

"Uh, sorry, Mom." I shuffled my feet and looked around at the guys. They didn't know what to do. Were we in trouble or what? Then I asked my mom, "You really think it looked real?"

"Oh, yes. Real enough, believe me."

A big grin smeared across my face. I didn't mean to scare my mom, but her reaction was perfect, exactly what we needed to know. I turned to Jeremy and put my hand up for a high five. He slapped my palm and Brendan and Max ran over, everyone talking at once. Now if everything would turn out exactly the same when we actually filmed.

In the garage we started taking off our 'video' clothes. "Man!" Max said, scratching his cheeks making streaks in the chalk we'd spread on his face. "This stuff is itchy."

I dug out a rag and handed it to him. We might have to find something else to use the next time to get the gross effect we wanted. "Here, use this to get most of it off. I don't think my mom will like it if we mess up the bathroom." I took another one to give to Brendan.

"Give me a sec," he said, rubbing his chest. "Let me get out of this garb, check something out first." He unbuttoned his shirt and pulled it open then carefully removed the tape and what was left of the blood packs. He winced, sucking air between his teeth as he began wiping at the fake blood that covered his chest.

"Wow," the guys said as they looked at the bright red spots on his skin where the packs had been taped.

"That has got to hurt," I said. He would have a bruise, for sure. "But you didn't say anything."

"Guess it sort of knocked the wind out of me. Then, when your mom yelled like that, I thought it would be better to wait and check it out later."

We found out a few seconds later that the reason Max hadn't suffered the same fate was that he'd put flat pieces of foam behind the metal discs before taping them down.

"I felt a little 'punch' but not like that," he said, pointing at bright spots on Brendan's chest.

We may have come up with a great, realistic special effect but there is no way we're going to go ahead with something that could end up with one of my friends getting hurt.

I looked into Brendan's eyes. "Brendan, I'm so sorry, buddy. We'll just have to come up with something else."

"Are you kidding!" He looked around at the others. "It was perfect. You heard what your mom said. 'Too real.' We can't change it. No way, Patrick."

"But you're hurt."

"Hunh. This is nothing. You oughta see me after a game."

"Are you sure?"

"Heck yeah. When're we gonna do it? For real?"

That settled it, then. We put all our gear into a cardboard box and put it up on a shelf. The trick would be to find a good time and decide on a good place to shoot our next masterpiece.

CHAPTER EIGHTEEN

That night, I tossed and turned off and on and dreamed of Brendan and Max with gaping holes in their chests. I woke in a cold sweat and lay awake a long time. The last thing I remembered before going back to sleep was saying out loud, "I promise I won't let anything happen to my friends."

Everything was back to normal the next morning at church. All the guys safe and accounted for, we stood around talking before heading for Youth Group. Renee Woods and Alyssa Dwyer walked by going in that direction.

"Hi, Brendan," Renee said over her shoulder, all girlie-like, as she continued down the hallway.

Hi, Brendan? Hey, what about the rest of us? What are we . . . invisible? Not that I cared or anything that she didn't say hi to us.

"Uh, see ya, guys," Brendan said and turned toward the Youth wing.

"What in the . . . ?" My mouth wouldn't shut as I watched him go then turned and looked at my friends, a big question mark on my face.

"Aw, come on, Patrick," James said, poking me in the shoulder. "You didn't notice Renee hanging around Brendan last night at the picnic?"

I remembered her and Alyssa bringing their plates and sitting at our table. "She and Alyssa were hanging around *all* of us."

"Huh-uh, buddy," Max put in. "You were on the other end of the bench and old Renee squeezed herself right in next to Brendan."

"So?"

James put his hand on my shoulder while Max and Jeremy doubled over laughing. "We need to talk, dude," James said, steering me toward class.

I can be slow about some things but it didn't take much for me to get the picture once James painted the details for me. I felt like a real doofus, but how was I supposed to know that girls were like *looking* at Brendan? And he was looking back it seemed. Only made sense, though. He was a jock, after all, besides being older than the rest of us. Oh, and there were the chest hairs, too.

Brendan sat with us during services, as usual, but I noticed that he kept looking over to where Renee sat with the rest of the girls. And *she* was actually making eyes at him! Alyssa gave old Renee a sharp jab in the ribs and she turned and gave Alyssa a really dirty look.

A couple of seconds later, Alyssa looked over at *me* and rolled her eyes. I couldn't remember seeing that look before. I'd known Alyssa almost as long as I'd known all the guys.

We'd all gone to school together from the time we were in elementary school and attended the same church. I'd always thought of her as one of the guys. Good thing, too. She could punch really hard if we ever treated her like a girl. *She would have gotten a big kick out of launching that mouse.* Now, she was sitting with a girl who was making eyes at Brendan.

I sure hoped she didn't think whatever she was doing with her eyes was attractive. Or that I'd care anyway.

The morning couldn't end soon enough for me. All I wanted to do was go home with my family and have our normal Sunday lunch and a normal family day.

After we ate and the table was cleared, I went to my room and finished my reading assignment for the next day. Then I went to see what the family was watching on TV. I was ready for some outer space sci-fi action. Any mindless entertainment to get my mind off that morning.

My mind cleared up real quick when my mother said she wanted to talk to me before we started watching the movie. I wasn't sure if this was a good thing or a bad thing. The last time she and my dad had 'wanted to talk' to me, I'd found out there was no summer vacation.

"Patrick, sweetie," Mom started, "I know you were really disappointed that we didn't go on vacation in the summer."

Yep. Here it was. My parents were finally going to tell me the grand and glorious news. *Should I act surprised? Pretend I'm thrilled about going to one-horse junction? Act like I'm so happy for Taylor? Gag. Well, get on with it.*

"Fall Break is only a few weeks away and we thought you'd like to know we have some really special plans."

For one split second, I imagined my parents had changed their minds about *The Plan*. Maybe we were going to Disney World after all. I didn't hold my breath. Good thing.

"Son," my dad said, taking over now. "We're all going to Arkansas."

I decided on raised eyebrows for a surprised look, and waited.

Then my mom was sitting on the edge of her seat. "We are *all* going! Everyone, the whole family: Clint and Judith and the girls; Nathan and Liz and Abby. And we're all going to Daly, grandmother's home town, where she grew up. You remember going there, don't you?"

Oh, yeah. I remembered all right. Nothing, forever. I nodded my head all excited-like, and smiled really big like I was just tickled pink.

"We're thinking the family all getting together like this may change plans for Christmas, we might not be able to be together then. I hope you won't be too disappointed. But we just thought this was too good an opportunity to pass up."

"Tell him about the Fall Festival," my dad said.

"Oh, yes. I almost forgot. Daly has a Fall Festival every year in the middle of October, and we will be there. They have a parade, and booths, and lots of food. Oh, and games, I believe I remember. Doesn't that sound like fun?"

I kept nodding and smiling, waiting for them to tell the part about how Taylor's plans all fit into this trip. I had a lot more waiting to do.

CHAPTER NINETEEN

"Dude, you *gotta* go," Max insisted as we walked to class the next morning.

"No, I don't *gotta* go," I said. The Sophomore Formal was the next weekend and I had no intentions of going. "It doesn't sound like any fun at all."

"Nobody said you had to have fun, you just have to go. We're sophomores now, dude, you gotta go."

I kept walking and slipped into my seat before the bell rang for class.

"Everyone else is going," Max whispered loudly.

"Whatdaya mean, everybody?" I hissed back. My mouth hung open when he pointed to the front of the room and zipped his lip like *now* we were supposed to focus on what our history teacher was saying. I had a hard time concentrating, wondering what Max meant.

What he meant, I found out, was that he, James, Jeremy, and Brendan were all going to the Formal. When had they decided to do that? I didn't remember being included in that conversation.

"You got the same schedule as the rest of us," James said when I asked him how come I didn't know about this Formal thing. "We did it together, man. At the beginning of the year. Patrick, look at your schedule. I bet the Formal is blocked out, just like on the rest of our schedules. We did it together, man."

I looked in my backpack. The schedule was in the packet we received the first day of school, and, sure enough, I'd highlighted the Formal.

"Doesn't change anything. I am *not* going."

Famous last words.

My mom and Taylor couldn't have been happier than when I came out of my room wearing dark pants, a new shirt and a tie. I drew the line when they wanted me to change out of my high-top sneakers. And no way was I wearing a jacket. I'd only agreed to the tie because my friends were going to wear one. I stood still long enough for my dad to snap a picture or two.

"Come on, Taylor," I called as I bolted for the door. I'd talked my sister into taking me and James and Brendan to school. She let us out at the gym door.

"When do you want me to pick you up?" she asked as I got out of the car.

"How about in an hour," I answered. The Formal started at seven p.m.

James leaned in beside me and said, "It's over at ten o'clock, Taylor."

Taylor smiled at James. "Thanks. You guys have fun." She pulled away from the curb leaving me there, dreading the next few hours like a root canal. (Never had one, but I hear they are awful.)

Music was already blasting when we entered the gym, with some kids dancing in the middle of the floor. There were even some cheesy decorations hanging from the ceiling and there was a table with punch and cookies. *Punch, for crying out loud. Could things get any worse?*

Yes, yes they could. And did. Max and Jeremy had just made their way over to where we were standing when Renee Woods and Alyssa Dwyer and a couple other girls walked up.

"Hello, boys," Renee said, looking directly at Brendan. She took a step forward and stood in front of him. "Want to dance?"

I made a sort of snorting noise and mumbled under my breath to James, "Yeah, right. No way is Brendan going to go for that."

But the next second I was snorting out of the other side of my face. I couldn't believe it. Brendan said, "Sure" and followed Renee onto the dance floor. Then it got worse. Those other girls asked Max and Jeremy if they wanted to dance and they all went out on the dance floor.

I could have gagged.

That left me and James and Alyssa. Well, good luck, girlie girl, I thought, standing shoulder to shoulder with my best buddy looking at her. She smiled at James then looked me straight in the eye. "Patrick, would you like to dance with me?"

All the air was suddenly sucked from the gym. My mouth was so dry I couldn't get a sound out. She must have been real determined to get out there and dance with her friends because when I didn't answer right away, she turned to James and smiled again. He took the hand she held out and they walked out to join the others. He actually took her hand!

While they all looked like they were having a great time, all I could think was, *What is happening to my gang?*

I jammed my hands down into my pockets and made my way over to the refreshment table. I downed several cups of punch and was on my fifth cookie when Max and Jeremy came up beside me. They filled their cups and washed down a couple of cookies.

"Whew, I am so thirsty," Alyssa said as she and James joined us. "So, how's the punch, Patrick?" She filled a cup without waiting for an answer and handed it to James, filled one for herself and took a sip.

"Not bad, I guess. At least it's wet."

We all stood around drinking our punch. The music started up after a few minutes and I decided I was not going to be left at the refreshment table by myself again like some dork.

"Alyssa," I said, setting my empty cup on the table and holding my hand out to her. "Want to dance?"

Now, that's the way it's done, I thought, as we walked out on the floor.

CHAPTER TWENTY

The Formal had turned out to be fun after all. Dancing with Alyssa wasn't much different than all the times we'd played tag together. Well, maybe a *little* different.

Things were mostly back to normal by Monday morning when I met up with the guys outside school. Right then we needed to get back to our usual routine and concentrate on our video. "Lunch, guys," I said before we went to our separate classes. "We have some planning to do."

While we ate lunch we made sure everyone would be free for the weekend. Fall break was in two weeks but most of us had something going then. For me, my lovely trip to small town U.S.A. was finally going to happen. Oh, whoopee.

We breezed through classes every day during the week, and homework every night. All the equipment was ready in our garage, but we went over a check list of anything we thought we might have missed.

We spread out on sleeping bags in the front room and didn't sleep much as we talked about the next day. The smell of bacon and my dad's pancakes pulled me awake next morning.

"Thanks, Mr. Morrison," James told my dad as we dug into breakfast. Everyone mumbled their thanks through mouthfuls of pancake too.

"So, did you boys decide where you're going to film today?" My dad knew we'd had lots of discussions about where we should go. What he didn't know was that Max was against going over to the mound. But then, my dad didn't know it was a mound either.

We'd taken a vote and the rest of us convinced Max that we should go back into the big open field. It would be the best place to do the showdown scene. We wouldn't have to go to the mound.

"We're going back over to the open field on the other side of Mr. Nelson's pasture," I answered my dad's question. "Plenty of space. We thought it would look good with all the tall weeds and grass."

"Yeah," James explained, "when the aliens get shot and fall, it'll look they were disintegrated.'

"Well, after you fix it, that's what it'll look like," I said.

"Right."

"Sounds like you boys have another hit on your hands," my mom said, coming into the kitchen. She'd really liked the video we did earlier in the year. In her words, we were just the cleverest young men. Looking at her, I figured she must have been up before we came in to eat because she didn't have her normal Saturday morning bed head. My hair is just like my mom's, dark—almost black—and goes in all directions when we get up in the morning. It looked like she might have run a brush through it this morning. And she made sense when she talked."If it looks anything like what I saw on the patio the other day, I'm sure you do."

We wiped up the last bit of syrup and gulped down the final drop of juice, thanked my dad again, and headed for the garage. Instead of using the ground-up sidewalk chalk to make Max and Brendan look bloodless, I'd been lucky enough to find a tube of clown makeup in a box of some old Halloween stuff. They dabbed it all over their faces and Brendan covered his hair again. Max spiked his hair and we were set. They looked like they really could be a couple of space ghouls.

The last touch was taping the blood packs to their chests. This time we made sure to put a couple layers of thin foam under the metal discs the packs rested on. We crossed our fingers it would work. Then we made one final run-down on everything we had planned. It would be a long walk there and back if we forgot anything.

When we were ready, I opened the door from the garage into the house. "Hey, guys," I called out to my parents, "we're leaving now."

We'd just closed the garage door and we were on our way down the drive when my mom came hurrying out of the house. "Wait, Patrick!" She stood on the porch with her camera pointed at us, clicking. My dad stepped outside with Taylor shuffling behind him.

She took one look at us and said, "Oh, good grief. You got me up for this?" She turned and shuffled back inside. Good thing. With her wild, crazy bed head, she looked scarier than Max and Brendan.

"Be careful, boys," my mom called before closing the front door behind her.

Finally. We could get on with it.

We trekked across Mr. Nelson's pasture, over the fence and into the field. We waited while James looked around, checking out what would make the best backdrop to our scene.

"Hey, guys, let's go over that way," he said, and led us to a spot several yards away. We stopped when he did, and waited for him to do a sweep around again. He handed me the camera. "The weeds and grass are higher over there," he said, pointing to a spot with the mound in the background. "We can shoot it so it'll look like Brendan and Max are coming from that direction with you and Jeremy waiting for them right here. What do you think?"

I looked through the lens and panned the camera around as he explained then handed it to Jeremy. After Max and Brendan had a look too, we all agreed that, as usual, James was right. The shot was going to look great.

We rechecked our weapons, the blood packs, made sure the igniters were working, and took our places. I holstered my weapon and James took a couple shots of me and Jeremy walking through the grass.

Next, he aimed at Brendan and Max where they stood. "Okay, guys, walk toward me with your guns raised like you're getting ready to shoot." After he got what he wanted, he asked, "Are you ready for the real thing?"

We were ready.

"Action."

Brendan and Max blazed away, Jeremy and I brought our firearms up and we fired. Pop! Pop! Pop! Pop!

Max's gun flew from his hands as red stained his shirt, then he fell over. Brendan looked down at the holes that appeared in his chest, then back up, acting shocked to see the blood that covered his uniform. He sank to his knees, no clutching his chest this time, raised his gun again as if he was trying to get off another shot, then fell forward. These guys were good.

"Cut!"

The aliens jumped to their feet and gave each other a high five. We were all laughing like crazy. It felt good but I wanted to know for sure. "How did it look?" I called to James.

He gave us a weak thumbs-up and, instead of the usual grin when he was happy with the results of a shot, he looked toward the mound. He had this weird look on his face and shook his head with a couple of quick jerks, like he was trying to clear it of something.

"Well, let's take a look," I said as we walked over to him.

"We need to go, guys." He looked me straight in the eye and I knew something wasn't right. He picked up his backpack, stowed the camera as he walked rapidly back toward the pasture, leaving the rest of us staring.

"Hey, James, what's up?" I stared after him. No matter how realistic the scene might have been, James wasn't the kind to get freaked out over it. So what was it?

"We need to go. Now." James said over his shoulder and kept walking.

Creepy-crawlers inched up my spine as it sank into my head what James had said. Every hair on my body was standing on end. Jeremy's face had gone as white as Max and Brendan's and I was sure if I could have seen my own, it would be just as drained of color.

James had just said the exact same words I'd said in the drainage culvert several months ago. I'd seen something then that rocked me to my high-top sneakers. I'd gotten out of there as fast as I could go after telling my friends, "We need to go, guys."

My friends all remembered too. James was one laid-back dude and they knew he would never react like he did unless something had spooked him. Without another word, we all picked up our gear and hustled to catch up.

When I was finally in step with him, I asked, "You okay?"

He looked at me and nodded his head, but I could tell by the look in his eyes that he wasn't.

CHAPTER TWENTY-ONE

James does not lose his cool. Things don't shake him up like they do most people. He's so logical he could be a modern-day Mr. Spock. Some day he'll be good at a job where it takes a calm head, and never panic.

I wouldn't say he'd lost it then, but I've known James most of our lives and I could tell he was more than a little shook up. None of us pressed him to say anything until he was ready. He kept walking and didn't stop until we were back across Mr. Nelson's pasture. He ducked between the wires of the fence then suddenly dropped to the ground on the other side.

"What is going on with you, dude?" Max said between gasps for air after climbing through the fence. James had gone at a pretty good clip and we were all breathing a little heavy.

"You're acting just like Patrick did when he found the . . . Oh, my gosh!" Max's knees buckled out from under him and he plopped down on the ground a couple feet from James. His freckles were popping even through the clown makeup. His red hair stood out in all directions. Actually, his hair usually stood out in all directions; it just looked weirder than normal with all the makeup on his face.

I sat next to James. He looked at me and said, "Patrick, I really don't know what to say. How to explain."

"What!" Max squeaked, panic in his voice. Max always panics. "You're really acting weird, James. And, remember, Patrick said there wasn't going to be anything weird." He looked at me. "You promised."

"Hey, buddy," I said, holding my hands in front of me like a sign of surrender. "I don't know any more than the rest of you. Give him a minute. I'm sure James is going to tell us what's going on."

Brendan and Jeremy were still standing and I asked James, "You want to go back to my house, get out of this stuff," I said, pulling at my clothes, tilting my "Indie" hat back on my head. "We'll get cleaned up, go to my room—"

"No."

"Okay, then." He really was serious. What could have happened? "Want to at least go sit around the cul-de-sac?"

James shook his head and wouldn't look at anyone. After a while he said, "Let's just stay here for a few minutes. Okay?"

We agreed that if that's what James wanted, it was fine with the rest of us. Brendan and Jeremy sat down. A cow waddled over and looked at us like she was checking to see if we might be trying to go after some of her grass or something. I tossed a handful of dirt and twigs at her to shoo her away.

James looked at the camera in his hands. He took a deep breath, held it for a second then let it out, looking up at us.

"Okay, this is it," he started. "When we set up the shot . . . you remember the mound was in the background? And I shot a few frames of Brendan and Max then some with Patrick and Jeremy?"

James eyes fixed on a spot in front of him as he described the scene, like he was living through it all again. "So . . . we start the scene, the vampire aliens walking toward the heroes, guns blazing. I pan over to the heroes, they draw their sidearms and return fire. I pan back to the aliens to get the blood packs exploding."

He stopped and looked up at Brendan and Max. This time he was grinning. "That was great, by the way. The blood packs worked really good."

Max and Brendan slapped a high five.

"Anyway," James went on, looking around at us as he talked, "I call 'cut,' but just before I push the off button, something caught my eye." James looked down and turned the camera over and over in his hands. "I looked up really quick, to where I thought I'd seen something and . . ." He stopped and shook his head. "You're going to think I'm crazy."

"Oh, c'mon, James," Max blurted out before James could finish. "You're just pulling our leg. If you think you're scaring me, then you're not. Quit fooling around."

James wasn't fooling around. He was dead serious. I knew him well enough to know that there was more to this story and I could tell he was having a hard time figuring out how to say it. He gave Max a hard steady stare.

"So, what did you see, huh?" Max said, baiting James, trying to give him a hard time. "Some big old scary Indian? Huh?" He snorted and looked around at us like he thought he was being really funny. He was not.

James stared at Max for what seemed like forever then said, "Not exactly."

Max gulped.

Now he was starting to freak me out. "Uh, James . . ."

He turned to me and said, "Patrick, I told you I didn't know how to explain."

James was my best friend and he was asking me for help. I shrugged. "Just say it."

"All right, then." He nodded and took a deep breath and exhaled. "I'd called 'cut,' but just as I was pushing the off button, I thought I saw something . . . or someone, I don't know . . . running out of the woods."

Even Max's freckles turned pale at that.

"I looked away from the lens, out over the camera real quick, but there was nothing there."

Brendan cleared his throat and Jeremy looked down and plucked at some grass by his feet. Max just sat there staring at James, eyes bugged, mouth hanging open.

"Patrick," James whispered as he leaned toward me, "I know this sounds like something Max would dream up. But, seriously—"

"I heard that!" Max blurted out.

"Well, listen to this, then." James cut Max off before he could say anything else. All eyes and ears were on him. "Okay, so I looked down at the camera and noticed it was still on. I guess I didn't push the off button, I don't know. But somehow the camera was still running. While you guys were coming over, I hit Rewind . . . just on the chance . . ."

James turned the display screen toward us and pushed the on button. We watched as Jeremy and I blazed away at our attackers. Those blood packs worked perfectly, busting out of Brendan's and Max's chests, blood gushing everywhere. When they fell into the tall grass, just as we'd hoped, they seemed to have disintegrated, disappeared.

But something appeared in their place. In the distance, some *thing* seemed to be running out of the woods. It sort of looked like what had been in that bright flash in the pictures taken from the rocket. This time, though, whatever it was looked like it was heading straight for us, with waving arms. Then in the blink of an eye, it was gone. Just like the aliens, it disappeared, gone.

The screen went blank and James pushed the off button.

Max jumped to his feet. "I told you! That's what I thought I saw when we found the tombstones, but from the back. And it disappeared just the same way." He threw his arms out wide. "Poof!"

While Max was bouncing around being all dramatic and theatrical, the rest of us were taking another look at the video.

"Hey!" Max stopped moving. "And that could be what we saw in those pictures the rocket camera took." He stopped and whirled around, pointing his finger at Brendan. "Aha! I'll bet that's what it was. So, whaddaya think about my theory now? Huh?"

Brendan handed the camera back to James and squinted up at Max. "Well, like I said when we found that crap in the culvert and you were so sure it was a ghost who did it. Ghosts don't crap. And that stuff was real. Which is exactly what we found out. I don't know what you saw in the graveyard, or what was in the picture, or what that was coming out of the woods. All I know is, I think there is a perfectly good explanation just like there was about the culvert crap."

Ha! It had been a while since I'd heard 'culvert crap.' But it brought back memories of how I'd stumbled up on this huge pile of the stuff in the culvert with no explanation of what it was exactly. Even when I thought I'd figured out for sure what it was, there was no logical way it could have gotten in there. As it turned out, the answer wasn't logical, but we did get an answer.

I had to admit this whole thing gave me the chilly-willies, but I was sure there had to be an answer here too. And right then there was no way I would rest until I figured it out.

"But what about the grave, the stone with the name Feurey on it?" Max was really working himself into a first-class rant. "What about what I saw, and what we all saw in the pictures?" He pointed at the camera and said, "And that? How do you explain that?"

"Max, there's no reason to believe any of that, or this, has to connect together," I said.

"I agree," James said. "But I would like to find out what's going on over there. Wouldn't you?" He looked around at us, ignoring Max because he knew Max wasn't ready to give up on his crazy Indian idea. And he'd been so close, so close.

"I'd like to know," Jeremy said. "But before we go diving into this right now, what do you say we head back to Patrick's? You ready, James?"

"Sure," James said. He stood up and dusted his hands and the back of his pants, then slung his pack over one shoulder and he and Jeremy took off.

Following their lead, we headed back to my house. My stomach was growling anyway. I sure hoped we'd find something to eat when we got there.

On the walk back, James got in step with me, Jeremy and Brendan on either side of us. Max was out in front. Jeremy put his hand on my arm and pointed his chin toward Max. "Slow down a bit, okay?"

What was he up to? Obviously, he didn't want Max to hear. Then I knew why when he told us what was on his mind. "Listen, guys, now's not the best time to get into this, but I noticed something when we were looking at the video. Guys, I think our friend—whatever—was waving something over his head."

"Like what?" Brendan asked.

"You're not going to tell me you think it was a spear or bow and arrow, are you? Please tell me you're not." I didn't want to think what we'd be in for if Jeremy went over to the Max side of thinking.

"Nothing like that, Patrick. I promise." he said, laughing. "But, whatever it was, I noticed there was a short reflection before it was gone."

"What kind of reflection?" Brendan asked. "Like that glare in the rocket pictures?"

"No . . . I don't know, but like when the sun bounces off something. What if it was the stock of a rifle?"

I stopped in my tracks. "You're kidding, right?"

Jeremy motioned me to start walking again. If Max saw us stop he'd want to know what we were talking about and for sure go nutzo if we told him. It wasn't like we were keeping secrets from him, it would just be best to let him in on things a little bit at a time. Like when we had more details, whenever that was.

"You're really serious?" Brendan asked. When Jeremy gave him a nod, he said, "Then we have to get another look at that video.

"Yes, but we should wait until . . ." James looked up ahead. Max was slowing down and we were gaining on him. "Just later, okay?"

A few more minutes and we were home. We went into the garage and peeled off the layers of clothes that had been our uniforms. We ditched Max and Brendan's blood-soaked shirts in the garbage—we could always find more old shirts when we needed them—and packed the rest of the clothes back in the box we'd taken them from and I stowed it on a shelf before we went into the house.

I cannot tell you how happy I was when we went into the kitchen to rustle up some grub. My mom already had a stack of sandwiches, chips and soda waiting for us on the counter. What a mom! We attacked that food like we hadn't eaten in a week.

CHAPTER TWENTY-TWO

When we were finished eating, my parents paused the TV and wanted to know how the filming went.

"Great!" I said. There was nothing to say about the weird thing we thought we might have seen. I had no idea how I could explain it anyway. "The blood packs worked perfectly."

"So now what's next?" my dad asked. He actually did take an interest in our video projects, even to loaning us his camera if we needed it for special shots.

I looked around at my friends then said, "Well, we don't really have a complete story yet. We just thought we'd build a script around the shoot-out. Maybe."

"Yeah, we've got a lot of work to do before it's done," James said.

"Well, I'm sure it will be wonderful," Mom said, then turned back to the movie she was watching when we came in.

Max was scratching his face, wiping the clown makeup off on his sleeve. "This stuff is beginning to itch. I need to get out of these clothes and wash this stuff off."

I handed Max and Brendan some paper towels to wipe off the makeup. There were bright red patches all over Max's face. "It's still itching," he said, still scratching at his face. "I'm going home. You coming, Jeremy? Brendan?"

"Right behind you." Jeremy picked up his backpack and, before following Max to the front door, he turned to me. "Later," he mouthed and put his finger and thumb up to his face to let me know he'd call.

Max and Jeremy rode their bikes over together most of the time Brendan only had to walk a few doors up the street from my house. Same for James. I figured maybe they'd stay behind. Brendan got another paper towel and rubbed at his face. "Yeah, in a minute. When I get some more of this stuff off," he said.

James was sorting through stuff in his backpack. "I gotta get this thing straightened out first."

I walked Max and Jeremy out. "See ya, guys," I said, and waited on the drive until I saw them round the curve at the end of the street.

James held up the backpack and nodded his head toward my room when I hurried back into the house. I couldn't wait to get another look at that video. Brendan tore off another paper towel, ran it under the kitchen faucet, and followed right behind me and James.

"Hey, dudes, Max was right," Brendan said, rubbing at his face as he closed the bedroom door, "this stuff really does itch."

"You going to leave?" I asked.

"Heck, no! We are going to take another look at that video right now. Maybe we can make some sense of it."

James pulled the camera from his bag and turned it on. We watched the video over and over, looking for the "flash" Jeremy said he saw. About the gazillionth time–actually more like fourth time–there it was! James spotted it first, we backed it up and a couple times more and Brendan and I could see what we thought Jeremy was talking about.

I mean, it was all so quick. Whatever was coming from the woods was there one second, gone the next. There did seem to be some kind of flash, like a reflection, but it happened so fast there was no way to be sure.

"Okay, so I see *something*," I said, "but why did Jeremy get the idea it could have been from a gun?

"Maybe he was thinking about the story his Uncle Denver told him about his neighbor shooting at him and his friends. Let his imagination run away with him. Guess we'll just have to wait and ask him," Brendan said. "Right now, I gotta get home and take a shower."

James packed up the camera and this time I walked the two of them out and said good bye. I watched them for a few seconds then went back inside.

"Patrick?" My mom called when I shut the door.

"Yeah?"

"Can you come in here for a minute? Your dad and I want to talk to you."

What did I do? was the first thing that popped into my mind. I couldn't think of anything. There was no way my parents could know what had been going on with the video. So what could they want? I went to into the family room to find out.

"Sit down, sweetie," Mom said as I walked into the room.

I sat, wishing this could have waited until I got a shower. No such luck.

"So, Patrick, we wanted to talk to you about something."

Uh-huh, I believe that's what you said, I thought. And waited.

"Well, as you know, Fall Break is next week, I mean, actually after the one coming up." My mother sniggered at her own mistake. "Anyway, I know you aren't exactly looking forward to the trip to Daly."

Understatement of the year, I'd say. My grandmother's little country home town is not exactly the dream destination of the average teenage boy.

My dad looked at my mom and they did one of those *looks* at each other, smiling.

"Well, there is more to our going to Daly than just to visit." My dad came from the kitchen and sat on the couch by my mom. "You see, Taylor has decided she would like to go to college in Jonesboro and—"

There it was . . . finally. I'd tried to put the whole thing out of my mind since Taylor told me about The Plan, but now that they brought it up, all I could do was sit there and listen about *Taylor's* plans. *Taylor this, Taylor that.* I was so steamed and was about to tell them just how unfair I thought this whole thing was. Then . . .

"So," my dad said, looking at me, "your mother and I were wondering if you'd like to invite one of the boys to go with you. Maybe James? Does his family have any plans that you know of?"

Had I just been transported to another planet! Had aliens abducted my parents and replaced them?

"Are you serious?"

"Absolutely. Much of the time we're going to be involved with getting things squared away for Taylor and it didn't seem fair that you'd have nothing to do. Plus, we realized that you are going to be vastly outnumbered in the female department. One guy with all those girl cousins."

Oh, my gosh. I hadn't even thought about that. Four females—Taylor, Abby, Jillian, and Kate. I'd say that was being outnumbered. I'd been so busy dreading being "down on the farm" that I hadn't even thought about that. Yuk!

And all of a sudden, Taylor's plans didn't seem such a huge issue any more. I couldn't wait to call James but I acted cool. "Yeah, sure." I nodded, trying to act like it was no big deal. "Sounds like it might work."

I also knew for a fact that James' family had no plans. He'd been disappointed, especially knowing that I was going to be gone.

"Then why don't you call him and find out if he can come?" My mom smiled and patted my hand.

"Oh, yeah, sure. Okay." I stood up and walked out of the room. I had my cell phone in my hand before I was around the corner. It was hard not to yell before I got to my room.

James answered on the second ring. "Hey, what's up? You forget something?"

"What's up is, you think you can go with our family next week?" I'd told James all about the plans, how much I dreaded going, how bored I was going to be. If I'd thought about being with a herd of girl cousins, I would have told him I was freaking out.

"So you're asking if I'd like to go to this place you'd rather put your eyes out than go to?"

Guess I'd complained just a little bit too much. Not exactly the best recommendation, come to think of it.

I explained the invitation had come directly from my parents and practically begged him to say yes.

"Hey, it sounds cool," he chuckled, taking pity on me and ending my torture. "Let me check with my folks, and I'll call you back."

In about five minutes, the phone rang. "What do I need to bring?"

"Let me check with *my* folks," I said, laughing and relieved. "I'll call you back." I felt so much better knowing James was going to be with me on this trip. I thought I remembered some kind of creek or something running somewhere around the farm, and I figured there had to be something to explore.

After dinner and a shower, I finally had a chance to call James. Then we talked for nearly an hour about what my parents told me we should take. I was actually looking forward to the trip by the time we hung up. Now I just had to make it through the next week.

There was one small problem with my plan though. More like three—Brendan, Jeremy, and Max. What were they going to think about me asking James to go and not any of them? They all knew James and I were extra tight since we'd known each other all our lives, I mean *all our lives*, like since we were babies, but I didn't want to hurt anyone's feelings. And I for sure didn't want to not tell them and have it look like I was keeping a secret from them. After I turned out the light, I couldn't go to sleep. Then I remembered Jeremy saying that his family was going to see his Uncle Denver over break. One part of the problem solved, and it was enough so I could relax a little.

The next morning at church, before Youth Group began, Brendan told us he'd been picked for a spot on the scrimmage team and would be at practice every day, all week. Problem two out of the way.

And Max was going to visit his grandparents. Bingo! Number three gone. Max would probably tell his grandpa all about the mound and the grave marker. I wondered if he'd say anything about the end of the video and seeing something coming from the woods. For sure, I expected we'd hear some new story from his grandpa.

Now, with no reason to worry about my friends' feelings, I could tell them about James going on our trip with my family.

I had just started explaining when Renee Woods and Alyssa Dwyer walked by on their way to the Youth wing.

"Hello, boys," Renee said. "You all coming to class?"

It could have been my imagination but I was pretty sure Alyssa smiled at me.

I fell into step with my buddies as we followed the girls to class.

CHAPTER TWENTY-THREE

All week I studied. I had a test in every single one of my classes and sweated getting an English essay finished in time. I'd worked on it most of the school year up to now and couldn't honestly answer why it wasn't done until the last minute. Could have been that I had rockets, mounds, and spooky, blurry images on my mind more than school work. Time off for a week couldn't come fast enough.

On Thursday, my friends and I went to a cookout at a nearby park for the Youth Fall Break get-together. It was still hot, but it was Texas and there had to be a big fire to roast the hotdogs and toast marshmallows. After we ate, we cooled down by having a water balloon fight. I didn't even try to out-run anyone throwing one at me. Although my back smarted like crazy after Brendan plastered me.

Alyssa Dwyer threw a balloon at me and missed. I got her really good, right on the back of her head. But not too hard. She laughed and brushed the water from her face then grabbed another balloon looking for someone to bust. She aimed for Renee who squealed like, well, like a girl, and ran behind one of our sponsors. What a weenie.

When it was time to go, Taylor picked up me, James, and Brendan and we all went to my house. James had brought his gear by earlier. He'd been ready for days. When we got to my house, we stayed up and watched a couple of movies then James and I walked Brendan to his house.

"You guys have a blast," Brendan said as we left his yard.

"Yeah, you too," I called back to him before he closed his front door.

I shouldn't have worried about my friends' feelings. They all had better things to do anyway.

Everything was packed and in my mom's big SUV and we were headed out by six o'clock Friday morning. The extra day added to fall break would get us to small-town-ville sooner. Whoopee.

It was way too early. But I figured James and I had plenty of time to catch up on sleep on the drive.

When we stopped at a restaurant, my folks didn't exactly rush through breakfast, but, since it's about an eleven hour drive from our house to where we were going, my dad kept reminding us we needed to eat and get on the road. James and I wolfed down our pancakes (not even as good as my dad's), washed them down with glasses of milk and piled into the car. After being awake so late the night before, and with a full stomach, I was out in no time.

When we stopped for lunch, my mom told me I had missed a lot of beautiful countryside and scenery. I'd had to trust her on that. From what I could tell when we got back on the road, there were just lots of trees, fields, and a surprising number of cows. It was so exciting I fell asleep again after about a half hour and didn't wake up until we stopped for gas, snacks, and to use the restroom. James and I pulled out our phones and played some games until it was time to stop for dinner.

While we were eating, my mom and dad talked about how much longer it would take to get to Grandmother's home town.

"We'll be there by bed time," my mom said, all excited. "A late bed time, but Mom will be so glad to see us."

I almost dropped my phone. What was she talking about? "Aren't we going to stop now? Like at a motel?"

"No, honey, we're going to go on to Daly."

There was no motel in Daly. It was too small. So where were we going to sleep tonight? Where were my grandparents going to spend the night? The rest of the family that was going to show up for this get-together? Was anyone using their heads?

"So we're going to stay in Jonesboro?" I asked. Jonesboro is at least ten miles from Daly. It's a sort of big town or a small city, I guess, with a university. There would surely be hotels there.

My mother's face was in danger of breaking she smiled so big, like she'd just been waiting for someone to ask. "That's what's so exciting about all of us going to Daly. We're all going to stay at Grandmother's old home

Wow! My mom was just full of surprises these days.

As for Daly, I'd seen that place. When we'd visited Daly, a long time ago, we drove out in the country to see this big old two story farm house, with an even bigger barn. From what I remembered there was an orchard and cotton fields all around it. Like I said, out in the middle of nowhere—in the middle of nowhere.

"Hello? I seem to remember that someone lives there?" I was sure I'd heard my mom say something about my grandmother, her brother and sister, rented the whole thing— house, barn, orchard and fields—to someone who lived in the house and farmed the land. "What're they gonna do? Put us all up in the barn?"

"No, silly," Mom said, still grinning. "The house has been empty for a while and Grandmother and Uncle Jack and Aunt Ellen have been renovating it. There is lots of room, room for everyone. Well, maybe someone will have to sleep on air mattresses, but that sounds like fun! Doesn't that sound like fun?"

What it sounded like was, all the kids got to have fun . . . sleeping on an air mattress.

"So, let's eat up and get on the road."

I groaned at the thought of spending at least three more hours in the car. I figured James was beginning to regret coming on this trip with me. Besides, my butt was numb from riding in the car all day long.

"Mom, my butt is numb."

"Oh, waa-waa." Taylor made sounds like a baby. "Everyone is tired of being in the car, Patrick. Quit being such a whiney baby." She smiled one of her squinty-eye, pretend-sweet smiles.

I wanted to punch in her face.

Before I could say anything, my dad said, "Come on, guys, it's only a few hours longer. We'll take a shortcut from here and be there before you know it."

Did he not hear about my numb butt?

"And Grandmother will have everything ready for us." Mom reached over and patted my shoulder. "Maybe even some chocolate chip cookies."

James poked me in the ribs and raised an eyebrow when I looked at him. "Dessert, dude."

Maybe he was right. My grandmother did make some smokin' good chocolate chip cookies.

My mom was absolutely one hundred percent right about it being late by the time we got to Daly. My dad's 'shortcut' took us on two-lane, hilly roads, in the pitch black night for over an hour before we came out on an interstate that would get us near Daly. Did I mention bumpy? There was no sleeping—my insides were nearly totally disconnected by the time we got there.

We drove off the bypass and onto the highway that went past Daly. When we reached the farm, it looked like every light in the house was on. Grandmother must have been looking for us; she was waiting in the yard when Dad pulled into the driveway. Papa stood on the porch, his hands in his pockets.

Mom jumped from the car and she and Grandmother hugged and laughed until Taylor and James and I got out of the car. Then it was our turn. You'd have thought it had been years since she'd seen any of us, instead of the couple of months it had been. She pulled James into a big hug then pushed him away and held him at arm's length.

"Jennifer, have you been hiding Patrick's twin?" She had met James at our house before when she and Papa visited and always said something about how much James and I looked alike.

"Grandmother, this is my friend, James," I said coming to his rescue. She still had one arm around his shoulder. I looked at my mom. Hadn't she even told my grandparents that I was bringing a friend? Good grief.

"Oh, Patrick, honey," Grandmother said, turning loose of James and grabbing me again. "I know this is James. Unless you decided to bring someone your mother didn't tell me about. But you two do look enough alike you could be brothers."

We'd been hearing that all our lives. James smiled and yawned.

Grandmother must have thought that was some kind of hint because she hurried us all into the house. "Let me show you all where everyone will be sleeping," she told my mom, "while Doug and your dad bring in your things."

What about the chocolate chip cookies?

Mom didn't let me down. "Uh, Mom, I think the kids were hoping for a late snack. Maybe some cookies and milk?"

That's all my grandmother needed to hear. She herded us out to the kitchen while my dad and Papa brought in our bags and stuff. She must have just taken a batch of cookies out of the oven because they were still warm. I stopped after four and a glass of milk, half asleep already, waiting until someone pointed me to where I was going to sleep.

James wiped milk on his sleeve and smiled at me, his head slowly bobbing up and down.

"Dessert, dude. Dessert."

After sleeping nearly the whole trip, I didn't know how I could be so tired and so sleepy. But, right then, I was ready to lay my head down on the table if someone didn't tell me soon where a bed was.

"Okay, kids, ready to turn in?" Dad said from the hall. "Taylor, I've got your bag. Boys, grab your stuff by the front door and we'll head upstairs."

James and I picked up our duffel bags and followed my dad and Taylor up the stairs. I grumbled to myself about having to carry my own bag while Taylor didn't, but right then, I was too tired to say a word. By the time we reached the third floor of the farm house, I wasn't sure if I'd ever go back down, even for food.

My dad was saying something about sleeping arrangements being temporary, but the sight of a bed in one of the bedrooms at the top of stairs blocked everything else out. James and I tossed our bags on the floor. I flopped on one of the twin beds, James on the other. I kicked off my shoes and sighed when my head hit the pillow. Closing my eyes, I stretched out with my clothes still on as my dad turned out the light and closed the door.

"G'nite, James," I mumbled. If he answered, I didn't hear him. I was already asleep.

CHAPTER TWENTY-FOUR

A blinding rainbow flashed over my head, right into my eyes.

"Hey, Dude, why you got a rainbow on your face?" James mumbled from the bed across from me. He squinted from one eye, the other half hidden in a pillow.

"Same reason you're wearing one on your head, I guess." Holding up my hand to block the glare, I looked around, trying to figure out where all this brightness came from. A stained glass window at the end of the room threw colored rays of light all over the walls and ceiling.

"Oh, yeah . . ." My head began to clear. Who could sleep with a light show going on anyway? I pushed up on one elbow and saw James sitting up looking at me. "I don't know about you," I said, "but I really need to pee. Just one problem."

"Me, too. What's the problem?"

"I have no idea where a bathroom is."

"Yep. *We* have a problem. But, we're not going to solve it sitting here." James stood up and went across the room.

"Hey! Look what I found." Instead of the door to our room, it opened to a bathroom.

James has been my best friend since we were in diapers. We have shared just about everything, including bathrooms. That's all I have to say about that.

When we found the actual bedroom door and opened it, the smell of coffee and bacon hit us like a tornado. And we made it down all those stairs a lot easier than we came up.

"Well, now," Grandmother said. "Look who's up bright and early this morning."

My grandmother is a big joker, so I figured she was giving us a hard time for sleeping late and that it had to be around noon. Especially with all that light in our room. A big clock on the wall showed six o'clock, either it was broken or we'd slept all day! So why was my dad at the stove flipping pancakes?

"Uh, we're having pancakes?"

"Of course, Patrick," Dad said. "It's Saturday morning. Pancakes."

James sat on a stool at the granite island. "Whoa. Did we mean to get up so early?"

"It was that stupid window and all that rainbow stuff," I mumbled as I sat next to him. I'd been wide awake when we came downstairs. Now, knowing the real time, I felt like going back to bed.

My dad hummed while he cooked, just the way he did at home. "You boys get the first ones while they're hot," he said, scooping up one pancake after another and plopping them on plates for me and James. Grandmother set a small glass pitcher of warm syrup and a dish of soft butter on the counter in front of us, along with a plate full of strips of crisp bacon and tall glasses of milk. She brought knives and forks from a drawer and set them by our plates. "Eat up boys, before it gets cold."

We didn't need to be told twice and dug in.

"Would you look at those boys eat." Papa was reading the morning paper at the kitchen table and put it aside to comment on the amount of food James and I were inhaling.

"You just forget how much our boys ate when they were at home," Grandmother said, and poured seconds of milk for me and James.

The last bite on my plate went into my mouth as my mother came into the kitchen. She had her usual Saturday morning blank stare and bed head. Grandmother must have recognized the look. She handed a cup of coffee to Mom as she shuffled by and went to sit in a big leather chair in the family room.

Papa got up from the table and clapped his hands together. "All right, boys, time to get this day started. Go upstairs and grab your gear."

"Where are we going?" We'd just got there. I looked at my dad. Maybe he could tell me what was going on.

"Everyone else will be here soon," he said, filling in the details, "and you and James need to clear your things out of the bedroom before Kate and Jillian get here."

"You mean *we* get kicked out of the bedroom so *they* can have it?"

My dad explained that all the granddaughters would have the entire third floor. *Because girls needed their privacy.* Like I hadn't heard that my whole life. My cousins just got bumped back down to the 'spoiled little darlings' on my list. Taylor and Abby weren't far behind.

So I figured it was air mattresses for me and James, somewhere in the house. No use arguing. We slid off the bar stools and started the climb up the stairs. James didn't say a word. He had sisters and they always got first choice too. All the time. Taylor came out of her bedroom at the same time we got to the top of the stairs.

"Good morning, guys," she said, all cheery like.

Her eyes popped when I growled and glared at her as I walked past her into the bedroom with the crazy window, slamming the door behind me. I shouldered my duffle and backpack and told James, "Well, at least we won't have unicorns pooping rainbows all over our heads every morning."

My dad met us at the bottom of the stairs. "Papa is waiting for you on the back porch," he said, pointing to a door leading from the kitchen.

It was worse than I thought. We were going to have to sleep outside on the porch! "Dad?"

"Just go on," he said. "Grandmother and Papa have a surprise for you."

We were surprised all right. When we stepped out the door, Papa turned and told us to follow him. He was walking toward the barn! It looked like it was in pretty good shape, but, still, it was a barn, for cryin' out loud.

"You gotta be kidding," James muttered.

"Hey, I'm sorry about this," I said, embarrassed I'd invited my best friend to come with me and end up staying in a barn.

Papa walked ahead of us down a path leading past some fruit trees. At the barn, he opened a tall door, waiting for us to catch up. I couldn't even look at him as I brushed past him and stepped inside. Expecting smells worse than the culvert crap, I was confused by the scent of pine and what looked like a mountain lodge or a big log cabin. One of those wood-burning stoves was in a corner and chairs and couches sat around the big room. And a HUGE flat screen TV!

I was still trying to take it all in when Papa said, "You boys go on up and pick out your room."

Was he serious? While I stared, he explained. "When your grandmother and her brother and sister decided to fix up the place, Jack got it in his head to include the barn. They have plans for the house, but your Uncle Jack and Kay live out here. Their room is at the end of the hall in the back, but the rest of the place is yours while you're here."

"But . . ."

"You will have to share some of the time, like if all you kids want to watch movies or play some games or things like that. Oh, and there's a fridge in the kitchen," he said pointing to the back of the large space. "I think Grandmother has it pretty well stocked, as well as the pantry. Feel free."

Papa went to the door then turned. "You two can share a room," he told us, "or you can each have your own, with your own bathroom. Whatever you want." He winked at me and grinned before stepping through the door. "Girls don't get to have all the fun."

"Patrick, look at this place," James said after Papa was gone, his voice barely a whisper.

"I know," I said, almost like I was in church or something. Then I yelled, "I KNOW! Can you believe it?" I did a three-sixty, yelling, "Eat your heart out, Taylor Elizabeth Morrison!"

We dropped our bags and ran to the kitchen and checked out the fridge and pantry. I couldn't have asked for more. We checked out the flat screen TV, looked through the cabinets for movies and games, and sat on one of the leather couches and drank a cold bottled water with some Oreos. Yep, this was living.

"Our rooms!" James and I said together and dashed up the stairs and looked into each of three bedrooms. We decided that we'd come there to spend the time together and chose one of the rooms with twin beds. It was the first room off the top of the stairs, as far away from Uncle Jack as possible. I took the bed closest to the door. We tried the shutters on the corner windows to make sure there wouldn't be any wild colored windows like in the house.

After getting a feel for the beds, we agreed we both needed a shower and some clean clothes. Our room had its own bathroom but since we didn't have to share, I said I'd take the bathroom in the room just next door so we'd each have our own. I let the hot water run over my head and shoulders until it started to get cool. I figured James was beginning to run out of hot water too, so I turned off the water and stepped out of the shower and reached for one of the big yellow towels. I could get used to this real quick.

James was standing at the window when I got back in the room. "That is a lot of cotton out there," he said.

He was right. The window overlooked acres white with cotton, ready to be harvested. In the distance we could see several wagons in the middle of the field, and some kind of giant machine sat nearby. We couldn't see any people.

"Patrick?" I heard my mother calling from downstairs.

I was just about to answer when I heard my sister. "Holy Cow!" she screeched. "Look at this place."

Yeah, Missy Prissy, take a good look at it, I thought, and eat your heart out. She could share a room on the third floor of the house and all those steps, this was all mine. Ours, mine and James. Except for Uncle Jack's room.

We stepped out of our room and I heard my mother say, "Why, it's beautiful. I had no idea."

"Pretty cool, huh?" I said as James and I walked down the stairs. Passing right by Taylor, I sat in a big chair, plopped my feet up on the footstool and leaned back, gloating.

Mom was already in the kitchen, opening the refrigerator then the pantry. "Well, it looks like you boys have everything you need," she said coming back into the main room. "How is your room? Or rooms, should I say?"

"Rooms?" Taylor squawked like a chicken and looked up the stairs.

Just then, someone from up there said, "Do I hear one of my favorite nieces down there?"

"Uncle Jack!" my mom cried and met him at the foot of the stairs for a big hug.

Uncle Jack, my great-uncle, is Grandmother's brother. He's younger than her and she tells some hilarious stories about taking care of him when he was little. He's retired military, a Vietnam veteran, and from what I've heard my parents say, he's sort of a loner. He sure seemed friendly enough right then, hugging my mom, making Taylor blush from his compliments and shaking my hand, which I wondered if I'd ever be able to use again.

"How's Aunt Kay?" my mom asked him.

"Oh, she's working."

"Well, we'll miss her."

Aunt Kay is Uncle Jack's wife. While he's retired, she's a lot younger than him. I am a first-class eavesdropper and from the conversations I'd listened in on, she does some kind of classified work for the government. I wondered if Mom and Uncle Jack were talking code for 'Kay is on assignment,' I figured I'd find out if she didn't show up sometime while we were there. And maybe with some creative listening on my part.

While they were catching up on news, I got up from my chair and strolled to the kitchen. "Want something while I'm in here, James?" I called loud enough to make sure Taylor would hear, just to rub it in.

"Patrick," she said, coming to the kitchen, "you shouldn't be eating anything. Grandmother sent us out here to tell you that lunch is ready. You better not be getting something to eat."

I pulled a snack cake from the pantry, slowly tearing the wrapper as I walked back into the room. "Oh, yeah? Who says?"

"I do," Mom said. "Taylor's right, Patrick. Clint and Judith and the girls will be here in a few minutes and Grandmother wanted us to all have lunch when they get here." She nodded at the treat I held in my hand. "Put that in a baggie, Honey. I don't want you spoiling your lunch. You can eat it later."

I really didn't mind not eating the snack cake, I only got it to get at my sister. What I *did* mind was the smirk on Taylor's face. I thought about stuffing the whole thing in my mouth, even better, cramming it in her face, but it went back in the pantry. Because my mom said to.

Uncle Jack was holding the door for my mom and Taylor when I stepped away from the pantry. I looked at James and shrugged and we followed them out the door. A white Trailblazer turned into the drive just as we reached the back door of the house.

Kate and Jillian spilled out of the car before their dad could undo his seat belt. Grandmother came out of the house and held out her arms then there was a lot of hugging and laughing and talking going on. I just wanted to go back to my barn.

After a while, I noticed Uncle Jack said something in my grandmother's ear. She smiled up at him and nodded her head. I don't think anyone else but me saw him slip away from all the noise and walk toward the barn.

As usual, Grandmother made enough food for the whole town of Daly. Only it was just family and everyone had all they could eat. As soon as we finished eating, Papa and Uncle Clint went to his car to bring in their things. Taylor took Kate and Jillian upstairs to see their room. James and I headed back to the barn.

There was no sign of Uncle Jack when we got there.

"You want to walk around some?" I asked James. "See what we can find?"

James was all for it. We grabbed a couple of bottles of water from the fridge and I checked the pantry for Oreos. There was a good supply, but we were both still stuffed from lunch so we just took our water and went out the back door of the kitchen. And walked right into a cotton field.

A black, late-model F-150 pickup was parked on a graveled space between the barn and the field. I figured it must be Uncle Jack's ride. Sweet.

After checking it out, we took a right and walked toward a line of trees at the end of the cotton rows. We followed a dirt road headed away from the house and kept walking until we reached a small ditch. There was hardly any water in it, but who knew what was in there. It looked like a breeding ground for snakes to me.

So, we followed the ditch until we found a wooden bridge that didn't look all that safe, and crossed into another field of cotton. There was no road on that side, but we could see another tree line and walked down the middle of the rows until we came to the end and the trees.

Another cotton field and three big wagons were on the other side of a fence, and we climbed through it and sat on the ground in the shade of one of the wagons and finished off our water. We could see farm machinery around a house where the field ended and decided to check it out.

"We should be able to get back to your grandmother's from there," James said looking back in the direction we'd come. The roof of the barn was still in sight.

Some dogs barked at us as we reached a big cotton picking machine and a couple tractors behind the small farm house.

"Git over here!" an old man sitting under a big tree yelled, and the dogs shut up and trotted over to sit on the ground by him.

"Reckon we might as well say 'howdy,'" James muttered under his breath and we walked over to where the man sat. He had a big metal pan full of some kind of peas or beans in his lap.

Exactly what are you supposed to do when you just wander into someone's yard? The old man cleared that up real quick.

"Afternoon, boys. Where you headin'?"

No 'who are you,' 'what are you doing on my property,' no 'where did you come from'? Just 'where you headin'?'

"Well, uh, you see . . ." I stammered. "I'm Patrick Morrison and this is my friend, James Moore. We're visiting with my grandparents—"

"Over at the old Ledbetter place. I know, everybody around heard you all was coming." The man turned his head and spit a stream of brown saliva on the ground next to him. He took a big dark blue rag from his back pocket and wiped his mouth then leaned toward me, studying my face. "You look just like your mother, young man. You both do. I'd have known you anywhere."

"Yes, sir," I replied, grinning. "I hear that a lot." I didn't bother explaining that James and I weren't brothers just because we looked alike.

He waited, scratching his jaw, watching us.

"Uh, well, we were just out looking around." I thought he might be waiting for us to answer his question. "Saw your place over here and thought we'd come this way."

"Well, all right, then. You boys enjoy your walk," he said and went back to shelling peas into the big bowl.

"Okay," I said, taking a step. "We'll just go on now." James fell into step with me and we walked toward the front of the house. We waved from the road and picked up our step. When we were well away from the house, I stopped to be sure we still had the barn in sight.

The blacktop road ran alongside a deep ditch. I remembered Grandmother telling about fishing in it when she was a girl. She'd let Uncle Jack fall in once and told her parents he'd run away from the house and fallen in when she'd chased him down. She and Uncle Jack both got "whuppins."

I also remembered driving from Daly to see the farm one time we were there when I was little, with the ditch on one side of the car. We were headed in the right direction, I was sure. All we had to do was walk until we got to the bridge that crossed the ditch, turn left and we'd come right back to Grandmother's house.

Kicking at gravel as we walked along the road, we passed a field of dried corn stalks which seemed out of place with all the cotton fields. "Hey, Patrick," James said, stopping. "Check that out. What does that remind you of?"

I looked to where he was pointing and came to a screeching halt. "Whoa." I could have been back home, looking across the field from Mr. Nelson's pasture. The trees in the middle of the cotton field looked almost exactly like the mound at home. Two groups of trees. Two mounds?

"I don't remember ever seeing that before," I said.

"But you were kinda little when you came here, right?"

"Yeah. And we just drove by the house so we could see where Grandmother lived. I was probably bored and didn't care about the whole thing, and never noticed that."

"Let's get back to the house and see if we can find out anything about it," James said. He started walking then stopped. "Hold up a minute. Let's take a picture and send it to the guys. They won't believe it."

He reached for his phone. It was not in his back pocket where he usually carried it. "Oh, no," he said, his voice a hoarse whisper, a look of panic in his eyes.

I went for my phone then and felt my heart hit my shoes. Mine was gone too. "Oh, my gosh. James, they could be anywhere!"

There was nothing to do but scuff on down the road and try and decide if we should retrace our steps. After a few steps, James grabbed my arm, stopping me. "Wait! Patrick, I don't think I even brought my phone. Didn't we leave them in the bedroom, charging?"

I felt air come back into my lungs and I started to grin. "Yes! When Taylor and my mom came out to the barn, I got so mad at Taylor all I wanted to do was get out of there. We didn't even go back upstairs, just snuck out the back door."

"Let's hurry and get back," James said. "Just to make sure."

We were out of breath when we reached the farm house. We'd jogged all the way.

CHAPTER TWENTY-FIVE

"Patrick! Where have you been?" my cousin Jillian shouted, bursting out of the house as we were heading for the barn. Her blonde pony tail bobbing behind her, she ran at me and nearly knocked me off my feet, jumping up to grab me. Her arms around my neck, her face in mine, scolding, "We missed you. We looked all over the place. You didn't even answer your phone."

"Yeah, I know." Setting her down on the ground, I hurried toward the barn with her tagging right along with us.

"We looked for you in there," she said when we reached the barn door.

"Is anyone out here, Jillian?" I asked before opening the door. I wanted to be sure James and I weren't ambushed before we had a chance to check our rooms for our phones.

"No. Grandmother and your mom and my mom are in the kitchen, cooking. Again." She followed us inside.

I looked around to be sure there was no one there and James and I took the stairs two at a time and opened the bedroom door.

"There they are!" James rushed across the room and grabbed his phone off the bedside table. He unplugged mine and held it out to me. "Let's go get that picture."

Jillian was running into the yard shouting by the time we made it down the stairs. "I found them, Aunt Jennifer." She yelled at the top of her lungs, before she was even in yelling distance of the house.

"Let's hurry," I told James. We bolted from the barn and ran to the front of the house before anyone had a chance to stop us.

We could see the mound clearly from the middle of the road. We each took some shots, and decided James would text Jeremy, with a couple photos, and I'd send some to Brendan.

"Who's going to text Max? Me or you?" James asked.

Max would freak out. There'd be a ton of questions that neither of us could answer. Not until we got some answers ourselves.

We decided I'd send Max a picture and a short text. Being sure to say we'd send more information later.

While we were deciding on who was going to do what, my dad walked up. "Where have you boys been?"

He didn't look upset or anything. Me and my friends had done some pretty crazy stuff in the past, but he was used to it, and was usually pretty cool.

"Um, well, we took a walk."

"You were gone for quite a while."

"It was a long walk."

"Oh, yeah?" He was grinning at me and I knew everything was okay. "And where did this long walk take you?"

We told him about taking off down through the field over to the farm house and meeting the old man shelling peas.

"I don't know who he was, he didn't tell us his name, but he didn't act bothered that we came through his field and yard. Oh, and he seemed to know Mom."

"Probably so. They all used to come here when she was a kid. They were all over the place, from what I understand."

"Jillian said you all were looking for us."

"*Jillian* was looking for you. You know how she always wants you to play with her, and Taylor and Kate were busy doing something together."

Right on cue, Jillian came running from the house, making a beeline toward us. I hadn't noticed that Uncle Clint was sitting in one of the rockers on the front porch. He and my dad must have been taking it easy together. Before Jillian could make it down the steps, he called her back and sat her on his lap, talking to her and keeping her out of our hair for a little while.

"So you walked all the way around," Dad said, pointing out back of the barn. "From that house over there and up the ditch to here?"

"Yep."

"What are you doing out here now? In the middle of the road?"

"Well, we hadn't noticed that mound over there until we were coming back this way . . ." I stopped, realizing he didn't know anything about our discovery about the woods at home actually being a mound. Or any of the mystery we'd uncovered.

"It looked interesting and we were just taking some pictures."

"Oh, yeah." He looked at the mounds. "Story is those are Indian burial mounds."

Chills ran down my spine and I looked at James, trying to stay calm.

"I'm sure Grandmother or Uncle Jack . . . for sure Uncle Jack can tell you all about them."

This was getting better all the time.

"But for now, better come inside and get washed up for dinner." He turned and walked back to the house.

"Okay. Be right there," I said. "Just let me get a couple more pictures, okay?"

Dad waved over his head and went up on the porch and took a seat in the rocker next to Clint and Jillian.

I turned around, looking at the *mounds*. "Oh, my gosh, James!"

"I know! Can you believe it?"

We kept our voices low and our backs to the house. If anyone had seen our faces right then, they'd have known *something* was up. We'd have to play this really cool.

It turned out that Aunt Liz and Uncle Nathan's flight had been delayed and they wouldn't be there for dinner after all. They were renting a car from the airport and driving from

Memphis rather than have someone pick them up. Maybe they'd be in Daly before bedtime.

Grandmother, Mom and Aunt Judith had fried chicken, mashed potatoes, made gravy and fixed biscuits. There was other stuff on the table, but I couldn't tell you what any of it was. With all her family around, my grandmother went all out. She even baked a pie. But I remembered a whole stash of ice cream sandwiches in the fridge in the barn; my grandmother's standard dessert.

When dinner was over, the table was cleared and the dominoes came out. It was a tradition when all the family was together. We played in pairs, making it simpler with so many people. Taylor offered to be Jillian's partner. Kate teamed up with her mother, but she didn't really need any help. James had never played Mexican Train with our family. It was a real eye-opener for him. His family is very quiet compared to mine.

No one actually won because we never keep score, we just play for the fun of it.

After several rounds, it was time for Jillian to go to bed. Kate got to stay up. She acted so much older than she had at Christmas, like she'd grown up a lot in the past months. And much quieter than she had been, almost shy now. Taylor asked her if she wanted to watch a movie.

"There's a huge flat screen in the barn," I said, inviting them to come out there before I realized what I was doing. Oh, well. "There's lots of DVDs, want to watch something out there?"

Taylor looked at Kate and asked. "You want to?"

Kate nodded, smiling, pleased to be one of the 'big kids.'

We found a movie we all agreed on much quicker than I expected. We made popcorn and I got the box of ice cream sandwiches from the refrigerator. It really did seem like Grandmother's house now.

After the movie was over, Taylor and Kate went back into the house. James and I grabbed our phones. It was ten, but not too late to text the guys the pictures of the mounds.

And, just as I expected, there were texts flying back and forth in no time. We used up so much data on our phones taking the pictures of the mounds we'd have to plug them in before we went to bed so they could charge overnight.

"We'll find out everything we can tomorrow and let you know," I told them. "Goodnight."

We turned out the lights, but I couldn't go to sleep. Neither did James.

"Patrick? Do you think we can go over there tomorrow?"

"To the mounds? Did you think we wouldn't?"

I knew James was smiling in the dark just like I was.

CHAPTER TWENTY-SIX

Some things are the same wherever you are. Which was true about going to church the next morning. Grandmother made sure everyone was up, dressed, and ready to go with time to spare. She grinned all the way through the services. Afterward, she gathered all the grandkids together so she could show us off to her friends. She included James, said he could be Brett's stand-in. We were the last people to leave the church.

Afterward, we drove along the road beside the big ditch, over the bridge to Grandmother and Papa's house. I was surprised to see their car in the driveway, and that she was in the kitchen already.

"How did you get here before the rest of us?" I asked my mom, who had been in my grandparents' car.

"Oh, we took the field road," she said, stirring a pot on the stove. "It's shorter."

"What *field* road?"

"The one across the road out front. It goes straight into town. Quicker."

"Why didn't we all come that way? Why do we always go around through the country or by the ditch?"

"Oh, honey," Grandmother answered, "we're just so used to going around. We weren't able to use the road through the field for years, it was more like a dirt path. It's only been usable for a couple of years." She smiled at my mom and winked. "One of the reasons we decided to fix this old place up."

"Patrick, if you and James want to change before we eat," my mom said, "do it now."

Questions about the field road buzzed through my head, but I could tell she had her mind on getting the meal ready and I decided to wait. She slapped at my hand as I grabbed a handful of black olives from a dish on the kitchen counter and popped one in my mouth. I shared with James as we went out the door.

Stuffed again with roast, mashed potatoes, and all kinds of vegetables, we excused ourselves and went out to the barn. It was going to take a crane to get me off the couch after I finally sat down. We were safe for a few hours, at least. I just hoped that Jillian wouldn't come looking for us again.

After a while, I asked James, "Want to take a walk? Over to the mounds?"

He jumped up from the couch, and we were out the door in a flash. I checked the front porch of the house as we went around the corner. I didn't want company. The field road didn't have blacktop like the one in front of Grandmother and Papa's house, but there was something that looked like oil on it and the dirt was packed down so that vehicles and farm machinery could pass over it.

When we reached the mounds, the only way to get to them was a dirt path with deep ruts where the tractors and cotton pickers had mired down at some point. We broke into a run and stopped when we reached the smallest mound.

"You ready?" I asked James. He said yes and we started walking up.

After only a few minutes it leveled off and we stood at the top. We walked around for a while, looking for anything interesting and decided to go on to the other one when nothing turned up.

The mounds were separated by a narrow strip of land; wagons, more machinery, and a large fuel tank were scattered around. The bigger mound didn't seem to be as wide, or as big as the one back home, but, when we started walking through the trees, it was a lot steeper. Vines and undergrowth made it hard to get to the top.

It leveled off in a clearing and I got a prickly feeling at the back of my neck. A tree stump sat near the middle of the area, a couple more lay on their sides a few feet away. There was a spot that looked like it could have been where a fire burned once.

"Well, your dad did say this was an Indian burial mound," James said, looking around.

Then we heard a noise, twigs and branches snapping. I nearly jumped out of my skin and we froze in our tracks, looking in the direction the sound came from. We didn't see anything.

"Probably, just a rabbit or something," James said, barely above a whisper.

"You're probably right."

This would have been where I would have pulled out some bottled water and Oreos, but I hadn't brought any.

"Want to go down and see what's there?" I pointed to the side of the mound opposite from where we'd come up. James nodded and we'd taken a couple of steps when I heard someone calling my name.

"Patrick?"

Jillian! What was she doing here? Was anyone with her? Whatever, there was no choice but to retrace our steps and find out.

Before we reached the bottom, I could see her through the trees. It looked like she was alone and was crying. I shouted, "Jillian?"

"Patrick! Where are you?" She was running toward the sound of my voice.

"Wait where you are," I called, "we'll be right there."

She leaped on me as soon as we got to her. "Oh, Patrick, I was scared when I couldn't find you," she said, crying on my shoulder.

"Did you come over here by yourself?"

She nodded and wiped her nose on my shirt and looked up at me. "Everyone was napping or just sitting around talking and there was nothing to do. I went out on the porch to play and saw you walking over here, so I followed you to see where you were going."

I sat her on the ground and said, "Well, you shouldn't have followed us."

"I know. I got scared when I got to that place over there." She pointed at the small mound. "You just disappeared. I walked around to where the tractors and stuff were, but I didn't see you anywhere. Then I heard some noises." She started bawling again. "Oh, Patrick, I was so scared."

I was so ticked right then, I wanted to pinch her. But I'd be in trouble for sure if I did. And I couldn't just point her down the road and tell her to go back. There was nothing to do but to take her. We'd have to explore the larger mound another day. I looked at James and rolled my eyes, he just shrugged. I'm lucky he is so laid laid-back and such a good friend.

I started walking toward the farm road and nodded in that direction "Come on," I told Jillian, "we'll take you back to the house."

No one had even missed me and James until they started looking for Jillian. Of course, the minute she saw her mother she started bawling again. Grandmother got out milk and cookies for her, assuring Jillian's mom it wouldn't spoil her supper. Tsk, tsk. Poor little thing. Precious little darling, just as always.

Then Grandmother sat out a hero's helping of cookies and milk for me and James which almost equaled things out in my opinion.

No one even scolded Jillian for running off from the house and not telling anyone or anything. But when all the drama died down, I got grilled.

After I'd explained to my dad, he said, "Well, next time, tell someone where you are going."

"Dad . . . Really?"

Fifteen and we'd have to tell every move we made? Just because a little snoop ran off. *She* was the one who should be warned. I was fuming.

"Patrick," he said, "just give someone a head's up. That's all I'm asking. Okay?"

I agreed, but I grumbled.

There was no basketball to shoot some hoops, but we did find a couple baseball gloves and a ball. James and I tossed some balls around until supper then went to the barn. I didn't invite anyone to come with us. We watched a movie that night—by ourselves.

CHAPTER TWENTY-SEVEN

I was glad to see my dad in the kitchen when we went in for breakfast the next morning.

"Can we go back over to the mound?" I asked him. "We didn't get to check things out at all yesterday.

"You guys finish up here and head out before anyone knows you're gone." He winked at me and looked around, checking on who else might be in the kitchen.

"And can *someone* make sure we aren't followed this time?"

"You betcha. And, Patrick, be sure and check in once in a while."

I nodded and took my last bite, chewing on it as we headed to the barn. This time I wanted to be sure and take some water and cookies. I grabbed my backpack and took some from the pantry, and we got away without anyone seeing us. As far as we knew.

The cotton pickers and wagons were gone when we got to the strip between the mounds. Someone had moved them, but no one was around. We headed up where we'd been the day before, before we'd had to rescue the 'precious little darling.'

Everything seemed the same. Same tree stumps, same spot that looked like old ashes. We stood still for a couple of minutes, listening. No noises.

"Hey, James, check it out," I said, pointing through the trees toward the farm. I hadn't noticed the day before that we could see Grandmother and Papa's house from up there. In fact, it was a good place to see pretty much all around, in every direction; the big ditch, and Daly, farm houses here and there, and fields of cotton that went on forever.

Taking a seat on a stump, I pulled out the Oreos and bottled water and shared with James. After a while, we took our time going down the other side from where we'd come up. When the ground leveled off, there was more of the cotton field. Like there was going to be anything else?

We decided we'd walk around the mound, like . . . get an idea of how big it might be. We'd only gone a few yards when James stopped. "Uh, Patrick . . ."

I turned to see what he was looking at and felt the air being sucked out of my lungs. A small patch of well-trimmed grass surrounded three white tombstones!

"All right this is way past being spooky," I said.

"No kidding."

"So what do you want to do?"

"Check the names on the markers," we said together.

Being careful where we stepped, we bent to read the stone slabs. Just like on the stones at home, it was almost impossible to read names or dates. But one thing for sure: none of the names came close to Feurey.

James and I stood up, stepped back, grabbed our cell phones and clicked away.

We looked around to see if there were any more tombstones, but didn't find any. Walking on around the base of the mound, we came back to the area where the farm machinery and fuel tank were. With not much more to see, we decided to head back to the house and see what was for lunch. My stomach was grumbling.

On the way back to the house we talked about sending the latest pictures to the guys. They were never going to believe what we'd found.

"Wonder how Max is going to fit his crazy renegade Indian into this?" James joked.

"I'm sure he'll have something to say about it all." I laughed imagining the look on Max's face when he saw the pictures we sent. "Maybe we should tell him and Jeremy together. Max will probably hyperventilate when he hears."

"About time you boys got back," Grandmother said when we came into the kitchen. Everybody seemed to be there, either at the table or at the kitchen counter.

I looked at my dad. Hadn't he told them where we were?

"Oh, your dad told us you were out exploring again," Grandmother said, laughing. At least my dad was off the hook. "He also told us you boys sometimes get so wound up in what you're doing, you forget the time. Go on now, get washed up and get a plate and something to eat," she said, filling a couple glasses from the ice dispenser in the refrigerator door.

While we ate at the bar, we learned there was a trip to 'town' planned. From what I remembered, there wasn't all that much to see or do in Daly. I'd rather stay in the barn and text or talk to my friends.

When I tried to beg off, my mother insisted. "Patrick, your grandmother's friend owns a boutique in town and she wants to show you kids off. That's what grandmothers do."

Good grief! Who knew Daly even had a *boutique*? I felt another one of those moments coming on when I'd rather have a root canal than step foot in a *boutique*.

"Patrick, you boys just go put on clean shirts and come right back," my mom said. "And don't take forever, we're ready to leave."

"There's not room for everyone, Jen," my dad told my mom. He winked at me and said, "Why don't the boys ride into town with the rest of us guys?"

"That sounds great," she agreed, picking up her purse and heading out the door. "Just don't take too long."

"Don't worry, son," Papa said when all the ladies were well out of the house and headed to town. "After your grandmother shows you off, all us guys will go over to the Shake Shop. My treat."

Sounded like a bribe to me, but, what the heck, I was not going to get out of going. We went to the barn and put on clean shirts.

Before we left the barn, we sent a text to the guys and asked if any of them would be together that evening. As we expected, Brandon had practice (didn't sports jocks ever get any time off?), but he'd let us know when he would be home. Our message to Jeremy said to see if he and Max could be together and we'd either text or call later. His text back said, "will make it so."

Papa, my dad and the two uncles were waiting in the Suburban, with the motor running, when we came out of the barn. James and I piled into the back and we headed into Daly.

"Why don't we just take the farm road?" I asked Papa who was driving. "Like you did yesterday."

"Could have," he said, "but I noticed the pickers weren't over at the mounds this morning. That means they'll be picking in that upper field close to town and we might get in their way."

Made sense, I guessed. So we drove around the country road. The ride in the very back of a big SUV, even when the surface of the road is tarred, is really bumpy. I was more than ready to get out when Papa stopped in front of Betsy's Boutique. There were at least a dozen cars parked outside the shop. I wondered if everyone in town was in there.

There were several people, make that women, inside the shop, and I was pretty sure not all of them were customers. After being on my best behavior for about as long as I thought I could take it, Papa stuck his head in the door.

"Livvy," he called to my grandmother, "you done with those boys yet? We're headed over to the Shake Shop, thought they might like to go."

She looked around and when she was sure no one had missed seeing us she said, "Oh, I suppose so."

We couldn't get out of there fast enough. But not before she called, "Don't you all spoil your supper, now, you hear?"

Instead of getting back into the SUV, we walked to the Shake Shack, easy walking distance from the boutique. After all, Daly is not a big town. I wasn't really hungry, but, like any healthy fifteen year old guy, I wasn't going to pass up a shake and fries. James and I sat by ourselves in a booth by the window and sent a text to Brendan. No telling when he'd get around to reading it, but at least he'd be up to speed when we did get a chance to talk tonight.

"How are we going to handle this with Max and Jeremy?" I asked between sips of vanilla shake.

"Text Jeremy and find out if Max is there."

Jeremy answered my text within seconds.

Jeremy: "Not now. Spending tonight at my house. Text then."

Me: "Cool. Later."

We finished up our fries and the last sip of shake just as my dad told us we were leaving. On the walk back to the boutique, we passed the Daly City Hall, the Post Office and a small grocery store. Next to an empty building on Main Street there was a machine shop which, Papa explained, serviced the cotton gins in the area. Betsy's Boutique was a little over a half a block away. We didn't see another person anywhere. Must have all been at Betsy's.

"Not much going on right now," Papa said, "but you wait 'til Saturday, things'll be jumpin' then."

"What's happening on Saturday?" James asked me.

"That's the Fall Festival," Papa explained. I remembered my mom saying something about a festival, but that's all I knew. "Won't be able to stir people with a stick then."

He told us about the fish fry on Friday night at the school cafeteria. On Saturday, booths would be set up along Main Street with people selling everything from zucchini bread (at least I knew what that was) to T-Shirts, to fishing lures. A parade would kick the whole thing off. The festival was big doings to these people.

It all sounded like fun, but right then, I just wanted to get back to the farm and get in touch with my friends. I couldn't get the mounds and those tombstones out of my mind.

We'd walked back to the boutique and there were still a lot of cars parked in front. Maybe more than had been there before. I really didn't want to go back in there, but before I knew it Grandmother was holding the door of the store open and waving for me to come inside.

She put an arm around my shoulder and led me through the door, motioning for James to come, too. Every lady who lived in Daly must have been in that store! James and I had always looked so much alike . . . black hair, blue eyes, same height . . . and I looked just like my mom, and everyone seemed to think he was part of the family. Grandmother introduced him just like he was. All we could do was smile and wait until they let us out of there.

When no one was watching, I looked at James and jerked my head toward the door. We made it outside without anyone noticing. My dad, Uncle Nathan, Clint and Papa were all leaning against the SUV, grinning from ear to ear, when James and I rushed through the door of the shop.

I looked over my shoulder thinking someone might grab me and drag me back inside. I would rather face a space alien vampire any day than those women in there.

I hurried over to my dad."Can we go home now?" I pleaded.

"Are the ladies ready to leave?"

"I don't know." I sounded like a whiney little girl but I couldn't help it. "Dad, please." I tried to get out of sight so no one could see us from the shop. Then I had a brilliant idea. "We can walk back to farm by the field road. Please, Dad?"

He asked Papa if it would be safe for us to walk through the field and I could have kissed them both when my grandfather said it would be fine.

"Just go to the corner there," Papa said, pointing to a street less than a half block away. "Turn right, go to the end, make a left and you'll be on the road. Can't miss it."

"Be careful," my dad called as James and I took off running.

At the corner, I looked over my shoulder and was sure all of them were having a good laugh. I didn't care. I just wanted out of there.

We found the road without any trouble and, when we were several yards down the road and I could actually see the farm house in the distance, I began to feel safe from all those females in that shop. And Papa had been right. Two large green cotton pickers were slowly moving through the field closest to town, leaving bare stalks with only ragged pieces of cotton hanging to them.

Skirting the machinery, we kept going until we got close to the mounds. Deciding we'd wait to go there another time, we walked on to the end of the road and crossed into the yard. No one was home. They were all in town. I could only hope we could get into the barn. I tried the door but it was locked. Even the back door. What were going to do now?

I heard someone calling my name and went back around to the front of the barn. Uncle Jack was standing by the back door of the house. "You boys want to come in the house, or do you need to get into the barn?"

"Either," I said. "Anywhere we can get a drink."

He held the screen door open for us as we walked into the kitchen. Something was cooking in the oven and it smelled good. I looked at the clock but it was hours until supper. I spied a cake under a glass cover on the counter. "Uncle Jack, think anyone would miss a couple pieces of cake?"

"Patrick, why don't you just call me Jack? And, if you'll cut me a slice, I'll get the milk." He took three glasses from the cabinet and filled them.

Uncle Jack wasn't much of a talker. I was glad. What do you say to an old guy you hardly know? I did have a question, though.

"Uncle Jack?"

"Jack."

"Uh, okay, Jack." I wasn't sure what my mom and dad were going to say about me calling him Jack. I figured I'd just wait and see. "My dad said you might know something about those mounds out there."

"Well . . . I might," he said.

"What can you tell us about them?"

"What do you want to know?"

Where to start? Should I tell him about the mound we'd discovered near our home? Should I mention the graves?

I put the last bite of cake in my mouth and washed it down with a big swig of milk. I looked at James. Maybe he knew where to begin.

Right then cars pulled into the driveway. Everyone was back from town and they were all coming into the house.

"Looks like we'll have to get back to this later," Jack said sliding out of his chair. He took our empty plates and rinsed them before putting them in the dishwasher. "Might want to get those glasses emptied and in here before they catch us," he said. He laid a key ring, with a couple keys attached, on the table. "You might be needing these."

With that, he nodded and walked out the back door. I watched him stop and say hello to the family as they made their way into the house, then he went to the barn. He walked around to the side and disappeared around the back.

Jillian hit the door like a west Texas dust storm, dancing and bouncing around all over the place. Taylor and Abby carried some shopping bags up the stairs. Grandmother, Mom and my aunts got busy in the kitchen.

"Clint," Aunt Judith said, "take Jillian outside and keep her busy and out of the way for a while. Please."

I couldn't wait to get out of the madhouse. *Before* Jillian saw us leaving. Trying to get around all those people in the kitchen, James and I decided to make our exit through the front of the house. Kate was sitting in a chair in the living room, a binder in her lap.

My hand was on the door when she called my name. "Patrick?"

No quick escape for me. I turned and looked at her. "Yeah?"

She bit her bottom lip and shook her head. "Nothing."

"Okay." I pushed the door open with James right on my heels.

"Can I come with you?" Kate blurted out like a squeaky mouse.

I didn't know whether to moan or groan. But mostly I surprised myself by saying, "Sure. Come on." I looked at James and said, "Sorry, man."

"Hey, man," he said, shrugging. "I'm good."

Kate looked at me like I'd just transformed into Captain America or Superman. She floated past me and down the steps, waiting at the bottom so she could tag along behind us.

We could hear Clint and Jillian right behind us. "Hurry," Kate said and sprinted past me and James to the safety of the barn.

CHAPTER TWENTY-EIGHT

We had a couple hours with no sounds but the beep of our phones. It would be after dinner before we could text with the guys. Kate huddled in one of the big leather chairs, focused on her binder. Her dark hair fell over her face as she concentrated on the sketch pad inside. *So that's what kept her so busy.*

"I'm getting water," I said as I passed by her on my way to the kitchen. "Want some?"

"Mmm."

She didn't raise her head but I took that as a 'yes' and brought a bottle to her. I tried to get a glimpse of what she was drawing, but she shut the cover of the binder until I walked away. I handed a water to James and joined him on the couch.

Ah. Peace and quiet.

But just for a little while. Jillian bounced through the barn door chattering a mile a minute about something. I made a mental note to be sure that door was locked behind us . . . *at all times.*

"Jillian!" Kate growled and glared at her little sister.

Whoa. What happened to the nice quiet person, happily drawing in her binder?

"Mom said to tell you guys supper is ready," Jillian chirped and made a bratty face at Kate.

Kate gathered her binder and stomped out of the barn, hurrying to the house.

"Patrick," Jillian happily informed me and James, "you're supposed to come, too."

"Okay. Right after we wash up." James took my cue and headed for the stairs. I put my hand on my cousin's shoulder and steered her toward the door. "Tell them we'll be right in."

I carefully led her out the door, closed it behind her . . . and locked it.

During supper, things got around to our true purpose for being there during *my* fall break. Taylor. I hadn't been having such a bad time up until I was reminded this whole trip was for my sister.

Up to that point, about all I knew was that Taylor and our cousin, Abby, were planning on going to school at the University in Jonesboro. And we were going there the next day so they could check everything out. It was news to me that they'd already applied and been accepted!

Wait just a minute! I thought. *What's with this "we"?*

"We're all going into town," my mother said. "After we look around the campus, we can have some lunch and do a little shopping. It'll be fun."

I was fairly sure she didn't mean Daly. And I didn't see anything fun about their plan and anyone could have seen that by one look at my face. But no one was paying attention to me.

My dad has this certain "look" he gives when he is dead serious about something. I've come to know it well. Right then I got "the look" so I knew there was no use arguing.

When the table was cleared, the dominoes came out and I figured there wasn't much else to do but suck it up and join the game. After a few rounds of Mexican Train, Taylor and Abby turned in their place and went upstairs to plan what they were going to wear the next day.

Oh, gag!

That gave me and James a reason to head back to the barn. Not to plan what we were going to wear the next day—geesh—but to leave the game to the adults. Jillian was already getting ready for bed and Kate was curled up with her sketch pad in a chair in the corner.

On the way out the door, I sent another text to Jeremy to see if Max was there yet.

Jeremy: "Max is here. Brendan too. What's up?"

Me: "Cool. Will be right back."

Jeremy: "Sure."

When we got inside the barn, I put together a group text and sent the pictures of the mound. Jeremy called James as soon as they looked at them. James put them on speaker phone.

"Are you serious!" he yelled.

"As rain," I answered. "But, wait, there's more."

I downloaded the pictures of the tombstones and clicked "send." Nothing. No text back, nothing over the phone.

Then, it was like the bird house at the zoo. Mostly from Max.

"Hey, Max," I said on speaker, "before you ask, there was not a Feurey on any of them."

Even Max laughed. Then we all talked for a while. They all wanted to know when we were going back to get another look. I explained about the plans for the next day and, honestly, I wasn't even sure there was even anything else to see over there. Although, I had to admit, I did want to make another trip and see if we could turn up anything.

"So, are you having tons of fun?" Brendan asked. I could hear the smirk in his voice. He knew me well enough to know I hadn't been cool on this trip in the first place.

"Don't even go there," I said. "But hey," I said with a sudden stroke of genius, "if we find anything new, let's do a visual chat next time. Whatdaya think?"

Everyone was in for that. I sure missed those guys. I'd be glad to get home.

CHAPTER TWENTY-NINE

I will never understand why it is so important to old people to get up so early. The next morning, Papa woke me from a perfectly good dream.

"Patrick? You awake?" he yelled from the bottom of the stairs.

"Well, I am now," I mumbled into my pillow.

"Time to get up."

Who could sleep with all that yelling going on anyway?

"You boys come have some breakfast."

I actually did mumble something about getting up, but I guess he didn't hear me.

"Patrick!"

"Yes, sir," I answered lifting my face out of my pillow. "I'm up. We're up."

"Well, the biscuits are getting cold."

I heard the door close as he left. I groaned and rolled over and looked right into James's face in the other bed.

"When I get home," he said, "I am going to sleep 'til noon every day for a week, at least."

"Right."

Since they seemed in such a hurry for us to come eat, we slid on our shoes and went into the house in our pajamas. My granddad was the only one dressed, everyone else in the kitchen looked pretty much like me and James.

I was beginning to wonder if there was at least one box of cereal anywhere around. Eggs and bacon, biscuits and gravy, even pancakes on Saturday morning, all those are fine some of the time. But a guy needs his cereal and milk. I looked through the pantry but didn't find anything but oatmeal and bran cereal, stuff like that—old people food. Maybe my mom could get her mind off Taylor long enough to pick some up from the store. I could dream, couldn't I?

After biscuits and gravy, James and I went to the barn, got our showers, dressed and came back into the house. It was like a zoo inside. We took one look at each other and headed back out the door. Kate was right on our heels.

"Okay if I come too?"

Who could blame her for wanting out of there? I nodded and she was beside us in a second.

There was no time to get into a movie or anything, so we took out our phones and each pulled up a game.

"Hey, Kate," I said, "no sketch pad today?"

She blushed and shook her head, with a big sigh. "My parents said I have to leave it here."

Not much more to say on the subject.

It took two vehicles for all of us. Thank goodness, James and I were in the SUV with the men. Kate and Jillian were with Taylor and Abby, my mom, aunts and Grandmother in another car. This bunch liked this caravan stuff.

The drive was not as long as I'd worried it would be. I was surprised that the campus was a pretty impressive place. Big. We parked and everybody piled out. I wished I could be transported anywhere else in the universe.

"Guys," my dad said, "come into the Admin building with us. I understand there is a student hangout downstairs and you can wait there for us if you want."

That was the best news I'd heard all day.

"Yes, sir." I grinned at James and we hurried ahead of the thundering herd.

"Just keep us posted, okay?" my dad called after us.

"Maybe things aren't going to be so bad after all," I said, climbing the steps of the large gray building.

"Yeah," James said. "I bet we even find some video games or something like that. This is a school, after all. Students, you know?"

As soon as we were inside the building, I spotted the stairs and headed that way. My high hopes soon went flying. I heard the 'little darlings' and their dad enter the building right behind us.

Okay, I figured, I'll have to change that to 'the little darling.' Kate wasn't all loud and squealing and bratty anymore like her little sister.

James and I tore down the stairs as fast as we could. We spied the "Mens" door and made a straight shot to it, and inside. We waited until we thought maybe Jillian would have her dad doing something. When we stepped outside, Kate was peeking out the "Ladies" door.

She looked around and asked softly, "Are they gone?"

"I don't see them anywhere." I was sure she meant her dad and sister,

"I asked my dad if I could hang out with you," she said shyly, coming to stand by us. "If that's okay with you?"

James' shoulders lifted when I looked at him for an answer. "Sure, I guess so."

Kate grabbed my arm to stop me from going the direction I was headed. "Not that way."

Then I noticed her dad and sister at the yogurt bar, and turned to follow Kate. What a switch. If anyone had told me a few months ago that I'd be following my cousin anywhere, I'd have told them they were nuts. We ducked into an arcade area and stayed busy for a while.

I got a text from my dad to meet them upstairs where we'd come into the building. We were all going to have lunch in the main cafeteria.

Me: Can't we just stay here and grab a bite?

Dad: No.

No explanation, nothing. I figured that meant no argument too. Lunch with everyone was the usual crazy circus. The burgers and fries weren't even all that good. We might as well have stayed in the food court.

The one good thing that came from the whole trip to "town" was when Papa suggested that the guys go back to the farm while the ladies shopped. I couldn't get to the car fast enough.

Back at the farm house, James headed to the barn and I told him, "Hey, I'll be right behind you."

"Dad, can I talk to you?" I said as I walked along beside him. He nodded.

"Is there some way that James and I don't have to tag along to everything the rest of you do? I mean, you know how James is . . . he would never say anything, but we invited him to come to hang out, with _me_. You know how laid-back he is, but even he is going to get tired of, well, you know."

"This bunch can get pretty overwhelming, huh?" he said, stopping at the porch and looking toward the barn then back at me.

"Yeah."

"We'll handle it."

"What about Mom?"

"We'll handle it."

"Thanks," I said and turned to the barn. James had the TV on, watching some weird reality show. I sat down on the couch and watched with him. After a while we heard cars in the driveway, followed by female voices. As they faded away, we heard a soft knock on the door and then it opened. I'd forgotten to lock it!

Kate slid through and quickly closed the door behind her. "Please, can I just hide out here with you guys for a while?"

If someone thought James and I were siblings, they might have supposed Kate was our sister. I wondered if anyone else had noticed how much we all looked alike.

I jerked my head toward a chair for her to sit. We all watched some backwoods kind of guys catching fish with their hands.

We just about jumped out of our skins a little while later when the door flew open and Jillian bounced in. Man, what a contrast to her sister now.

Kate looked at me. "Sorry, I forgot to lock the door."

"No problem. I do it all the time." When I wasn't upset, relief was written all over her face

"Guys! Guys! Come out front!" Jillian bounced all over the room. "We're going to play ball!" Everything was full throttle and at maximum volume with this kid.

"You know they're not going to leave us alone until we go see what's going on," James said.

"True."

We turned off the TV and I patted my pocket to make sure the key was there before I locked the door and left the barn.

There was a lot going on when we went around to the front of the house. Jack had dug out some equipment while the rest of us were in town and he, my dad and uncles had set up for a ball game. The front yard was huge, plenty of room to smack a whiffle ball around and run some bases.

At least we wouldn't just be vegging out the rest of the day until it was time to eat again then go to bed.

Papa split everyone into teams, making sure things were even; men and women on both sides. Abby and Taylor were split up, and Jillian and Kate. So were me and James. We grinned when he told us we'd be rivals. Hah! Game on.

James and I were best friends, but we were also very competitive. We could be brutal rivals.

It turned out to be a lot of fun, James and I keeping score on who had more hits and runs. After a while, though, my dad and uncles were playing something that looked a lot like tag football. That's when my mom and aunts decided it was time to take a break.

We all took a time out that lasted until supper. While James and I tossed a ball around waiting for the game to start again, all the women disappeared into the house, and the guys hung out on the patio in the shade of a big tree.

Jillian got a time-out for something and was sent to her room. Squalling at the top of her lungs, of course. Abby and Taylor asked Kate if she wanted to come to their room with them. I was glad they'd decided to take an interest in her.

We looked around. James and I were the only ones left in the yard. He said, "Well, that was fun . . . while it lasted."

"Yeah, if the guys were here, we'd still be trying to beat the socks off each other."

I looked toward the mound. "Think we might go have another look around?"

"Probably wouldn't have much time to explore. You know, before it's time to eat again."

He was right. We threw the ball gloves on the porch and drifted back to the barn. Maybe there'd be something on with a bunch of rednecks trying to catch something with their hands.

When we didn't find anything good on TV, we dug through some games on the shelves next to the TV and found a Battleship game. It had just started to get interesting when my phone vibrated. A message from my dad told me it was time to get ready for dinner.

Here's the thing: What is there to "get ready"? You go get the food, you eat it.

When we started into the house, I found out what "get ready" meant. Lugging ice from the house and dumping it in a big tin tub on the patio, then hauling out pitchers of lemonade and tea. Papa had the grill going and sent me in the house for the burgers and hotdogs.

I don't remember when the conversation got around to Taylor and Abby and school, but I began to pay attention when someone started talking about them living at the farm and what a savings it would be.

All I heard was that our grandparents had kept the farm and fixed up the house . . . for them. Seriously? Sounded to me like the trip back to the old home town had not only been about checking out the college, but had also been so my sister and our cousin could check out the farm house to see if they would want to live there instead of on campus.

Seriously?

Couldn't they have just left me out of the whole thing?

"Well, now Livvy," Papa said, "all this fixin' up wasn't just for those two girls." He looked at me and winked. "Patrick, there, may want to go to college here too, someday. Maybe James could come with him."

Finally! I didn't know what I thought of his idea, but at least not everything was about Taylor, after all.

"And there's those girls, you know," he said, nodding toward Kate and Jillian who were paying no attention, just glaring over the table at each other about something.

James just smiled and lifted one of his shoulders like "Who knows? Maybe" at what Papa said about him. James coming to school here too would be about the only way I'd consider it. I nudged James and leaned toward him, talking real low so no one could hear me. "Maybe all the guys could come too. We could form our very own fraternity."

"With our own frat house."

No one noticed us laughing.

CHAPTER THIRTY

Rain hitting the tin roof of the barn woke me the next morning. I rolled over and checked the time on my phone. Five-thirty was way too early to be up and I laid back down and pulled my pillow over my head. I've heard that some people like the sound of rain on the roof. It helps them sleep. Even with my pillow over my ears, I could still hear it beating on the metal. I wished it would stop.

An hour later I heard Papa yelling up the stairs that breakfast was ready and to come eat it while it was still hot.

I was starved. James and I dressed and dashed through the rain to the house.

"Wonder what you do on a rainy day on a farm?" James said, leaning toward me.

"No clue, buddy, but it doesn't look like much of anything." It looked like this was going to be one miserable day.

People came in and out of the kitchen, and Jillian showed up with some cards. I figured we might as well play with her. Nothing else was going on. The game got more interesting when Kate wanted to be included, and then Taylor and Abby asked to be dealt in.

I expected it to get old after a while, and was already wondering what James and I could find to do. Then Papa came into the kitchen.

"You boys want to go into town?"

Which town? Little town or big town? Daly or Jonesboro? I didn't really care, anything to get out of the house. On the other hand . . .

"Who's going?" If a trip into town meant putting up with all the girls, I'd just as soon stay put and me and James find something to do by ourselves.

"I asked you boys."

That sounded like just me and James.

Jillian began to put up a fuss, I mean a real pain in the . . . well, she was being a pain.

Papa gave her a look that would have stopped a Tyrannosaurus Rex in his tracks. She got quiet, but looked she might start in any second.

"Oh, you don't want to go off with those old boys," Grandmother said, taking Jillian's hand and leading her to the table. "All of us girls are going to do something all by ourselves today. Aunt Liz, Aunt Jennifer, your mom and I have a project all planned. Just for girls."

That got Jillian's attention. Kate even looked more cheerful when she heard that.

It turned out Papa's plans were to go to the mall in Jonesboro. James and I knew malls, we could find something to do. Seemed like that was what Papa counted on. Stopping in front of a department store, he told us he had some shopping to do and to meet him in the food court in a couple of hours. He winked at me, turned and walked into the store.

"There's got to be an arcade around here somewhere," I said, spying a standard mall directory. Chills 'N' Thrills Arcade was by the food court. We got our tokens and found our favorite game.

Two hours later we met Papa. "You boys want some lunch?" he asked. "No sense in waiting until we get back to the Shake Shop."

"Is it all right if we have pizza?"

"You know, that sounds good. I might even have some myself."

We ordered a large pizza with everything on it and the three of us ate the whole thing by ourselves. With James and me putting away the biggest part. When we had finished off the last slice, Papa asked if there was anything else we wanted to do while we were out.

"I don't know what else there is to do," I told him. I was just so glad we'd had at least a few hours out of the house, off the farm.

"Well, then, I guess we'll just head back to the house."

Once we were in the truck Papa took a different way back to the farm."There's things to do around these parts, you know," he said. "You just got to know what it is you want to do and where to go and do it."

Whatever he was talking about, I'd just have to take his word for it.

But I was soon to find out. I could tell we were not too far from the farm, traveling on some of the back roads when Papa pulled off the road. He turned off the motor and got out of the truck.

"Are we supposed to get out?" James asked, leaning over from the back seat.

"I have no idea."

We watched Papa walk around the truck to the passenger side where I'd been riding shotgun. I jumped, my heart racing when he opened my door.

"Climb on over under the wheel, Patrick," he said, motioning me to move.

"Uh . . . Sir?"

"You heard me," he said, waving toward the driver's seat. "Get on over there."

I did as he said and crawled over the console and sat behind the wheel. It was a very big truck.

Papa got in and shut the door. "You got your permit, right?"

"Not yet. I'm supposed to take my test to get it when we get back."

He looked in the back seat at James. "How about you, son?"

"No, sir. Same as Patrick."

Papa looked back at me. "Well, you practice sometimes, don't you? With your folks?"

Was he saying what I thought he was saying? I whirled around to see a big grin spread across James's face. I felt my face might break.

"Why, yes, sir, we sure do."

"Well, I don't suppose you can get too much practice." Papa settled back in his seat. "You ever driven a truck like this?"

"No, sir. Mostly my mom's car."

"Well, that's a fair sized vehicle. You should be able to handle this truck." He pulled on his seat belt and snapped it into place. "Start 'er up, Patrick."

I buckled my seat belt and had to adjust the seat. My grandfather is a big man. And this was a very big truck. I checked the mirrors and looked to see if there was anyone on the road.

"After that rain, there won't be hardly any traffic out here on these roads," Papa told me. "They're mostly used for farmers going from one field to another."

I figured that was his way of telling me I shouldn't worry about other vehicles. I slowly pulled out onto the surface of the road. I couldn't believe this was happening. Our trip to the country just got a hundred percent better.

We drove past one field then another; I'd drive a few miles, pull off the road then James would take a turn. A couple of times a truck passed going the other way and I'd lift my hand from the steering wheel in a little country greeting, the way I'd seen Papa do. I could tell that James was having as good a time as I was. What a blast! Who knew my grandfather was so cool?

After about an hour or so driving around, Papa said, "You boys ready to head back to the house? They'll be looking for us soon."

Was he kidding? Of course I wasn't ready to stop driving! But it did surprise me that we hadn't heard from anyone already, not even a text from my parents. I'd been having too much fun to notice.

I pulled off the road and started to kill the motor.

"What're you stopping for?" Papa asked.

"So you can take over? Drive home?"

"What for? You've been doing just fine."

"You sure?"

"I'm sure. Go north then turn left when you come to the next road," he directed. "It's straight home from there."

I started the motor and eased back onto the road.

When I turned into the drive, my uncles sat in the rockers on the porch, my dad leaned against a post. Before I could wonder what my dad thought about me driving Papa's truck, he flashed a huge grin and a thumbs-up at me. He put a hand on the back of my neck when I walked up onto the porch.

"Have a good time?" he said, rubbing the top of my head.

"The best."

"Good." He put an arm around my shoulder, and I saw him wink at my grandfather. I was pretty sure he'd known all along what Papa was up to. "You boys go get cleaned up now, supper's almost ready."

He didn't have to tell us twice, I was starved. Driving a big pickup truck can make a person mighty hungry.

We rushed to the barn and back and my mouth watered when we went through the back door into the kitchen. The food tasted better than anything I'd eaten all week. I didn't even mind playing games with everyone after supper was over. If my mom knew we'd been driving Papa's truck that afternoon, she didn't let on. Never said a word.

Even though we hadn't had a chance to go back to the mound, James and I decided to call the guys and have a visual chat anyway. We had something more exciting to tell them anyhow.

But Jeremy was the only one home and he didn't have much time. He was going to Six Flags with Max. Before our side trip with Papa that afternoon, I imagined James would have been wishing he'd stayed home where there were a lot of fun things to do. Not anymore.

"Too bad you didn't get to go back to the mound," Jeremy said when we explained it had been too wet.

"Aw, not so bad at all," James told him, turning to me and grinning.

"Oh, okay." Jeremy was getting antsy to go. "Maybe tomorrow."

"Yeah, actually we did something better," James said, ignoring Jeremy's brush-off. "Patrick's granddad took us out driving."

"Um-huh, sounds like fun. Look, guys, I gotta go. Max'll be by any minute."

"Oh, well. You guys have a good time," James said. "Oh, and when you see him, tell Max that Patrick's granddad let us drive his truck."

"Huh! What did you say?"

Now we had his attention.

"Yep," I said, "drove that big old pickup all over the farm country around here."

"Are you serious?" Jeremy squealed.

"As serious as Batman. Me and James. I drove first then we switched back and forth for over an hour. Man, it was a blast."

"Oh, wow."

"It was really cool when Patrick got to drive home," James said. "Right up the drive so his dad and his uncles saw him."

Yeah, that was pretty cool. I knew I'd never forget that feeling.

Jeremy turned his head away, and we could hear a doorbell ring. "Listen, guys," he said, "that's Max. I gotta go. Oh, man! Wait 'til I tell Max."

Sweet. "Okay. Later, dude."

"Oh, I'll tell Brendan too." Jeremy added. "They're not going to believe this! You know they're going to want to hear all about it. Maybe we can chat again tomorrow?"

"Sounds good. Tell them we said Hi." I closed the laptop and sank back into the sofa. It had been a really good day.

CHAPTER THIRTY-ONE

Papa had said there were "things" to do but you couldn't prove it by me. I was sure he wasn't going to take me and James out driving again. It was too wet to go back over to the mound, we'd be knee deep in mud. I didn't know what more I expected to find over there. At least it would have been something to do.

But exploring was our thing. So we decided to explore.

"Where do you want to go?" James asked as we walked around the front of the house.

"The ground's too wet to go back to the mound." I looked across the field as we stood in the road. We'd already been around by the big ditch, so I looked in the other direction. "We haven't been that way."

We fell into step down the middle of the road. There were fields on either side of us and the road straight ahead. After about a half of a mile, we came upon a narrow road, and saw a small house which we discovered was abandoned and empty. The door of the house was hanging open and we went up on the rotting porch and looked inside.

"How long you think it's been since someone lived here?" James asked.

"Who knows," I replied, poking at a pile of broken furniture and litter.

In another room, we rummaged through an old chest filled with pictures and albums, letters and keepsakes. "Wonder why anyone would just go off and leave this stuff? I know my family wouldn't."

"I know, neither would mine," James said.

"Feels sort of creepy." We shut the chest, dusted our hands and went through the kitchen and out the back. Old garden tools lay around in the yard, and there was a barn that looked like it could fall in on us. We didn't go inside.

Just then, Papa pulled up in front of the house. My dad, Uncle Nathan and Uncle Clint were with him. As they got out of the truck, a Jeep Wrangler with Jack at the wheel pulled in behind them. No wonder we never saw him driving his truck, he had other transportation. I had no idea where he kept it, but it was a good looking ride.

"Hi," I said, looking around at them.

"We saw you heading over this way," Papa said, getting out of the truck. "Thought we'd come over and see what you were up to."

"We were just looking around," I explained. "Why? Did we trespass or something?"

"Not at all. Not at all," Papa answered, leaning against the truck. "In fact, this place is all part of the farm."

I looked around and wondered why it had taken all of them to check up on us. If something had happened, my dad could have just sent me a text. Nothing in the way they were acting felt like we were in trouble. "So, what's up?"

Jack rubbed his chin. "You boys ever been muddin'?"

"What?"

"Remember how I told you there were things to do around here if you knew where to look?" Papa said.

"Yes."

"Well, you got to wait for the right time, too. Right after a good rain is a good time for muddin'."

"I thought you and James might be interested in a favorite pastime among the young folks around here," Jack said.

Mudding. Hum.

James turned, standing close to me he said very quietly, "You don't think they mean for us to whip up some mud pies or something, do you?"

A loud snort blew out my nose.

"Um . . . so what is this . . . *mudding*?" I managed to say after a bit.

"Muddin'!" My five grown male relatives corrected me at once.

"Okay . . . muddin'. What is it?"

For an answer, Jack opened the door of the Jeep and Uncle Nathan, my dad and Uncle Clint climbed in.

Papa got into his truck and said, "Hop in, boys."

We got in and followed Jack around the side of the old barn. Papa stopped. Jack kept going, driving right into a huge puddle of water.

The Jeep didn't stop, split the water, throwing mud and water to the side and spinning from the rear wheels. It splashed over the top as it came out of the water and was flung in all directions several yards. Then Jack spun the Jeep around and drove back into the water, churning up the mud even more. I could see through the part of the windows not covered with mud that my dad and uncles were laughing like crazy. Even Jack had a big grin.

"This is beginning to look interesting," I said and opened the truck door. James and I stood outside, watching the Jeep churn the mud into one huge, mucky, oozy puddle.

After three or four turns back and forth through the muck, Jack pulled the Jeep over next to us. Dad and the uncles got out, still laughing and talking.

"Your turn," Jack said to us from behind the steering wheel. James and I couldn't get inside the Jeep quick enough.

Before I closed the door, Uncle Clint said, "Remember, you have to get out and push if the Jeep gets stuck."

I wasn't worried—nothing had slowed Jack down yet. We bumped and slid through the mud, out and back into it, over and over. "Wait 'til we tell the guys about this!" I yelled to James.

Whoopee! One more turn.

Then we weren't moving anymore. The Jeep was stuck and Jack was shifting like crazy, trying to rock the Jeep loose. It moved just enough so that mud flew from the back wheels, straight toward my dad and uncles who stood next to Papa's truck. Everyone scattered in all directions as the truck took a direct hit and mud smeared over the windshield and hood.

Jack looked through the window and laughed, a big loud belly laugh. "Those guys got just a little too cocky, in my opinion."

"Uh, guess we get out and push," I said weakly, looking at James.

"That means we'll be walking home," he said.

"Oh, yeah." Papa wasn't going to let us get in his truck all dirty and muddy. And we couldn't get back into the Jeep covered in mud. I could only imagine what my mom was going to think about our clothes.

"Sit tight, boys. Nobody's taking a mud bath today." Jack shifted into reverse. He pressed the gas, shoved the gear into drive, the wheels reaching for traction. "Hmmph," he snorted, "get stuck my eye."

The next minute, we were pulling out of the mud like we'd been taking a Sunday drive. Jack rolled down his window. "See you boys back at the house," he called to the men, saluting them. He took his foot off the brake and pulled away.

I took in a deep breath and sat back in my seat for the short drive home. Jack pulled around to the back of the barn to let us out. I don't know how we were able to get out of the Jeep without getting mud all over us. Somehow we did.

"That was the best fun ever," I told Jack, holding the door open. "Thank you so much."

"I will never forget it," James said.

"You guys have been real patient with all the doings going on around here. I figured you deserved some fun. I hope you had a good time."

"The greatest."

"I'll be back for supper," Jack said. "There's a place in Daly I can get all the mud knocked off."

The Jeep crunched through the thick gravel and disappeared around the back of the barn. We let ourselves in the back door and went upstairs to our room.

We stretched out on our beds and just lay there for a few minutes, not saying anything. James heaved a sigh and said, "Awesome. That was the best."

He was right. There was nothing more to say. The battery was low on my phone. I plugged it in to charge and plopped back down on my bed and looked to see if there were any messages. There were none. The guys would have been busy—just like me and James. I laid back and closed my eyes and the next thing I knew, someone was calling us from downstairs to come in for supper.

Of course, everyone had heard of our muddy adventure and we heard all kinds of stories about muddin' while we ate. There was more talk about my sister's and cousin's move, but I couldn't imagine either of them actually enjoying being here even though they both seemed pumped at thc idea.

"Hey, Taylor," I said when we'd finished eating and were clearing the table, "want to watch a movie?"

Might as well, I thought. It would fill the time until it was time to go to bed again. Huge, bored sigh.

"Depends."

"No chick flick. Action."

She looked at Abby who said, "I'm in."

I noticed Kate was sitting on the edge of her seat, listening to us. I jerked my head toward the door inviting her to come with us and she was out of her seat and right behind the older girls in a flash.

Jillian squawked about not being included until Grandmother distracted her, saying they'd watch their very own movie, in the house, all by themselves.

Did I say yet that Grandmother is cool?

Everybody had their own bag of microwave popcorn and something to drink and we settled in and popped in my favorite superhero action movie, followed by the sequel. My kind of movie night. We were all yawning by the end of the second one. The girls headed into the house and James and I headed upstairs and turned in.

"So, are we going to the mounds tomorrow?" James asked after we'd turned out the lights.

"I'm ready, aren't you?" I said.

"Better than sitting around all day."

"Totally."

"Nothing planned for tomorrow? No trips into town, or something?"

"Haven't heard of anything. I don't care. *I* am going to the mound."

"Cool."

"There might not be anything new, but we can at least take videos so that when we get back home the guys can see what it's like here."

"Yeah," James said, yawning. "Compare notes."

CHAPTER THIRTY-TWO

After breakfast the next morning, we loaded up some bottles of water and a pack of Oreos and headed to the mound.

On the way, we walked around some puddles left from the rain. The climb up the mound was messy where the underbrush and leaves hadn't dried out yet, but nothing was caked to our feet when we got to the top. We sat on the stumps and looked around while we had some water and cookies.

"Didn't you already look up stuff on Indian burial mounds?" James asked, looking around.

"Yeah, but something's not the same."

"That's because this is not a burial mound," Jack said as he stepped into the clearing.

I nearly jumped out of my skin. *Where did he come from?* I hadn't heard a sound.

He came over and pushed one of the stumps with his foot, rolling it closer to me and James. He turned it up on end, took a seat and asked, "Got any more cookies?"

Still wondering where he'd come from, I pulled the Oreos out of my backpack and handed the package to him. He took a handful and popped one in his mouth.

"Water?"

I pulled a bottle out and held it out to him.

After washing down the cookie, Jack screwed the cap back on the bottle and set it on the ground. "So?" he said, bracing his hands on his knees, eyeing me. "What do you want to know?"

"Uh . . . um . . . I don't know where to start."

"I'd say it's best to just start. Anywhere, just start."

I swallowed hard and told him about the mound back home. "It's bigger, taller, and steeper, but there's a clearing at the top, just like this," I said, looking around. "Stumps, fire pit, everything. Just the same. We wondered if it was some kind of sacred place, special."

"Why would you think that?"

"Someone told us it was an Indian burial mound. I guess it would be special, like a graveyard or something."

"First of all, this *is* a mound made by Native Americans, Indians. And a place like this," he said, his arms spread, taking in where we sat, "this *would* be sacred to the Indian. Wherever they gathered around a fire and shared food and brotherhood was sacred to them. But *this*," he said looking around, "is *not* a burial mound.

"There *are* some burial mounds in other parts of the state, scattered around the country even, but not many survived.

Many were destroyed by modern development or plain old vandalism. Some were destroyed by treasure seekers."

"Treasure?" It went through my mind that there might be a connection to Max's story about a giant crazy Indian who killed a lot of people and buried the stuff he stole from them.

"There were some who thought gold or silver was buried with those who had died." Jack made a noise in his throat like he had something that tasted really bad stuck there. "Like the mounds held some hidden treasures."

"You mean like the pyramids in Egypt or the Mayan ruins? Something like that?"

"That's right. But these people didn't value those kinds of things. They had no need of them. Weapons, things they could use for survival in the afterlife, everyday simple things like a bowl or tools were all that was buried with them. And it was all that was ever found in the sites. But the treasure hunters kept looking and digging. They plundered everything they came across until there were very few left. Not many of the artifacts the mounds held survived.

"The only thing that stopped the raiders was when preservationists, historians, and universities stepped in and made the mounds protected sites under the law. Only legitimate exploration was allowed after that. By then, very few were left."

"But these two survived, they're protected?"

"They are protected, because of their significance to Native American culture. They have historical significance. But, as I said, these are not burial mounds."

"So, if they were built by Indians, but they're not burial mounds . . . what are they?"

"Hunting mounds." Jack took a minute to let that sink. He stood up and looked toward the farm house as he explained. "Great vantage point from up here. They could spot anything they were after or that was after them.

"But what about the other one?"

"The other one was probably the same size, built along with this one. Farmers may have come along and removed a lot of the dirt from it to make room for their fields. Or maybe treasure hunters tore a big portion of it down. Before they got caught and were stopped.

"A small part of the tribe could set up camp, protected between two mounds, where animals could be dressed out and meat and hides preserved. When the tribe had what they needed, they would move back to their camp or on to another one."

Jack sat back on the stump, picked up his water bottle and drained it.

"So, do you think the mound that we found is a burial mound or a hunting mound?"

"Oh, if it's as big as you say it is, I'd say it is a hunting mound. Unless you saw signs of digging, some kind of excavation around it."

James cleared his throat, my cue to explain that we had never gone around the mound. We had no idea what was on the other side.

"Well, you see . . . we don't really know about that. We never went all the way around it." I was embarrassed to tell my uncle that we'd been scared off by some graves and tombstones. Well, it had mostly been Max—the others of us were ready to check things until he freaked out.

Wait . . . the tombstones! I'd forgotten about them.

"See," I explained, "there were several tombstones, at the bottom on one side of the mound. One of our friends was totally freaked out by them—"

"One of your friends?" Jack asked with a doubtful smile.

He was right, sort of. "Okay, I guess it spooked the rest of us, too. But, Jack, there are graves by this mound too."

"Patrick, those graves down there are what's left of the family that lived and farmed the land around here a long time ago. A very long time ago. From back in the 1800s. The house is gone now, but back then families just made their own grave yards near where they lived. More than likely, if they'd heard the stories about this being a burial ground they figured it would be a good place to bury their own. "

I looked at James. "The 1800s. That's the date on the tombstones on our mound!"

"Most of them," he said. "What about . . . you know."

I did know. The tombstone with "Feurey" on it. The one that freaked Max out and convinced him there was something to the Indian legend after all. And the reason he wouldn't go back to the mound. I really didn't want to tell Jack that detail.

Jack didn't seem to notice what James had said. "Probably the same with the graves you found. Whole families could be wiped out by some illness and, remember, people were pretty isolated back then. They did the best they could with what they had."

There was a lot going through my mind at that point. Max's grandpa had told him he thought the mound was an Indian burial ground. If some homesteaders in Texas had heard the legend about the one there, then they may have done like these people and just used the mound for their own graveyard. Was Feurey one of those families? Did any of this have anything to do with Max's story? And, would I be able to learn anything when we got back home?

Jack stood up and brushed the seat of his jeans off. "Any more questions?"

I had quite a few, but I'd have to wait until we got back home where I could get to a computer and do some research.

"You've told us plenty for now," I said. "Thanks."

"Well, then, I think I'll head back to the barn. You might want to come back pretty soon yourself," he said. "There's a fish fry at the school cafeteria tonight and your grandmother will want her whole bunch there, spit and polished."

One thing for sure, there would be no getting out of Grandmother's plans. By the time James and I got off our stumps Jack was already gone.

He had left just as quietly as he'd come.

CHAPTER THIRTY-THREE

Seemed like my grandmother knew everybody at the fish fry. And she had to introduce us to all of them. She still included James like he was one of the family. All right by me, and no one seemed to care one way or the other.

After nodding and smiling at what seemed like every little old lady in the place—and eating all the fried fish, French fries and coleslaw we could hold—I noticed James looking around. Like maybe for an escape route.

If he found one, I'd be right behind him. I couldn't imagine spending the next few hours sitting around watching the old folks. Worse yet, having to come up with something to say. Even worse, put in charge of amusing the 'little darling.'

I looked across the table at my dad and said, "What now?"

He stood up and, down at the end of the long cafeteria table, so did Uncle Clint. Dad motioned for us to follow him. Uncle Nathan had joined us before we walked out the door, and into the gymnasium.

The gym was empty and Uncle Nathan found a basketball. He hurled it to Uncle Clint. He passed off to my dad who made a layup shot.

James and I looked at each other, grinning. Maybe, just maybe . . .

"Patrick," my dad called, "let's me, you and James show these guys how to play."

Woot! The game was on.

We were up one game when my mom and my aunts tracked us down to let us know it was time to go home. I was glad. I didn't think I could make the backboard one more time. Those old guys had more energy than I would have thought.

James and I went straight to the barn when we got back to the farm. After the game, I needed a shower and we'd been told we needed to be up early next morning for the Fall Festival. It was late to text the guys, so we settled down with games on our phones. I turned off the light when I noticed James was asleep.

No cereal for breakfast again the next morning. Another reason to go home. I mean, a guy has to have his fiber.

But, since today was our last day on the farm, might as well enjoy the Daly Fall Festival. I asked if James and I could walk through the field road. Taylor and Abby decided they'd come along.

"It's farther than you think," I said, glaring at Taylor. So far, I'd avoided doing anything with her after the trip to the campus. Why break a perfect record now?

"I think we'll be fine," she said in her fake sweet voice then turned to Kate. "Hey, Kate, you want to come with?"

Groan. This was getting worse by the minute.

At least Aunt Judith said 'No' when Jillian started begging to come with us too.

We took off on foot before anyone else left the house. We planned to meet up with them outside Betsy's Boutique; which was okay, just so long as I didn't have to go inside.

As we walked through the stripped cotton fields, we talked about the parade we were on our way to see. Abby lived close to Pasadena, California, and had told us about seeing the Rose Parade many times. I'd watched it lots of times with my family on New Year's Day, but it was still fun to hear about it straight from someone who'd been right there. The night before the parade, Abby and my aunt and uncle go down to where the floats line up, close enough to see everything.

"The next day, to start the Parade," Abby told us, "a Stealth bomber flies straight down Colorado Boulevard. The noise is deafening, but it's so cool."

"We've got to see that someday," I said to James, promising myself that I'd make that happen.

"Once," Abby told us as we walked on through the field, "my dad and I were able to listen to the radio communications from the bomber to air traffic control."

"We are *so* doing that," James said, walking close by me. "Maybe not the radio thing, but the parade and the bomber, that's for sure."

Just as Papa had predicted, Main Street was crowded with people. There were tables filled with food and T-shirts, and stuff that looked like some things every female relative of mine, from Grandmother to Jillian, would be interested in.

Across the street, alongside the railroad tracks, hotdogs and hamburgers were grilling behind a makeshift stand. People stood around a short platform where a band was playing country western music.

Taylor, Abby and Kate went inside Betsy's Boutique as soon as we got there. James and I hung around outside until my family showed up. Grandmother's friend already had a space blocked off for us in front of the store. We were going to have front row seats.

Soon the crowd began to line the street, looking toward the high school where the parade was supposed to begin. Everyone seemed really excited. Then they all got quiet, and looked up in the sky.

I looked up, trying to see what all the people were watching. All I saw was what looked like a very large bird circling over the school.

I heard the sound of a motor but couldn't tell where it was coming from.

Then it sounded like the motor died and the bird, a big yellow bird, was swooping toward us. I mean, this thing was coming right at us! No one but me seemed worried about it.

They were all whooping and hollering and waving. I looked around frantically for a place to duck for cover. Then all of a sudden a small yellow plane barreled just feet over our heads, right down Main Street! *Rusty's Supreme Crop Dusting* was printed on the side in bright neon blue letters. The motor roared to life as the engine caught again and the plane shot upward, banked to the right and out of sight.

James looked at me, his mouth hanging open. "Do you believe that?" he yelled over the noise of the crowd. I was still shaking my head in disbelief.

My whole family was in front of the boutique when I turned around. Abby and her mom and dad looked as if they weren't sure what they'd just seen.

"Well, not exactly your stealth bomber," I said to Abby.

Uncle Nathan grinned and rubbed his chin. "Nope. But you gotta hand it to the town, though. They go all out with what they got."

Papa laughed so hard he wheezed to catch his breath. He'd known all along what was coming, but hadn't told any of us. He'd been waiting for our reaction. "You boys looked like you were ready to run for cover," he said holding his sides.

My dad hid a grin behind his hand. He must have known, too.

"You could have told us," I huffed, feeling red up to the roots of my hair.

"Oh, no," Papa said, laughing louder. "Would've taken all the fun out of it."

For you, maybe, I thought.

"Here comes the parade!"

The crowd began clapping and I turned to see an old-model pink Cadillac convertible pass by, a really pretty girl wearing an evening gown and a crown on her head sitting on the back of the rear seat. A sign on the side of the car said, Miss Daly. She waved to everyone. The rest of the parade that followed was made up of the town fire truck, old-model cars and trucks. Tractors pulled floats, flatbed trailers with people from different school or community groups riding on hay bales and decorated with fall colors. Everyone waved and threw candy to the crowd, the little kids scooping up hand-fuls, cramming some in their mouths and stuffing their pockets.

James and I managed to get a few pieces ourselves.

After we'd eaten some great barbeque for lunch I asked my mom, "When do you think we might be going back to the house?"

"Oh, probably in another hour or so."

"James and I thought we'd walk around town, check things out before we head back."

"Are you going to walk back by the field road? I think the girls want to ride back."

"Sure. See you back at the house then." We took off before anyone noticed we were gone. Or maybe they just didn't care.

Daly wasn't a big town, it didn't take us long to walk through most of it. There were lots more older homes than new ones, and lots of churches for such a small town. We'd made it all the way around the town and back to Main Street, heading toward the boutique when a car pulled alongside us, going really slow. I turned to look and it was Taylor driving our car. Abby and Kate were with her.

Taylor leaned over and said through the open passenger window, "Hey, want a ride?"

James and I looked at each other and nodded. Might as well, not much else of the town to see. We climbed in the back seat next to Kate.

"Which street do we take to get to that field road?" Taylor asked me as she drove slowly down Main.

"You sure you want to go that way?"

"Just tell me, Patrick."

"The one past Betsy's," I said. Whatever would get me back to the barn and out of the car sooner. It only took a few minutes in my sister's company and my teeth were already on edge. "Then turn right."

"Since the railroad is on the left," Taylor said, snorting, "that's the only way you *can* turn, isn't it, dork?"

"You want me to tell you how to get there or not?" I growled at her. She made me so mad.

"Fine."

We were almost in front of the boutique and I leaned over the front seat and pointed to the street at the next corner. "Turn right there and go to the end of the street . . ."

Before I could tell Taylor the street turned into the field road, Abby yelped, "Pig!"

We all jumped and Taylor slammed on the brakes, stopping right in the middle of the street. I lurched forward so far

I thought I would end up in the windshield. Good thing no one was behind us.

"PIG! PIG!"

Abby pointed wildly out the window where one of the biggest pinkest pigs I'd ever seen—not that I'd actually seen many pigs—trotted down the sidewalk heading straight towards Betsy's Boutique. We watched its wild escape as some teenagers ran behind trying to catch it.

The car began to move again but we were all so stunned we couldn't talk. I mean, a humongous pig making a break for it down Main Street was the last thing any of us would have expected to see.

As Taylor turned the corner, Abby turned to her and said, "Well . . . that's not something you see every day in L. A."

That cracked us up and we laughed all the way to the corner and the field road.

We were almost at the mounds when I decided I really wanted to go there one more time before we went back to Texas.

"Want to take another look?" James said. "Maybe get some more videos?"

"I was just thinking the same thing!" I slapped the back of the driver's seat. "Hey, Taylor, let us out here."

"We just want to get some more shots over there." James pointed toward the mounds.

"Sure." She stopped and we stepped out of the car.

Kate was watching us. I looked at James to see if he minded if she came with us and he nodded. I motioned for her to come along and she bolted from the car, racing over to us. She didn't ask any questions and kept pace with every step we took.

We climbed the larger mound and sat on some of the tree stumps watching the sun as it got lower and lower in the sky. A fire had been built recently in the ring of stones.

"You think maybe that was Jack?" James asked.

"Probably," I replied.

My phone beeped. A text from my dad saying it was time to get on to the house. We hiked back down the mound and walked toward the farm house.

I couldn't wait to get back home and to my friends and tell them about what Jack had told us about the mound. I had a feeling the one at home would be a lot like this one, some things we would never have thought about.

CHAPTER THIRTY-FOUR

"Thanks for letting me come along," Kate said as we crossed the road and walked across the yard. "It was fun."

"Sure." I'd told her about the mound at home, how Jack had explained things that we thought would clear up some questions we had.

My dad was on the porch with Papa and my uncles when we walked up. He said, "Better go on inside and wash up for supper. The women have been waiting for you to get back."

As usual, there was lots of food, lots of laughs, and lots of tales by Uncle Clint. And *on* Uncle Clint. I'd learned the hard way to be careful about trying some of the things he said he did. They never turned out good for me.

"Oh, yes," said Grandmother. "If we weren't worrying that he was going to burn something down, we had to keep our eye out to make sure he didn't blow something up."

"Sounds like Patrick," Taylor put in. "And some of his crazy stunts."

"Oh, yeah?" Uncle Clint looked at me, like he'd just noticed I was sitting at the table. "So what has Patrick been up to?"

"Tell him, Patrick," said Taylor, grinning. "About the rockets and stuff."

Everyone's attention turned to me. I said, "Uh, well, one of my friends got some rockets from his uncle and we shot them up." I shrugged and looked at James. "It was fun."

"Hah! And they almost started a fire when one of the rockets misfired. But they finally got one up that took pictures, and everything." She started laughing like crazy and said, "Oh, and then there was the mouse."

I couldn't believe she'd blabbed! Something I'd told her in secret. I shot Taylor a look.

Her face turned white, like she suddenly realized what she'd done. "Oh, Patrick, I . . ."

"What fire!" my mom gasped.

I would never trust my stupid sister with another thing as long as I lived.

"What fire, Patrick?" my dad asked. Rather calmly, I might say.

"Well . . . you see, uh . . ."

James cleared his throat. "It wasn't really a *fire*, Mr. Morrison," he said, coming to my rescue, "as much as some sparks in some grass and a little smoke. We made sure it didn't spread."

Uncle Nathan leaned his elbows on the table, his attention on me. "I'd like to hear more about the pictures."

"I'd like to hear more about the fire." My dad was doing that thing he does looking over the top of his glasses and he was going to have more questions about the fire, I knew. But, at the moment, he seemed willing to put it off until another time. "Later, young man."

I was glad to explain how we took the pictures and jumped right into the story. At the end, I explained, "The film was old, the pictures didn't come out very good. But we hope we can try it again sometime."

"Now, what about a mouse?" Uncle Clint nailed me with his eyes. He wasn't going to let that get past him.

And I couldn't figure out a way to get around it. Taylor wouldn't look me in the eye when I glared at her. My parents knew about our launching the rockets, even that we'd put a camera on one. I'd just never shared about the *almost* fire, and for sure I hadn't said anything about shooting a mouse up in a rocket. James only gave me a shrug and a lame smile. I was on my own with this one. And it wasn't even my idea. *Thanks a lot, you guys.*

"Okay, well you see, it was like this . . ." I started. I had never seen my Uncle Clint speechless and, I have to say, that got me into enjoying telling about our mouse launch. Everyone—even my parents—were laughing so hard when I finished with the first landing, I couldn't help myself . . .

"Patrick! You *didn't*!" my mother shrieked when I began describing the mouse's second trip.

"Oh, come on, Jennifer," Uncle Clint told my mom when he finally stopped laughing. "It was just gonna be snake food anyway." That sent everyone into another fit of laughter.

And me into the final episode of the mouse launch adventure.

We skipped church the next morning. Everyone either had a long plane trip or a long drive home.

"Maybe we can do something fun next time we come to Grandmother's," I told Kate.

"Okay," she said, grinning ear to ear.

After a gazillion hugs and kisses with everyone, we were the last ones to leave. Even Jack had come out to tell us good-bye.

"Let me know how it goes with your mound," he said, gripping my hand.

"Yes, sir . . . uh, Jack. Thanks for everything."

James and I settled into the back of the SUV. No way was I sitting anywhere close to my sister. Maybe ever.

CHAPTER THIRTY-FIVE

We got home late Sunday night and I had to be at school bright and early the next morning. James spent the night with me so were able to head for school as soon as we got up and dressed.

We didn't catch up with the other guys until lunch. They were talking about what a fantastic break they'd had and looked at me and James like they felt sorry for us having to spend the whole time out in Podunk, U.S.A. Hah! Were they in for a surprise.

"So, what's the deal on that burial mound you saw while you were in the sticks?" Max sniggered.

"Actually, we learned a lot," James said, waiting a second before he added, "when we weren't driving Patrick's grandfather's truck." He looked at his arm like there was a watch there. "But, oh my, just look at the time." He stood and picked up his lunch tray. "Time for class. Gotta run"

Way to go, James, I thought as I picked up my tray and followed him from the cafeteria.

Max, Jeremy and Brendan stared after us when I looked back at them. Their mouths hung open as we dumped our trays and headed for class.

After school, I barely made it inside my front door when my phone beeped. Three times. I knew it was the guys and, instead of answering, I made a group text to see when they could come over. Even Brendan didn't have any kind of practice and they were all there within minutes.

James and I were waiting in the cul-de-sac and we all sat on the curb. The two biggest things about our trip to the farm were what we'd learned about the mound and driving Papa's truck.

"So, what do you want to hear about first?" I looked around at their faces, pretty sure which they'd pick.

Driving. I went through every minute of our time behind the wheel and they hung on every word. I was feeling pretty proud of myself right about then.

"Aw, I bet my grandpa would let me drive his car," Max said, "if he lived in the country."

"Patrick's grandpa doesn't live in the country, Doofus," Jeremy corrected Max. "He lives in Oklahoma City."

"Well . . . anyway."

"*Anyway*," James said, "after we drove around for a while, we went 'muddin.' It was a blast."

Muddin' was new to the guys too, and for a while we talked about when we got cars—or Jeeps—we'd try it someday.

"But what about the mound?" Jeremy asked. "What did you find out about that?"

We told them what we'd seen there, the tree stumps, the fire ring, the graves. We showed them the videos we took, and everything Jack had explained about the mound.

"So, then the one here isn't a burial mound after all?"

"I'm not saying it's not, I don't know. I'm thinking probably not. Maybe we can all get together and find some more information about mounds, other kinds of mounds, instead of just burial mounds." I needed some help with this. I'd had mounds on the brain too long. Everyone agreed we'd start later in the week.

There was lots more to tell about our week in Daly, but I wanted to hear about all the stuff they'd done. We'd get around to it all eventually.

Over the next couple of weeks, there weren't many chances to share much of anything. Our teachers dumped loads of homework on all of us. If fall break hadn't turned out to be so much fun, it wouldn't have been worth having the time off.

James and I had rehearsals for fall concert, Max and Jeremy had a science project to complete and present, and Brendan had football games. Before we knew it, it was time to decide what we were going to do for Halloween.

We hadn't done the Trick or Treat thing for a while. Instead, our church threw a big Harvest Festival for kids, all ages, with games and candy and prizes, a pumpkin patch, more candy, and a maze.

But we still dressed up for the Festival. We weren't ready for that to end yet.

"What are you guys going as this year?" Max asked one day at lunch.

My friends and I had always tried to come up with killer costumes for the Festival.

This year might be our last time for disguises and all that stuff —after all, we were growing older. We decided it had to be something special, our best ever: blood-sucking flesh-eating zombie alien vampires like from our video. The timing was perfect. We needed a couple more shots for the final scene and if we got into costume a couple hours before the Festival, we could wrap that up and then head back over to the church for all the fun and games.

I finished my chores and James came over after lunch. We'd just taken down the boxes with the things we'd need when Max and Jeremy showed up. Brendan had practice but he'd be at my house in time to get ready, over to the field, and back to go to the Festival with us.

"Uh, guys," Max said, peeling tape for a box. "Do you really think we oughta go back to the field?"

"Why not?" James stopped pulling things from a box and turned toward Max. "Where else are we going to film the last scene? We'd have to start all over if we change places."

"I was just thinking about the last time we were there, you know, what we saw in those pictures, in the film."

"What we *thought* we saw, you mean." I'd had time to think about those pictures, especially after talking to Jack, and I'd come up with a whole different view of things.

"Are you still hung up on that ghost stuff?" James asked.

Max gave James a look like he still wasn't sure. James groaned and plopped down on a stool.

"Oh, for cryin' out loud, Max! You can't be serious!"

"It's okay, James," I said, sitting on a plastic container beside him. "Look, Max, we didn't have the pictures, but James and I talked about them a lot while we were gone. You know, buddy, we looked at them so much, I think we sort of talked ourselves into thinking we actually saw something in the pictures. I think we let our imaginations run away with us. The film was probably over-exposed, but whatever was there wasn't anything solid."

Max started pacing back and forth. Max did a lot of pacing when he got excited. He was working himself into being really excited right then. "But what about the video! There was something there and you know it."

"Yeah, about that," I said, looking at James for some back-up. He gave me a nod and I went on. "We did have the video and we watched it a lot too. Seriously, I think we were looking for something to be there. And I believe we let ourselves get spooked again."

"That's right, Max," James added, looking around at all the guys. "Hey, I thought I saw something coming out of the woods, but that's it, I *thought* I saw it. When I looked again, it was gone. By the time we all looked at it, we'd talked it up so much we were convinced somebody was coming after us. We can all look at it again, if you want to. As long as you keep an open mind and stay calm."

"That sounds like a good idea, Max," Jeremy told our friend, trying to talk him down. "We'll look at the pictures and the video again. They're probably right."

"Okay, all right, you win," Max said, scuffing his feet.

Oh, wow. He was really worked up now.

"I'll look, and you think you'll convince me." Max glared at me and got close to my face. Too close. "But how do you explain that tombstone? Huh? How are you going to explain *that* away, Mr. Smarty-Pants?"

"There were tombstones at the mound by his grandparents' too." Jeremy, always the rational one.

"Oh, yeah? Well, did any of them have Feurey engraved on them?"

"Not that we could make out, Max, but I'm pretty sure it wasn't," I said. "And there might be a perfectly logical explanation about the gravestone here. Can you just give us some time to check it out? See what we can find about it?"

Brendan came into the garage just as Max opened his mouth to say something. It wasn't hard to see that Max was about to go off. Brendan's 'happy to see you guys' face turned into a 'what dumb thing is Max up to now?' face. Brendan had no patience with Max and his dramatics.

"Hey, there, buddy." I jumped off the crate and walked over to him. "About ready to be a big bad alien?"

"Just in the nick of time?" he whispered to me, the scowl leaving his face.

"You got it."

We had everything ready to go and we couldn't wait much longer or the light would be gone for filming. I put on my gear as fast as I could and helped Brendan and Max get into their gear and ghoulish makeup. When we were ready to leave, I walked into the house, grabbed some bottled water from the pantry and tossed it into my backpack. I didn't bother with the Oreos, we'd have plenty of treats at the Festival.

"We're heading out," I told my mom. "We'll be back as soon as we finish up."

"Call me or text me, Patrick," she said, following me to the garage. "I'll take you boys over to the church when you get back. Don't stay too long, I need to be there early. I have the ring toss booth tonight."

She stopped in the doorway when she saw all the guys. "Oh, you boys look positively frightening! Remember, Patrick, don't be late."

CHAPTER THIRTY-SIX

We ducked under the big garage door just as she hit the "Close" button. The sun would be going down soon so we hurried past the ravine and across Mr. Nelson's pasture. Once on the other side of the fence, we walked into the open field and checked out the light. It was fading fast, we had to hurry.

The final scene was that the hero—that would be me—and the new sidekick hero, Jeremy—would take one final look at the place where the zombies had fallen. Then as they turn to walk away, sure they'd finally finished them off, the zombies start to rise from the brush.

THE END

Yeah, we left it open for a sequel—you just never know when you might be in the mood for another zombie alien vampire movie.

We huddled around James to look at the footage and it was great. The light was really spooky, perfect. It was a good thing because if we didn't leave right then we'd be going home in the dark. And my mom would kill me.

"Hey, guys, check that out," Jeremy said. "What is that?" He pointed to the mound, the setting sun reflecting in his eyes.

Or was it the flicker of light we saw, like a fire? I started walking toward the mound, like something was pulling me to get a closer look.

"Hey, there's a fire burning up there," Brendan said, walking next to me.

We could see flames through the trees as we got closer.

Then we heard screams.

We stopped dead in our tracks.

Then Max screamed. "Oh. My. Gosh! Oh. My. Gosh!" Max repeated over and over, rubbing his cheeks and smearing the paint on his face. If he hadn't been paralyzed with fear, I was sure he'd have been half way home by then.

The screaming on the mound cut off, but we could still see flames.

"Think someone fired up the old pit?" James asked.

"Think we should get the heck out of here!" Max yelled, stumbling backward.

Jeremy grabbed Max's arm. "Hold on, Max. Let's stay calm and think about this a minute. After all, it's just a fire."

"Jeremy's right. Probably some perfectly logical explanation," I said.

"Look, we've known from the first time we came over here someone had been lighting fires up there. We saw ashes and all," James said as we walked closer. "Whoever it was probably decided to come back and have a wiener roast or make s'mores or something. Simple as that." He stopped. "Patrick, remember what your mom said. We need to start back."

"James is right. We should go. But, what about, maybe . . ." Max sputtered.

No way was Max going to be satisfied without an answer to the sounds we'd heard. "That sound, you know, the noise?"

"Probably just an animal or something, Max." I said. "No big deal."

Brendan shot another look at the mound. "James is right. We're letting our imagination run away again, and we promised Patrick's mom—"

The screams came again, earsplitting shrieks. And loud yelling like a giant was on the loose up there.

"There's nothing imaginary about *that*," Max said, his voice hoarse. Close to panic now, he could barely croak out, "I'm telling you guys, it's the ghosts of those people buried there. And maybe *you-know-who*."

Of course we all knew he was talking about. Fury—the wild crazy Indian in a story his grandpa had told him. He just wouldn't let go of that whole thing.

The sounds stopped, just like that. Just like it had before.

"Okay, that does it!" I said, whirling to face the direction of the mound. I was tired of all the mystery and wild stories. I wanted some answers. I headed for the mound.

"Patrick!" Brendan yelled and came running after me. "Where are you going?"

I stopped and turned to look at my friends.

"What are you doing?" Brendan asked.

"I'm tired of all this bunk about ghosts and stuff, guys." I pointed at the mound and started marching toward it again.

"Patrick, don't do it!" Max yelled. "What if—"

"What, Max?" I stopped and turned around. "What if *what*? Huh, Max? If there really are ghosts—which I do not believe in—what can they do to us? Really?"

"Well . . . uh . . . I guess . . . but—"

"Max, buddy, I'm tired of guessing and you making up wild stories about what it could be. I'm ready to know what's going on and I am going to find out. *While* something is *actually* going on and I can see it with my own eyes. You can come or stay here. It's up to you. I don't care." I turned and was nearly to the tree line when Max called after me again.

The rest of them ran to catch up with me, Max trailing behind. Our weapons in hand, weapons that would do us absolutely no good against any real danger, we charged up the slope to the top. As we rushed up the hill we heard a 'whump, whump, whump' noise, like someone beating a drum:'

We were panting and out of breath when we broke into the clearing. And came to a screeching halt.

Dancing around the fire ring was a group of very short, black-haired, black-eyed people. Kids? They took one look at us and began screaming.

Loud blood-curdling whoops sounded over the noise the kids were making. A very large man, dressed in buckskins, black hair in long braids, a spear raised over his head, rushed into the clearing. He skidded to a stop when he saw us, lowering his arm and staring.

"FURY!" Max screeched. His eyes bugged like they were going to explode from his head and he was shaking from head to toe.

I think he might have peed his pants. I almost did.

Dozens of little black eyes turned on Max. They turned up the shrieking a notch and ran toward the tall warrior, huddling close to him and hiding their eyes in his leather pants.

What were they doing running to him like that? Didn't they get it, that we were there to save them? Some of them were crying hysterically and clinging to the man and each other.

James put his hand on my shoulder and whispered behind me, "Patrick, look." He nodded from me to Jeremy then Max and Brendan. In the firelight, the gray paint made their faces look really weird, like they glowed. The fake blood seemed to be dripping off their jackets. The way they were holding those phony weapons, it looked like they were ready to pull the trigger and blast the whole crowd.

At the same time, if I looked anything like Jeremy, his face mostly hidden by his hat pulled down close on his head, we were a pretty scary sight too.

The big Indian grabbed the kids and pushed them around behind him, shielding them from the assault team of blood-sucking, flesh-eating, zombie alien vampires.

One brave little kid peeped around the long legs, his dark eyes big and unblinking as he looked at me. Then he took a step toward us.

"Patrick?"

I looked at him and dropped my side arm before he tackled me.

"Jimjoe!"

My hat fell off as I picked up our little friend from the apartment complex day camp. He wrapped his arms around my neck. Then more than a dozen little kids squealed and rushed us.

"Patrick?"

"Mr. Meeker?" I said, recognizing the tall Indian.

I set Jimjoe on the ground and took a step toward the big Indian. Or should I say, my youth leader from church. I was about to ask what was going on, but stopped in my tracks as another Indian walked into the light of the camp fire. I sucked in a huge gulp of air.

"Dad?

"Mr. Morrison?" one of my friends squeaked out, staring bug-eyed at the two men. I was having trouble breathing.

"Patrick, what are you doing here?"

I could ask you the same thing was on the tip of my tongue. But before I could get a word out, I noticed another Indian and a cowboy near the edge of the circle.

Seriously? For real? Was someone back there in the trees cloning these guys or something? What was going on?

The little kids hopped up and down pulling at our hands, shouting, "Come play with us."

James eased up beside me while the other guys bunched as close as they could with the kids crowding around us.

"Patrick, what is going on here?" Max asked.

"You're asking me? Are you kidding?" How come they thought I always had the answers. "I don't know any more about what's going on than you do."

"But . . . your dad . . ."

"Aren't you boys supposed to be on your way to the Festival?" My dad came around the fire ring walking toward us. "Patrick, weren't you supposed to wrap up your filming and go home?"

"Yes, sir, we finished shooting the last scene, but then we saw the fire and heard screaming and we thought . . ."

Mr. Meeker started to walk toward us, but those other guys hung back.

"Dad? Would you please tell me what in the world is going on here? Why is Jimjoe and the other kids here? Why are you dressed like that, and who are those men?"

He started laughing. They all started laughing.

I did not see anything funny about any of this.

When we started talking, the kids moved away from us and started skipping around the fire, playing.

"Dad?" This whole thing was very confusing and I wanted some answers.

He looked around at Mr. Meeker and the other men, smiling. "Well, Clyde here got the idea to bring the kids over here so they could play."

Mr. Meeker stepped forward to explain. "Patrick, you guys know they don't have much of a place to play around the apartment complex. These kids were used to being in the forest so I thought they'd like it here with all the trees. I've been bringing them here to play sometimes."

James leaned close to me and muttered in my ear, "Why are they in that get-up?"

"You talking about the kids or my dad and Mr. Meeker?" There was more than one story here.

"All of them."

"Yeah, and who are those other guys?" Jeremy added under his breath.

Where would I start? My friends were shooting more questions at me than I could manage. I eyed Dad and my youth leader, including the men watching the kids play around the fire ring.

I pointed to Mr. Meeker. "Okay. So you've been bringing the kids over here to play?"

He nodded he had. I interrupted him when he started to say something. I turned to my dad and asked, "And why are *you* here?"

"Oh, well, I came to help Clyde. That's a bunch of kids, you know."

I knew.

"Why are they dressed that way?" I pointed to the kids. Some of them were still dancing around the fire ring. A few had taken seats on the logs. "And what about you, Dad? And Mr. Meeker? Why are you dressed like Indians?"

"The kids have asked questions about the fire ring and the stumps," explained Mr. Meeker. "It seemed a good time to tell them about the mound and the Native Americans who came here."

"Since we're taking them to the Festival at church we thought we'd just go in these outfits," Dad said, touching his fake buckskins. "And the kids' native clothing makes great costumes, don't you think?"

Oh, my gosh! I'd forgotten all about the Festival. My mom was going to kill me!

Just then my phone beeped that I had a text. I had a good idea who it was.

Mom: Patrick, I'm taking Taylor's car, going to church. Come home! Now! She will bring you boys in my car. NOW, young man.

There were still so many questions! I felt like my head was going to blow off my shoulders.

"You too?" my dad asked holding his phone. Mom had texted him too. "Hey, Clyde, we're supposed to be at the church with the kids. We better wind it up here." He started helping Mr. Meeker round up the kids. "Can you boys get back to the house okay? The church van and Clyde's SUV are full."

"Yeah, we're all right." I hoped we could make it back across the field and pasture without breaking our necks. My mom might do that for me anyway. "But, dad . . ."

"Patrick, this will have to wait until later. We really have to get the children to the Festival now."

"Okay, we're going. Just one thing first," I said, pointing to the two strangers. "Who are those guys?"

My dad looked at me, surprised. "Why, Patrick, you boys know Bill Nelson."

Mr. Nelson? Like in Mr. Nelson's farm? Mr. Nelson's pasture? That Mr. Nelson? How were we supposed to know? I didn't exactly recognize this native version of Mr. Nelson. So who was the cowboy?

"Oh, and that's his brother, Jim. They're helping with the kids."

"Patrick, we have *got* to go." The day campers were already running through the trees down the other side of the hill. There *was* a down side to the mound, where I'd wanted to go, to see what was there. And these little kids looked like they knew exactly where they were going. My dad ran after them, calling back over his shoulder, "See you at the church."

Kemo Sabe and Tonto started dumping dirt on the fire.

CHAPTER THIRTY-SEVEN

There was a full moon lighting our way as we made our way across the open field, making it easier to see where we were going. We climbed through the fence at Mr. Nelson's pasture and sprinted down the path to my house. Taylor was expecting us and we piled into my mom's car and headed out for the church.

Pumpkins and straw and hay bales were all over the activity hall, the place crawling with kids. It was easy to spot the kids from day camp, they were all dressed alike and sort of hung out together. My dad and Mr. Meeker were close by. Keeping an eye on them, I guess.

It was easy to spot my mom, too. She was the woman over by the ring toss booth with lightning bolts shooting at me from her eyes. I gave her a weak smile and a little wave and walked toward the booth.

"Uh, Mom, I'm sorry. We—"

One look from her shut me down. "Did you have your cell phone?"

Before I could answer, she looked around at my friends. "Did any of you have a cell phone with you?"

"Well . . . yes." Every one of us had a phone with us. "I know, Mom, you're right. We should have called."

"You boys were supposed to come here with me. Your parents were asking where you were and I had to tell them I didn't know."

The look of disappointment on her face made me feel about two feet tall.

"Mom, really, I'm sorry. It's just that we got caught up in something and—"

"Patrick, no excuses. I don't have time." She pointed behind us where there was a long line of kids waiting their turn. "We'll talk later."

We got out of line and decided to go through the maze. By the time we found our way through, which was easy, it was like we might as well go ahead and have a good time while we were there. It might be the last good time I had for a long time.

"Well, I figure it's a good thing we finished up the video now," I said, moving out of my mom's sight line. "I have a feeling I might not be able to see you guys until maybe Thanksgiving. If then."

The rest of the evening, I tried to forget the hot water I was in and had a pretty good time. After a couple of hotdogs with the guys, we played some of the games—except for the ring toss. Any prizes we won, we gave to the little kids.

And speaking of the little kids, they acted like they were afraid of us when we first came in, but they warmed up quick when we talked to them. Especially when we gave them the prizes or candy we'd won.

After a while, my dad looked us up. "Patrick, Clyde and I are going to take the children back to the complex now. You boys will need to get rides home."

"No problem, Mr. Morrison," Jeremy said. "My mom will take me and Max."

With Jeremy and Max having a way home, it was just me, James and Brendan. I asked my mom if there was anything we could do to help her clear up and she put us to work. Lots of people were pitching in to help clean and put things away, so it didn't actually take a long time.

Taylor had stayed to help too. She picked up a big plastic tub and said, "Mom, I'll take these things on home, if there's not anything else to do."

"Sounds good," Mom said. She turned to pick up a box then handed it to me. She called to my sister, "Taylor, take the boys with you. Okay?"

She handed the large container to me, pointed to a couple more on the floor. "James, you and Brendan each grab one of those, all of you go with Taylor."

We did as she'd instructed, glad to do something to make up for not calling her earlier. Hoping to get on her good side was more like it.

We dropped Brendan at his house first, then James.

"You are in deep doo-doo, buddy," Taylor said as she pulled into our garage and parked Mom's car.

"Thank you for your support," I growled at her.

"Well, it's your own fault." She got out and opened the hatch to the back of the SUV. We began unloading the boxes. She took a container and stacked it on top of one of the others. "You have to learn to be more responsible, Patrick."

I set the last container on top of the pile. "You don't know all the circumstances."

"It doesn't matter—"

"Give it a rest, Taylor," I shouted and stomped into the house. I went straight to my room and slammed the door. I peeled off my clothes, not even noticing where I threw stuff. In the shower, I scrubbed my face and hair then let the water run over me until it started getting cold. It was pretty safe to say my mom would be home by the time I got out of the bathroom and dressed. As late as it was, I just hoped she was tired and would wait until morning to address my problems.

As I went down the hall on my way to the kitchen for a glass of milk before I turned in, I heard my parents talking. My dad still wore the pants and fringed shirt of his Indian costume, but the wig had disappeared when I went in to tell them that I was going to bed and say goodnight.

"Mom, I'm sorry, I—"

"Patrick, your dad has told me some of what went on tonight." She got up from the couch and came and kissed me on the cheek. "It's late now, let's go to bed. We'll talk about it tomorrow."

My dad patted me on the shoulder, said good night, and walked behind my mom into their bedroom.

Leaving me standing in the kitchen wondering what had just happened. For sure, not what I'd thought would happen. I stayed awake for hours thinking about it.

The next day, I was sure my mom would pass up her Sunday afternoon nap and we would "discuss" the previous day. However, it didn't turn out like I'd thought.

My dad got the ball rolling. "Patrick, I'm sure you realize you should have phoned your mother and let her know what you boys were up to yesterday."

I apologized again, expecting my mom to give me another piece of her mind. What she did came as a complete surprise.

"Patrick, I knew you boys were together and I'm used to you all getting wrapped up in what you're doing. It was just that I had my car loaded with the stuff for the ring toss booth, and when you weren't here, and hadn't called me, Taylor and I had to unload it and put it in her car. I had to rush to get to the activity center and get set up."

"So you aren't mad at me?"

"I was very *disappointed* in you," she said, her smile showing me she wasn't mad at me.

Now I felt like a real jerk. I don't like disappointing my parents.

"I just wish you would have called. But, from what your dad tells me, it got pretty confusing last night."

"We really did mean to come right home, Mom, as soon as we wrapped up filming, but then we saw the fire . . ." I stopped and looked at my dad. "But I guess you've already told her all that part."

"Up to a point," he said.

My mom got up and ran her hand over my hair. "You and your dad can talk about this, but right now, I feel a nap coming on."

We watched her go into the bedroom and shut the door. She was giving me and my dad time to talk. I looked at him, wondering where to start. "So, can I ask you a few questions?"

"Sure."

"Okay, so Mr. Meeker has been taking some of the kids from the apartment complex over to the mound. When did that start?"

"Right after school started. Only a few of the kids were ready to go to school; like your little friend, Jimjoe. So Clyde would take some of the others over there to play while their friends were in school."

"Did you go with him?"

"No, son, he took them during the day. I was at work."

"But you've known about him and the kids all along?"

"Clyde talked to me about it. Yes."

"How come you never said anything about it?"

"That's something else Clyde talked to me about, but that will have to wait until another time. By the time school started, you had stopped going over there. You were working on another video and I thought you'd lost interest. But then you saw the mounds in Arkansas and you were interested again. I was going to talk to you about it when the time was right, but then you showed up last night before I got a chance."

"We never even meant to go back to the mounds. Not any time soon anyway. Max got scared off by some things we found over there, and . . . well, to tell you the truth there *were* some spooky things going on. So we decided to steer clear for a while."

My dad got up and walked to the patio door, looking out at the yard. Without turning to look at me, he said, "What kind of spooky things?"

I told him about finding the graves and how Max was okay until he thought someone had been watching him. I explained about the marker with the name Feurey on it. My dad already knew about Max's obsession with that stupid myth about a giant renegade Indian named Fury. I figured I might as well tell him everything, from the beginning.

"When we got the film from the rocket developed, we were sure we saw something near that tombstone in some of the pictures. We were ready to let that go . . . just back away. Max was too creeped out anyway. Then, when we were in the field filming, James thought he saw someone running out of the trees."

At this my dad turned to look at me and walked back and sat down. "Someone?"

"Well, someone or *something*, James was sure of it, but then it disappeared. When the rest of us looked at the video, it looked like it could have been a person. It happened so fast, there for a second, gone the next. And Max was already worked up by the whole thing, he was ready to dig up that crazy Fury story. We just decided to let it go, stay away from the mound. At least for a while."

"But then you saw the mound at Grandmother's?"

"Right. That got me and James thinking about it again . . . well, I never really stopped thinking about it. But some of the things Jack told us just made sense, and we thought it would explain some things to Max and we could go check it out more, do some exploring and stuff.

"But, Dad, listen . . . all that's okay, I mean, it can wait, we can go back and look at the video, we can do some more research. But for right now, can we go back to last night?"

"Of course, son. What about last night?"

"I understand Mr. Meeker taking the kids to play. You explained that he asked you to help last night. I got that." I started pacing around the family room, trying to sort through things. I turned and said to my dad, "But how did Mr. Meeker *know* about the mound? All the time we were over in the field, I never even knew about it. Did you? And how did he, and you, get there?"

My dad walked over and sat on one of the bar stools. "Clyde grew up around here. He's always known about the mound. As for how did we get there . . . let me ask you this. Where all on the mound have you boys been?"

"James and I talked about exploring it the first time we went over there. But we wanted to wait for the other guys. Then when we all went over together, we didn't have much time and Max got bored. So we came home. But the rest of us planned to go back, even if it meant without Max."

"So you know about the meeting place at the top, the tree stumps and fire ring, and the grave sites. What else do you know?"

"Not anything, really. We talked about it lots, but sometimes things . . . like a scaredy-cat friend . . . can mess up all kinds of plans." I didn't have to explain to my dad who that was. He'd known Max for a long time.

"You never went all the way around the one here like you did the one at Grandmother's?"

"Huh-uh. We never had time and besides it's a lot bigger and . . ."

Wait just a minute . . . maybe it wasn't that much bigger. I had nothing to prove that. We'd never explored it, never got that far. That got me to thinking, but my dad was talking.

"Well, Patrick, instead of being surrounded by cotton fields like at Grandmother's, this one has the open field where you boys have done your filming and rocket launches, the mound, and a farm house on the other side."

I didn't know where my brain had been, but, for the first time, I wondered why we'd never explored any more than the field and never even thought about the mound. That's being a little bit too focused, even for me. I felt like a huge dip-wad right then.

"Seriously?"

"Seriously. Clyde and I took the kids over to the farm—"

"Wait, wait. How did you get to the farm?"

"Patrick, Blanton road goes by it and—"

"Dad! We go Blanton Road all the time, we used to go that way to take Brett to soccer practice. I don't remember ever seeing a farm house or a mound."

"You probably had your nose in some electronic device and didn't notice."

He gave me one of those looks over the top of his glasses, like 'Am I right or am I right?' followed by "May I go on?"

I zipped my lip.

"The mound really isn't noticeable from the road. It just looks like woods, the way it did to you on this side of the field, and the house sits some way off the road."

"Wow!" I came to sit on the stool next to my dad. I pulled my phone out of my pocket, and said, "I can't wait to tell the guys you know about people who live there. We can ask them about the graves and stuff. That will be so cool."

"Wait just a minute, Patrick. We need to talk."

What did we have to talk about? I couldn't believe our luck in having answers just fall into our laps. All because of my dad's connections. Go figure.

"But, Dad, I—"

"Sit down and let me explain a few things. Then you can call your friends."

Of course he would know that I would call my friends. I told them everything. I perched on the stool next to him and waited.

"I do know who lives in the farm house—"

"You do! Why haven't you said anything before now?"

"Hold on. Let me explain something first. All right?"

I nodded but what I really wanted to know was *who* lived in that house and when could I meet them? I had a truckload of questions and I was ready to get on with it.

"You see, the field, the mound, the farm house—that's all one property. It belongs to Bill Nelson and his brother Earl. Earl lives in the farm house by the mound."

"Mr. Nelson?" Our Mr. Nelson? My brain began to tilt. Mr. Nelson who chased us with a baseball bat when we tried to "tip" one of his cows? The Mr. Nelson whose granddaughter tried to run away? Mr. Nelson who talked my dad into letting us cut across his pasture to get to the field so we could make our video? I wondered what else there was to know about Mr. Nelson.

On top of that, I didn't even know Mr. Nelson had a brother. We'd run all over Mr. Nelson's property and I never knew it. But then why would I? I hardly knew Mr. Nelson.

"Mr. Nelson is a pretty cool old guy. He probably wouldn't mind talking to us about the mound."

"Patrick . . ." My dad drew my name out like when he is definitely not going along with what I have in mind.

I *have* been known to get just a little bit over-focused.

"Hey, did you know Mr. Nelson had a brother?" My mind was racing a mile a minute. "Do you know him? Dad, that would be so cool if we could talk to them."

"Okay, buddy, back up there. No one said you were going to talk to anyone."

"But you said—"

"Patrick, I know Bill Nelson and I know he and his brother own all that land. But I only met Earl Nelson last night."

"At the bonfire?"

"Yes."

"Oh, my gosh! Was that him with Mr. Nelson? Was he the cowboy?" Everything had been so crazy with finding the kids and my dad and Mr. Meeker on the mound I couldn't remember when Mr. Nelson and the other guy weren't there anymore.

"Patrick, hold on. Don't get ahead of yourself. You can't just decide you're going to talk to someone. You don't know all the details."

"You mean I can't tell my friends?"

"I didn't say that. I'm saying that for the time being you can let them know about who the property belongs to. But I do *not* want you going over to the mound again."

"But, Dad!"

"Promise me you won't go over there. I'll talk to Clyde and see if he thinks you could talk to Bill and his brother."

I was ready to argue my case, but I barely got my mouth open when my dad cut me short.

"Son, listen. Sometimes there are reasons not to do things that might not make sense to you, but they are very good reasons. Reasons you don't always need to know."

Was that what 'on a need to know basis' meant?

"Let me talk with Clyde and I'll let you know."

"When?"

"As soon as I can."

One look at my father's face told me it would be best if I let it drop.

CHAPTER THIRTY-EIGHT

"I'm telling you, that's all I know," I said as I ate lunch with my friends in the school cafeteria the next day. "Mr. Nelson and his brother own all that property over there."

I'd already talked to James the night before. I couldn't keep that kind of news to myself.

"Even the mound?" Brendan asked.

"Yep. Everything."

Max put his sandwich down and crossed his arms over his head like he was having to hold the top on. "Oh. My. Gosh! We have been trespassing all over the place."

"I don't think you'd call it trespassing if he knew and said it was all right for us to cross his pasture to get to the field."

"But . . . but . . ."

"It's cool, Max," Jeremy said. "Eat your sandwich."

Max ate his sandwich, and his chips, and his cookies, and half of Jeremy's.

The question we all had then was when my dad might find out if we were going to be able to meet with Mr. Nelson and his brother Earl. Our answer came that night.

I was in my room studying when my dad knocked on the door and came into my room and sat down on the end of my bed.

"You think you could get all the boys together this next Saturday morning? Meet at the top of the mound?"

"Are you serious?" I slammed my book closed and reached for my phone.

"If you want, have them stay over Friday night, I'll make pancakes as usual. We can get an early start." My dad grinned and stood up. "Don't stay on the phone too long," he said, pulling the door closed as he left my room.

I did a group text. Brendan he had a game later in the day, but he could come if he could leave by noon. Max was worried it might not be safe.

Jeremy: c'mon max!

James: are you nuts?

Brendan: that's crazy

Me: agree. you r nuts. no worry. My dad will be with us.

Max didn't respond, but told us the next day he'd "think about it." I guess he heard us talking about it so much that by the end of the week he was in.

My dad had more than one reason for saying my friends should stay over the night before we were to go over to the mound. We were all bunked down for the night and he came in to talk to us.

"Patrick, could I talk to you boys for a minute?"

We all sat up and turned our whole attention to what he had to say. "Sure, Dad. What's up?"

"I want to ask you all to be especially respectful to Bill Nelson and his brother."

"Well, sure, Dad." I looked around at my friends. We could do some wild, crazy kind of things, but we had all been taught to be polite and courteous. Especially to grownups. "That's the way you taught us."

"I know, I know. What I'm saying is don't throw a lot of questions at them all at once."

"But how are we going to find out anything? How can we get—

"Patrick, I don't mean you can't ask questions, just keep it simple. Don't all of you start talking at the same time."

He was watching each of us. Then he turned to Max. "Max, I know you're sort of edgy about the mound, that you've got lots of misgivings about going over there. But I'm going to ask that you stay in control, don't act, uh . . . let's just say, don't lose it. Okay?"

Max turned all shades of red and stuttered, "Okay, Mr. Morrison."

"It's just that Earl Nelson is a very quiet man. He keeps to himself and doesn't get around people much. He agreed to let you boys come to the mound because his brother Bill asked him to. You've got Clyde Meeker to thank for that."

Jeremy held up his hand "Can I ask a question?"

"Of course, Jeremy. What is it?"

"Are the Nelsons mad at us? For coming over to the field and going up on the mound?"

"No, Jeremy."

"Should we apologize or something?" James asked.

"I think you'll find out that is completely unnecessary."

Then Max asked the question that was on all our minds. "Uh, is something *wrong* with this Earl Nelson?"

"No, Max."

My dad tugged at his ear and rubbed his cheek, concentrating on what to say. "Here's the thing. Earl is a veteran. When he came home from Desert Storm, it was hard for him to integrate back into the world. He decided to stay in the house nearest the mound, with the fields and woods sort of like a buffer from the outside world. His own private place."

"Dad, is that like that stress disorder thing people talk about?"

"That is what it is like. So I'm asking you, don't pressure him. Bill and Earl know you're coming loaded with questions. They're good with that. Just go easy is all I'm asking. You boys can be a bit overwhelming at times."

He was right about that and we knew it. But we wanted to find out about the mound and the graves so we'd be on our best behavior.

"We can do that," I said, looking around at my friends. "Can't we guys?"

Everyone was in agreement. My dad said goodnight and turned off the light. We lay in the darkness, the only light from the street light outside filtering through the blinds.

We'd all heard about guys like Earl Nelson. I wondered if that was the reason Uncle Jack stayed to himself. No one said anything for a while, then quietly we started talking about the next day.

CHAPTER THIRTY-NINE

The next morning, we were dressed by seven and in the kitchen eating pancakes. When the last one came off the griddle, my dad asked, "Did you boys want to come in the car with me or would you rather go through the field like you usually do?"

Of all the things we'd talked about the night before, none of us had thought about how we were going to the mound.

"Well," Brendan said, looking around at us, "I think I'd like to go across the field like we've always done. It'd feel sort of funny going over to the house and see the mound from that view for the first time."

We all liked his idea and were ready to leave the house when Dad closed the garage door and drove down the street.

Being early November, the temperature had dropped and frost covered the grass and brush. Our shoes were wet by the time we reached the treeline and trudged through the leaves covering the ground as we climbed to the top of the mound.

I could see through the trees now, all the way back to the fence at Mr. Nelson's pasture. There was a clearer view up to the top of the mound, too. We could smell wood burning and when we reached the clearing, a fire was going in the ring of stones.

My dad and Mr. Meeker sat on the logs surrounding the fire pit. An older man I didn't recognize sat next to them. He had a ring of white hair around his head and a pot belly. All he needed was a red suit and a bag of toys and he'd be a dead ringer for Santa Claus. His eyes even lit up when he saw us.

"*Granpa!*" Max gasped.

Although I'd heard a lot about him, I'd never met Max's grandfather. So Santa Claus was the one feeding Max all those stories about giant Indians and ghosts that haunted these parts. In some sort of weird way, it made sense.

He grinned and lifted a hand in greeting. "Hey, there, Maxie, boy."

"What are you doing here?" Max asked.

"Well, I hear you boys have a mystery you're trying to solve and these fellas thought I might have something to add."

I choked on a groan and hoped he didn't see my eyes roll. What could he possibly say to help? Was he going to tell one of the wild tales like those he'd told Max? What *was* he doing here?

My dad told us to take a seat. Someone had pulled up a big long log and we sat down side by side on it like birds on a telephone wire waiting to see what would happen next.

Bill Nelson had stood up when we came into the clearing, and now introduced each of us to his brother who stood next to him. As they shook hands with us, I noticed Earl

Nelson looked very much like his brother, the same height and weight, same brown hair and greenish eyes. He acted a little shy and brushed his hands on his jeans after he shook hands with us.

He started to sit back down, changed his mind and asked, "Would you boys like some hot chocolate? Didn't figure you drank coffee so we brought things to make hot chocolate."

I looked at my dad to see if it was all right for us to accept. My friends were looking at me for direction, and I nodded it was okay when my dad gave me the go-ahead.

Earl passed around some metal cups and plastic stirrers and a big can of cocoa mix with a long long-handled plastic scoop inside. Bill Nelson came around with a camp kettle that had been heating over the open fire and poured hot water into our cups. As I stirred the mix and water together I thought, *Why, we're having our own campfire tea party. Isn't that special?*

"So, I understand you boys were surprised to learn that all the land around here belongs to the Nelson family," Bill Nelson began when he sat down, getting right down to business.

"Yes, sir. We thought you owned the farm with the pasture and all," I answered. "We had no idea about the rest of it."

"Well, Patrick, I manage the part around my house, Earl here takes care of all the rest. His house is back over there." He jerked a thumb over his shoulder toward the surrounding trees.

Then there was a silence big enough to drive a truck through. Max was squirming and began stealing glances around at the rest of us. I motioned for him to stay still and be quiet.

"Now if you're wondering about the mound," Bill Nelson said, as if he had read our minds, "yes, it is part of the property."

I wondered if my dad had told Mr. Meeker some of the things we were curious about and he'd passed the information on to the Nelsons.

To my surprise Earl Nelson started talking, his voice real quiet, but steady.

"Our family homesteaded this land long before the land runs in the West. They brought some cattle and farmed a bit. Our great-great-grandfather built the house I live in. Some say the mound is a burial place made by the Indians, but, from what they told our family, we knew it wasn't."

If I'd been sitting on a chair, I would have been sitting on the edge of it. I couldn't wait to hear what Earl Nelson said next, what he would tell us about this mound

"You probably already know that the Indian believed the land belonged to the earth. Not to humans."

I did know that, from American History class and then Uncle Jack had explained that too.

"See," Earl continued, "they were nomadic and the hunting parties came here and set up camp when they were looking for food, gathering up their stores for winter. From up here, the warriors could see any enemies coming their way. It was a perfect view for tracking animals as they crossed the open range. Their women and children stayed at the base, where the house is now. That's why my family knew it was a good place to build their house."

I knew it! It was just like Uncle Jack told us about the mound at Grandmother's.

"It is not a burial ground, but it is a sacred place in the Indian culture. Our family has tried to preserve that, to make sure it wasn't disturbed or desecrated. My great-great grand-father became friends with a member of the tribe who came to this mound, and he promised him he would do everything he could to preserve this place.

"Over the years, people have tried to come and excavate and dig around for relics and, as was promised, we've tried to make sure they didn't. With it being private land, and the house so near, the treasure seekers didn't have access to it and it's stayed pretty much intact."

I knew from what Uncle Jack told us that the same thing had happened to the mounds in Arkansas. People looking for relics, digging around, had almost completely destroyed one of the mounds, and whittled down the other, larger one a great deal. Even though they were on private land too, no one had bothered to keep them away from the mounds. They had been stripped of almost all historical relics until the preser-vation people stepped in.

"That's almost exactly what my Uncle Jack told me about some mounds just like this in Arkansas," I said, interrupting. I stole a look at my dad, hoping I hadn't totally stepped out of line.

"I told them, Patrick," my dad said, letting me know it was okay.

"We weren't meaning to trespass or be disrespectful or anything. We didn't know this was an Indian mound or that there might be treasure or something like that. We knew it wasn't just an ordinary hill, but we couldn't figure out what it was. Then James and I saw the ones in Arkansas and Uncle Jack explained what they were. There were even graves at the base of one of those, just like there are here."

"That was fairly commonplace. You see, this place was pretty isolated back when it was first homesteaded. When someone died they didn't take them into town to bury them in the graveyard there. They made their own."

"That's what Uncle Jack said too."

"And I knew you boys weren't after anything over here," Earl said. "Except getting those rockets up."

"You know about the rockets?" I didn't know if I should be worried. My friends' faces showed they had the same concern.

"I had the best view in the country," he said, a smile creeping around his eyes. "You had me a little worried there for a bit when that one got away. Until . . . Max isn't it?" Earl said to our red-headed friend. "Quick response there, Max. That could have gotten out of control if you hadn't been on your toes."

Now our mouths were hanging open. He'd been watching us the whole time!

"The one with the camera really shot up there."

"Yes, sir. We thought we'd lost it there for a while. That's how we discovered the graves, when we were looking for the camera."

Earl chuckled softly. He picked up a stick and poked at the fire. "Yep. That was a close one."

"Sir?"

"Well, you see, I think that rocket got a lot more height on it than you knew. I saw it coming down and knew if you got to looking for it, you'd see the house and get to wondering about it. I wasn't ready for that," he said, rubbing the back of his neck and sort of squinting up at us. "So I ran down and got it and tried to get it over by the tombstones. Max got there before I made it, so I ducked behind a tree until he wasn't looking and threw it as hard as I could. When he saw it and picked it up I started to leave. I thought he might have seen me so I dropped behind a marker."

Jeremy looked at me and said, "That blurry shot, what we saw in the pictures, there *was* someone in that picture!"

"And I was sure that camera wasn't there when I first looked," Max broke in, his voice rising. "I *told* you guys there was someone watching me!" He turned and pointed at Earl and said, "*You*."

"Guilty." Earl, his head bent, nodded. "On both accounts."

Max turned on me, his face turning redder by the second. "You guys tried to tell me it was all in my head, that I was just seeing things. You didn't believe me."

"We weren't sure *what* to believe, Max," James said, trying to calm our hot-headed friend. "There just didn't seem to be any logical explanation."

I couldn't blame Max for being upset. We were always accusing him of being over-the-top and getting carried away over the least little thing. Mostly, we just ignored him when he got like that. This time we'd been wrong. This time.

"We needed more time to think about it," I said. "Maybe explore some more, research things."

James picked up a clump of dirt and chucked it at the fire pit. He looked at me. I knew that look; he was trying to decide something. He cleared his throat and looked across the dying flames. "Mr. Nelson, can I ask you a question?"

The brothers looked at each other then looked back at James, unable to decide who he was talking to.

James nodded at Earl who nodded back.

"You say you've been watching us."

"From when you first started exploring around here." He gulped and his eyes widened. "I . . . uh, I mean . . ." His face glowed red and I was sure it wasn't just from the reflection of the camp fire. Earl had said more than he'd meant to.

Which made me wonder about something else, and I had a sneaking suspicion Earl Nelson might have the answer to something we'd been curious about. "You mean from when we first started going into the culvert?"

Earl nodded. "Yes, Patrick. The first time I saw you go in there, you didn't stay long. Then, later, I was by Bill's barn and saw you boys going into the culvert again. When you didn't come out for a while, I was worried you'd get hurt so I got in my truck and drove into the housing development. With all the noise you boys were making, it wasn't hard to figure out where you were, you know."

That had to be the time we'd taken noise makers, horns, even some of my mom's baking tins, anything that made noise into the culvert thinking we could scare whatever might be in there away.

"The racket you made echoed through those pipes for a ways, but I was able to figure out just about where you were. I picked up some big rocks and rolled them into one of the storm drains, hoping the sound might scare you off." He actually showed teeth when he smiled at me then. "It worked. You all came running out of there like you were running for your life."

"We thought we were." I didn't know whether to be mad or relieved.

"I am sorry for that. I just didn't want you to come to any harm."

James jammed his elbow into my ribs. I looked around at my friends. "Well, at least now we have an answer to the missing piece of the Culvert Crap puzzle."

We could finally lay that mystery to rest. Everyone was smiling from ear to ear.

James wasn't finished with his questions yet. "So, when we were shooting the new video out in the field, did you run out of the woods, like when we were finishing the last shot?"

"Yes."

James looked at me and smiled. "Well, that's a relief. We weren't seeing things then either."

"I was surprised when I saw you with guns." Earl pointed at me. "You had a bow and arrow before. The guns looked so real, I was afraid someone was going to get hurt. Without thinking, I started running to try and stop it."

If he knew I carried my bow and arrow in our first video, Earl Nelson had been watching us even then. "You saw us shoot our first video?"

For a second, Earl looked like he was going to panic. Bill put his hand on Earl's knee and said to me, "I told my brother about you shooting a video, so if he saw you out in the field, he wouldn't be concerned." He squeezed his brother's knee. "It's okay, buddy."

Earl looked into Bill's eyes and took a deep breath before he went on. "Well, this time, I started running down the hill and had just come out of the trees trying to get your attention."

"Were you by any chance waving something over your head?"

"Yeah," he admitted, lowering his eyes to the ground then sneaking a look at his brother. "A bat."

Huh. Seemed like a baseball bat was the weapon of choice for the Nelson brothers. Bill Nelson had chased us from his field with one when we tried to tip one of his cows.

"What kind of bat?" I was hoping his answer would clear up another question we had.

"What kind?"

"Yeah."

"Well, uh, it was aluminum. Why?"

"Oh, just curious."

Aha! But it did explain the reflection we thought we saw. I was going to explain, but right then Brendan shot a look at me and James. "You guys only *told* us you'd given up the idea of seeing someone at the end of the video," he said. "But you didn't, did you?"

"Honest, we wanted to, but it seemed so clear." Now I really felt bad about not telling the guys. "We were going to have everyone look at the film again and decide what to do together."

Brendan shrugged and nodded. He held his fist out for a bump. We were cool.

Earl Nelson had turned white as a sheet. "You mean you filmed *me*?"

"By accident, Mr. Nelson. Honest," James said. Earl looked like he might barf. This dude was like spooky kind of shy. "It was right at the end before I hit Off. I thought I saw a person, but it was there for just a second and then it was gone."

"Oh." Earl calmed down. "Well, when I saw the boys stand up . . . obviously they weren't hurt . . . I did what I'd seen them do. I dropped into the tall grass and lay there hoping you hadn't seen me and praying you wouldn't come looking for me."

"You didn't have to worry, that wasn't going to happen. We were already so spooked by graveyards and tombstones, and Max getting so creeped out by it all, and no explanation for any of it. Patrick and I decided the best thing was to get away from the whole thing and investigate it later."

"But later came sooner than we thought it would," I said. "When we came to the field to shoot the last scene of the video, we'd already decided we weren't going anywhere near the mound."

"Yeah, but then you got other ideas," Brendan said.

We could laugh about it then: Me, ready to lead the charge up the mound and face ghosts, or whatever, when we'd heard those screams. Finding Mr. Meeker and my dad dressed as Indians, and the day camp kids in a place we would never expect them to be. It was all pretty funny now, sitting around the fire.

But not for Max. He couldn't hold it in for one more second. "But what about those graves?" he blurted. "Who do they belong to? What about the crazy renegade Indian Fury!"

Bill and Earl Nelson looked at one another and chuckled. Bill said, "We heard that story was still around."

Max wasn't finding anything to laugh about. His arms were crossed over his chest, his lips a tight line, his eyebrows scrunched together.

Bill could see Max was serious and said, "Sorry. I guess it's not all that funny to you." He cleared his throat. "Well, you see that story got started a long time ago. The way it happened was the Indians who used this mound found a family traveling through here. They were real sick and the Indians brought them here to their camp. But everyone in the family died except one young girl. The tribe buried the family and moved on to their winter camp, taking the girl with them. A few years later the girl's family came looking for her but by that time she was the wife of one of the young braves and with a couple of kids, and she didn't want anything to do with the any of the original family."

"Those folks tried to take her and the kids, but the tribe took off with them," Earl continued the story. "To keep them from being followed, the young husband led the search party and authorities on a wild goose chase. But he was caught and thrown in the stockade, in hopes he would tell them where the tribe went with the young woman. But one night, he escaped and went to the camp where he knew his tribe and family would be. No one ever found any of them.

"There was some rustling going at that time, and people started blaming it on the Indian brave, saying it was revenge for losing his family. Well, he'd never lost anyone; he knew right where they were all along. But, anything bad happened after that got blamed first on the Indian and, as time passed, on his ghost."

"Our family kept the story going," Bill said looking at Max, "to keep people from coming around after our family homesteaded the land. But the tale kept growing and after a while the young brave was a giant. A lot of the old-timers picked up the tale as a good way of keeping outsiders from jumping their claims to the land. To scare them off. A few kept the yarn going."

Max bent his head, nodding, deep in thought. The only sound was pops coming from the burning wood and wind stirring through the leaves. I was sure he had more questions.

After a while, he looked up and eyed Mr. Nelson. "So you're telling me that my granpa told me some old story that never was true in the first place? He's just one of the old-timers who kept the yarn going?"

"Now, Max, it had some elements of the truth to it," Earl said. "I'm sure he didn't mean any harm."

For the first time, Mr. Brunner spoke. "He's right, Max. I didn't—"

"Maybe not, Granpa," Max said, turning to his grandfather, cutting him off. "But I believed that stuff you told me. And it scared the snot out of me."

The guys and I laughed. We knew firsthand how serious Max had taken his grandfather's stories.

"Max, son, I had no idea you still believed all those stories I told you." Mr. Brunner put out his hand to touch Max's arm. "About Indians and ghosts and things."

Max jerked his arm away. "I believed you, Granpa!" Max was near tears. "I never thought you'd lie to me."

"Oh, Max, my boy. Those stories were never meant to be a lie. Just old tales to entertain a little boy. I thought you'd outgrown them by now."

Was he kidding? Poor Max had been driving the rest of us crazy with those old tales for as long as I could remember. He'd never once doubted his grandfather.

I could feel his embarrassment. Knowing Max as I did, I couldn't be sure if it was from disappointment in his grandfather or that he was ready to blow his top. It could have been a little of both.

He rubbed his nose on his sleeve and said, "I have just one more question."

We braced ourselves for what our red-headed friend might say next.

"The grave yard. Those tombstones. The one with the name Feurey on it."

Jeremy grinned and elbowed Max in the ribs. "Uh, dude, that's more than just one more question. I definitely counted three."

By the look on his face, I knew Max was not in the mood for any joking from anyone. Finding out the story his grandpa had told him had all been just that . . . a story . . . this time he wanted the straight truth. "Maybe so, but I still want to know."

Earl looked at his brother. Bill nodded.

"Well, you remember the family came looking for the young girl who survived?" Bill looked around while we hung on every word. "She told them where the Indians had buried the rest of her family before she disappeared with the tribe. Our family later claimed the land and put up those markers that are on the graves. Everybody in the territory knew the story, how the Indians had found the lot of them and buried them. So when cattle started disappearing, any bad thing came along, they put the blame on the young husband. They'd just say, "It was the Feurey Indian.""

Max breathed out a big 'Whoa.' My mouth hung open just like his. It was beginning to make sense now. Crazy how things can get all turned around.

"Feurey was the name of the family, Max. It's not clear on the markers now, but it was there."

"Maybe it's not clear on most of them." Max kept pressing for more. "But there is that one that's bigger, and the name is for sure clear on it. What about that?"

Bill Nelson rubbed the back of his neck and turned to look at his brother.

Earl stood up and brushed the seat of his pants. He picked up a couple of small tree limbs and tossed them on the fire, sending sparks flying. Taking his cup, he walked around the log seats, holding his cup in one hand, the other tucked in a pocket.

I glanced at my dad, wondering if Earl was upset. What was happening? Was he leaving? Dad made a slight movement with his head, signaling me to stay calm. I turned my attention back to Bill Nelson, who had started talking again.

"Well, Max, that part of the mystery is a secret our family has protected all these years. You see, no one ever came around those graves so nobody ever asked any questions. Until now."

I could hear Max's heavy breathing. He jumped up and did that pacing thing we all knew meant he was about ready to go off like a rocket. *Ha, ha. Wasn't that what got us into this situation in the first place?*

"Oh, good grief!" Max said as he paced, a grumble in his voice growing louder with each word. "Now there's a *secret*? Here you've all just about convinced me there's nothing spooky about this Feurey legend and now you throw in a family *secret* out of the blue?"

Max was really wound up, his voice high and screechy sounding. We all knew the signs. He ran his fingers through his hair then clenched his hands into fists at his side as he paced. It was going to take some serious kind of explanation to get him calmed down.

"Max, let me finish, all right?" Bill Nelson calmly continued. "The thing to remember is back then our family had known these people, had been friends with the tribe." He looked at Max who just huffed loudly, but slowed his pacing.

"The Indian showed up many years later. He was very old and his wife had died. The markers were faded by then. Even so, he wished to bury her with the rest of her family, in the graveyard. Only our family knew he placed her there."

Max's lips were still tight, his hands clenching and unclenching by his side. "But that still doesn't explain what happened to *him*."

Earl Nelson stopped in front of Max, neither of them pacing any longer. Max had grown in the past few months, but he still only came to the man's chin. Earl took his hand from his pocket and placed it on Max's shoulder. "Want some more hot chocolate, Max?"

He was stalling for time! Why?

"No, sir, I'm good." Max ducked his head and shuffled his feet, not knowing what to do now. Irritated and frustrated, Max was still trying to be respectful.

"Let's sit down, Max." Earl didn't have to say it again. Max hurried back onto the log, a slightly embarrassed smile as he looked at me and the guys.

Earl took a seat. "The Indian never left his wife's side. He stayed on the mound. A few days after she was buried, the family found him dead next to her grave. They buried him with her, along with the mystery of whatever happened to the renegade Indian called Fury."

I nearly fell off the log at what happened next.

Clyde Meeker stood and looked at me and my friends. "As for the grave marker? Several years ago, my grandfather had it placed on the grave to honor our ancestors."

His ancestors! What was he talking about?

"The Feurey Indian was my great-great-great grandfather. The Nelson family has honored his memory all these years by not revealing who he was. He wouldn't have wanted people nosing around, digging up the old history. Both families were content to let the legends be told, and keep the truth to themselves."

Words hung in my mouth. I couldn't say anything. Who would ever have thought there was this kind of mystery around here? This story was a whole lot better than the one Max's grandfather had told him.

"Did you know, Granpa?" Max's voice was barely a whisper.

"Yes, Max, I did. But the story wasn't mine to tell. The old legend of the renegade Indian, the story I told you, had been around forever and didn't give away the true one."

I looked at my dad. "Did you know?"

"Not until Clyde told me just before we brought the children here for the bonfire. He knew you boys were just going to get more curious and would keep digging. It was best you all weren't over here poking around."

He glanced at Earl and remembered what my dad had told us about him. We could have made the man's life miserable if we'd nosed around the mound without his brother or someone.

"I wanted to tell you the real story." Mr. Meeker sat back down. He looked at Bill and Earl then at me and my friends. "But now that you know, I have one thing to ask. Will you be willing to keep this to yourselves?"

The whole thing was so fantastical. I looked around at my friends. "We're okay with that, aren't we guys?"

"Sure," "Absolutely," "Right," they answered. All Max could manage was a confused nod. That was all right. It was hard for me to get everything we'd just learned straight in my head, and I'd bet it was the same for the other guys.

The men stood and started cleaning up and putting out the fire.

"I've just got one request," I said.

"Patrick!" My dad did not look at all pleased with me.

"Just hear me out, okay?" I needed him to trust me with this one more thing.

"Those graves down there . . . they're, well, it seems like they could use some help. Like some cleaning up around them."

"He's right you know," Bill Nelson said looking at Earl and Mr. Meeker. They all looked embarrassed. "We haven't taken care of them like we should."

"Would it be all right, then, if me and the guys came over and cleaned them up?" I didn't have to check with my friends on this, I knew they'd back me up.

All the grown-ups looked stunned. The Nelsons and Mr. Meeker started thanking us, saying how thoughtful that would be. Max's grandfather smiled from ear to ear. The best part was the look of pride on my dad's face.

"I really do have to go," Brendan said and stood up and started for the trail.

"Let me give you a lift," my dad offered. "If it's all right with you fellows," he said to the other men, "I'll take the boys on back and get Brendan to practice."

They agreed and we headed down a path we'd never been on before. Brendan was already late so we had to hurry. There was no chance to get a good look at the house or anything. Maybe we could check things out when we came back to take care of the graves.

My dad stopped at Brendan's house and waited for him to grab his gear and a couple sandwiches. We all rode along to the football field.

"See you after practice," he called when he got out of the SUV and sprinted toward the field.

CHAPTER FORTY

My dad pulled into a burger place on the way home and we took our order to my house. When we got there, we piled bags of fries in the middle of the kitchen table and dug in. The next hour we went over and over what we'd heard around the camp fire. When Brendan came in after practice, we went over it all again.

All that mystery, and history, went on right in our own back yard . . . well, nearly. And to be charged with keeping the secret . . . that was huge.

But then, who would we tell? We were the ruling body of the Nerd Herd and there wasn't exactly a line beating a path to join our ranks.

"Uh, Max . . ." I wanted to say something but didn't exactly know what or how. "I don't know, um . . . about your grandpa . . ."

"You know, those stories he told me were pretty wild, huh?" Max wore a big grin, something I hadn't expected. I thought he'd still be upset with his grandpa. "Wow! He could sure make them sound real. I believed them when I was little and just never gave up on them. He didn't keep telling them, I just kept believing them. With all the weird stuff going on in the culvert and everything, I let it all just fuel my imagination."

"But you told him about our going to the mound, and said he told you it could be an Indian burial mound."

"But that's all he said. He never mentioned anything about that Fury legend. I sort of added that on my own." The tops of his ears turned red, and his mouth formed an embarrassed lopsided grin.

We'd given him such a bad time for so long, it was our turn to wait on what he had to say.

"But, you know what?" He slapped the table in front of him. "I like this new story a lot better And I like that Granpa is part of it, sort of."

Well, what did you know? Our little Max was growing up.

When we were just about talked out, we didn't want the day to end. We checked out movies and decided on one.

"Hey, Taylor," I said, knocking on her door.

"Yeah?"

I opened the door a little and she motioned me in. "If it's all right with everyone's parents, would you take us to the mall? For a 4:10 show?"

"Patrick, the only thing that starts at that time—you've seen it three times already."

Did she think she was talking me out of it, or just encouraging me? When I didn't answer her, she gave up her argument.

"Honestly," she said, flipping the magazine she was reading aside and sliding off her bed. "Your brain is a total mystery to me."

"So will you take us?"

Taylor's head jerked forward, fists planted on her hips. "What'd you think I got up for, Dip-wad?"

"Oh, well, I just wanted to know. The guys still have to check with their parents to see if it's okay."

A low growl came from her throat, her eyes slits as she stared at me. She pressed a palm against my chest until I stood outside her bedroom. "When you are absolutely sure you want a ride," she said, "let me know." The sound of the door shutting was a tad louder than normal.

A big bucket of buttered popcorn passed up and down the row as we watched one of our favorite superheroes defeat the villain and conquer the aliens. When the credits rolled and the lights came up, I didn't want it to end. I loved that character. Couldn't I just sit here and watch the whole thing again? And again?

What were we going to do now? Chasing adventures was what we did. Where could we explore next? Where would we find another mystery?

The guys turned to look at me when I didn't get up and follow them from the theater.

"Hey, dude," James said, coming to sit next to me. "What's up?"

"What are we going to do now, James? I don't mean like right this minute, I mean what are we going to _do_?"

What we did was go back to school on Monday. James and I had extra rehearsals all week for choir concerts coming up, and football on Friday night. My mom insisted I clean my room on Saturday–always a favorite of mine, right up there with the garage. My dad had an afternoon planned for us to bond over the garage. I needed something to explore, some adventure.

Where were the guys and a couple of rockets when you needed them? Not in our garage, for sure.

When Mr. Meeker walked into class Sunday morning, I couldn't keep a straight face. All I could think about was him in that wild wig and buckskins. From the sniggers I heard from my friends, I was fairly sure they were thinking the same thing.

His face actually turned red when he saw us, then he brought up the topic for discussion that week.

That feeling of having nothing special to do hung on all afternoon and through the Sunday night movie with the family.

As I was drifting off to sleep, scenes from the movie I'd seen with my friends ran through my head. I came suddenly awake and sat up in bed.

Aliens!

Our movie wasn't finished. With the whole mound thing, I'd forgotten all about our video. By the time I closed my eyes and fell asleep, I had figured out the perfect ending for our movie. This time, we'd finish off the blood sucking flesh eating vampire zombie aliens once and for all.

CHAPTER FORTY-ONE

Scenes and dialog filled my mind as I dressed the next morning. I sent a group text to tell the guys to meet early outside school, we had something special to discuss.

There were a few minutes to fill James in on some details before we picked up Brendan. Taylor dropped us off in front of the building. We waited on the sidewalk and within a few minutes Max and Jeremy showed up.

"So, what's up?" Jeremy said as we walked with them to the bike rack.

"Well, see," I started, "I've been wondering what we could do next. It was bugging me we didn't have something to explore, you know, to check out. Then last night, it suddenly came to me that we haven't finished the video."

"But, I thought it *was* finished," Jeremy said, Max nodding in agreement.

"What if we could make it better?"

That got their interest. I told them, "I'll explain at lunch. You're gonna love it!"

Half of my sandwich and a bag of chips sat on the table untouched when the bell rang for us to return to class. But the guys were in. I knew they would be. The plan was perfect.

All I had to do was talk to my dad. And get my dad to talk to Mr. Meeker. And ask Mr. Meeker to talk to Earl and Bill Nelson. The whole plan hinged on them.

"I thought you boys were going to clean up that little grave yard," my dad said when I explained what I had in mind.

"We are, Dad, we are. But we need to do this first." He would understand later why it was important that we wait to clean the graves. "Will you help me?"

"All right," he said after thinking about it for a bit. "When?"

"As soon as possible."

I couldn't believe things happened as fast as they did. My dad called Mr. Meeker and after supper Dad and I picked up James and headed to Earl Nelson's. I thought it would be easier for me if I had James there to cover my back.

It felt like roly-polies were rolling around in my stomach as we drove up the long lane to Earl Nelson's house. A silver-gray pickup, which I figured belonged to his brother, was in the drive next to the house. I recognized Mr. Meeker's van and we parked next to it and got out. My palms were sweaty and I wiped them on my jeans as I followed my dad up the steps.

Earl opened the door before my dad had a chance to knock. "Come in, come in," he welcomed us, and showed us into a large room that looked like a hunting lodge. In a way, it looked like Uncle Jack's place, I noticed.

My mouth was so dry I was afraid I'd never get a word out. Bill Nelson came from another part of the house carrying a bucket with ice and bottled water. I gladly accepted one as soon as he offered.

"So, I understand you have a favor to ask," Earl said when I'd chugged half the bottle of water. Guess he figured I needed something to get me going.

The plan poured out of me then. When I finished Earl looked at his brother then asked me, "But what do we have to do with this?"

"Well, you see, first of all I wanted your permission to shoot the video on the mound. Make sure it was all right with you."

He nodded.

"The guys and I want to get started cleaning up the graves and stuff before Thanksgiving, but we need everything to be just like it is for now."

"Okay," he said, waiting to hear what else I had to say.

I could tell by the look on his face that he wasn't getting the whole picture yet.

"Mr. Nelson," I said, scooting forward on my seat. "You watched the first video we made over in the fields. And you saw us when we filmed the next one."

"I did find it interesting." He looked embarrassed, but he was smiling. A little. "I enjoyed watching you boys."

"Well, this time, we'd like for you to have a front row seat. We'd like to film around the grave yard, by the tombstones, with all the weeds and grass and brush and stuff just like it is."

I heard my dad take a sharp breath. I'd explained that we wanted Earl Nelson's permission to film on the mound before we cleaned up the grave yard. I had not told him about actually using it as part of the filming.

James pressed his knee against my leg. I looked at him, relieved to see him wink to let me know I was doing okay.

The only sound in the room was the snoring of the hunting dog lying next to Earl, and the ticking of a big clock on the fireplace mantle. It seemed like forever before Earl Nelson spoke.

"And you won't be filming me—even by accident?"

A big breath of relief gushed out. I'd been holding my breath without realizing it. "Oh, no, sir! That's a promise."

"Then let me ask you a question. What is Clyde's part in all of this?"

He was right. I did plan for Mr. Meeker to play a big part in the final ending of the aliens. He just didn't know it yet. When I told them what I had in mind, I held my breath again waiting to see what his reaction would be.

The Nelson brothers laughed . . . out loud. My dad looked at me like I'd grown another head. James pressed his knee against my leg so hard he nearly pushed me off my seat while we waited for Mr. Meeker's answer. I jumped to my feet when he gave us his okay.

Now we had a project! I couldn't wait to begin work on it.

Every day after school the following week we worked on our costumes as soon as we got home. On Friday night we were so keyed up I didn't think any of us would sleep a wink but we all slept like logs. The smell of my dad's Saturday morning pancakes cooking woke me. I turned over to see Max staring directly into my face.

"Can we get up now?" he asked, the back of his hair sticking straight into the air like the tail of a bird. "I'm starving."

Sleeping bags were rolled up and stowed in the garage in nothing flat and we gathered around the table. We finished off the pancakes and nearly a gallon of milk before we headed to the garage to get ready to go to the mound.

This time, we took my dad up on his offer to drive us. No sense in taking any chances and have any of our gear messed up before we started filming. Mr. Meeker was waiting for us when we got there. Max's grandpa came along at our invitation. Seemed like the right thing to do.

We followed Earl and Bill Nelson to the mound and out by the graves.

According to the script we'd come up with, everyone took their places. The Nelsons were well out of the way of any sight lines. Max and I, the designated heroes, walked several feet away from the edge of the markers. Brendan and Jeremy, the vampire aliens, took positions only a few steps from the Feurey tombstone.

We all readied our weapons. I had the fake gun holstered on my hip, but I'd decided that "Rick, the Hero" started out with bow and arrow in the first film so he should end these monsters the same way. James and I wanted to shoot arrows into the aliens like we'd done with the darts that day in my garage. But we couldn't figure out how to do it with the arrows and had to drop it. Maybe we'd find a way to work that into another video sometime

The bad guys aimed their side arms at me and Max. Max aimed his pistol. I held my bow and arrow cocked like I was ready to shoot.

James called, "Action."

Brendan and Jeremy fired at me and Max. We ducked, then stood and began to walk toward them. I raised my bow and started to pull the string back. The aliens stumbled backward, on either side of the big headstone.

With a puff of smoke, Mr. Meeker playing the part of The Ghost of Fury: the Renegade Indian, rose up behind the marker, surrounded by a white cloud. Jeremy had made smoke bombs that Mr. Meeker set off before he stood up from behind the tombstone. He spread his arms and hooked each alien around the neck, then sank back behind the marker, pulling them with him.

"Cut!"

Jeremy and Brendan lay on the ground next to the tombstone, only part of their legs and feet showing.

"Action!"

Another puff of smoke and the aliens were pulled into the cloud then disappeared.

"Cut!"

"Does that mean we can move?" I heard Mr. Meeker whisper loudly from his hiding spot.

Jeremy and Brendan stood up with Mr. Meeker towering above them. "Now we look to make sure we got everything," Jeremy told him.

The whole scene couldn't have turned out better. After I'd explained the idea I'd come up with, Jeremy worked all week coming up with smoke bombs to create the effect we wanted. They worked perfectly.

After we'd seen that it was a good take, the Nelsons came out of the trees to take a look, together with my dad and Max's grandpa. They declared our video a success.

CHAPTER FORTY-TWO

Thanksgiving was just a few days away and we worked like crazy to cut and edit the video. We were giving a sneak preview for the Day Camp kids. The church hosted a big Thanksgiving dinner for them and their families in the activities hall.

Our families set up tables, decorated the hall, and served the guests of honor. Even a few extra people showed up. Earl Nelson sat at a table with my mom and dad and his brother, Bill. He didn't take his eyes off the screen when the film ran, and clapped along with everyone when it was over. He gave me a nod when I caught his eye after the credits rolled. I felt like I'd just won an Oscar.

Earlier in the week, I'd just happened to mention to Alyssa Dwyer that we were going to premier our video. Okay—I didn't exactly use the word "premier", it was more like, "Hey, you want to come see a video me and the guys shot?"

And she said, "Sure."

Dumb old Renee Woods came too. I mean, what could I say when Alyssa asked if she could. This time I could see what the guys were talking about her hanging all over Brendan. Bleck!

He didn't seem to mind at all. Double bleck!

The next week, Alyssa and I just happened to be going the same direction on our way to class.

"I heard you got your license," she said as she walked beside me.

I couldn't keep the grin off my face. After all the studying and waiting, I'd passed my test the week after Thanksgiving. "Yeah. It's cool."

She didn't say anything. "Uh, I don't have a car, though."

"Oh?"

"Yet. I've been saving for one."

"Uh-huh."

"My sister lets me drive her car. And my parents."

"Your movie was really great."

Air came back into my lungs and I could swallow again, relieved she'd changed the subject. She'd already told me that the night of the showing, but I liked hearing it again.

"I really enjoyed it. Do you want to make films, like for a career someday? You seem to have a real talent for making movies."

"Honestly? I haven't thought that far ahead before." The truth was the idea had been running through my mind as something I might like to do. I just didn't want to say it, so I just shrugged. "Who knows? Maybe. Someday."

The only plans I had were for the near future. First, the guys and I had set a date to go to the mound and clean up the graves like we'd planned. I would be driving us over.

After that all the family would be gathering for Christmas at Grandmother and Papa's in Oklahoma again after all. I thought I'd take the video along. I figured they'd get a big kick out of it. I hoped maybe Uncle Jack could be talked into coming too. I was sure he would find what we had turned up about our mound interesting, and how the mystery had been solved.

And I would know that at last the Renegade Indian called Fury had been laid to rest—along with the blood-sucking, flesh-eating vampire zombie aliens. I honestly didn't think I was going to miss either, and I was sure they wouldn't be resurrected.

That didn't mean I didn't have some other ideas bouncing around in my head. Maybe I'd discuss them with Alyssa Dwyer, see what she thought—after I ran them by the guys, of course.

You just never know.

-THE END-

ACKNOWLEDGEMENTS

Who knew when I was trying to keep our sons, Jim and Davis, from burning something up, tearing it down, or breaking their necks, that one day some of their wild adventures would end up in a book. Thank you, boys, for your boundless curiosity and fearlessness. Even when you were scaring me silly or running me ragged, you've been a source of pride and delight and inspiration.

Davis, I deeply appreciate your talent and skills.

Thank you Noelle Massey and my husband, Jim, for editing my work and for your continuing help and support and advice.

Caprice, you have no idea how it encouraged me to write the next page each time you called and asked, "How's it going, Mom?"

Janet Brown thank you for your confidence in me. Additional thanks to David Hargrove.

A special thanks to Drake Massey who started this journey.

ABOUT THE AUTHOR

BONNIE LANTHRIPE, playwright, award-winning actress, and novelist, has degrees in Theater and Creative Writing. She has written several one-act stage plays and "Estate Sale," a full-length published work. An independent editor, her short stories have appeared in inspirational, historical and devotional anthologies.

Originally from Arkansas, Bonnie and husband, Jim, made their home in California for several years before moving to Edmond, Oklahoma. With four children (grown) and six grandchildren, Bonnie says there is always a story just around the corner.

VISIT BONNIE AT:

www.Bonnie.Lanthripe.com

Follow her on Facebook: Bonnie Lanthripe, Author

BONUS!

DON'T MISS "THE RINGLEADER"! THE BOOK THAT STARTED THE ADVENTURES.

Fourteen-year-old Patrick Morrison makes a bizarre, unexplainable discovery while exploring a drainage culvert with his friends. Obsessed with identifying what it is and how it got there, his search turns up some surprising clues. Certain he has found an answer to the mystery, Patrick ventures into the culvert one more time for proof. Another obstacle arises when he is almost swept away when water rushes out of nowhere. Deciding further investigation is too risky, Patrick persuades the boys to take a break from the hunt and finish the video they had been working on.

While filming the final scenes of the video, a series of unusual twists uncovers all the pieces of the puzzle Patrick searched for, bringing a surprising resolution to the riddle.

PRAISE FOR THE RINGLEADER

"Bonnie Lanthripe's book engages me from the first words, gaining my attention with a tale with gusto, intrigue and suspense intermingled with animated dialogue. I smiled at the antics of the bright, curious, and delightful young characters. Her writing skills keep the story moving from one event to the next, creating a delightful, fun-loving book that is sure to capture the interest of many. I love to read anything Bonnie Lanthripe writes and hope to read many more of her books."

~KATHRYN SPURGEON, author of *Love from the Inside Out*

"The Ringleader promises to be a page-turning mystery novel for middle-school readers as they follow the fun adventures of the young heroes of this story."

~LOUISE TUCKER JONES, Gold Medallion Award-Winning Author/Inspirational Speaker/Columnist

CHAPTER ONE

The buzzer on my alarm clock screamed in my ear. Patrick Morrison, I thought, you have got to be nuts to get up at eight in the morning when you have a Friday off from school. Most four-teen-year-old guys would sleep in. But my friends and I were all about adventure, and we agreed the three-day weekend was exactly what we'd been waiting for: an extra day to explore the big drainage culvert at the dead end two streets over.

I groaned, reached out and hit the 'Off' button. I rolled out of bed and thought about the day ahead, excited about what we might come across this time.

Over the past several months we'd checked out a lot of neighborhoods, a nearby conservation area, and the farm on the other side of the ravine across from my house. Some pretty interesting things had turned up: an old-time brick incinerator, mud pits that sucked the shoes right off your feet, and some pretty mean cows. Not to mention one mad farmer.

Interesting couldn't begin to describe the discovery I made that Friday, or the way it would change my life.

The plan was for everyone to meet early at my house. James and Brendan lived up the street and around the corner from me. They were at my front door before I got my shoes on, and hung out while I ate breakfast. By ten o'clock we were outside, but still waiting for Max and Jeremy. Hey, I mean, I got it. Growing boys need their sleep. I sure could have done with a few more zzzzs. I had hardly slept thinking about what we might come across inside that culvert.

I pulled out my cell phone, wondering what could be taking them so long. Max was on speed-dial. He answered just before it went to voice mail. He sounded groggy, like he was just waking up. I knew it! He wasn't even out of bed yet. "Hey, dude, where are you guys?" I said.

"Morrison?"

"Yeah, it's me. I'm on my porch with James and Brendan. We're waiting for you."

He mumbled something about putting his shoes on and ready to go out the door. Yeah, right. Same phony-baloney I would have given.

"Okay. Just meet us at the culvert. Later." I disconnected and dialed Jeremy's house. The only one of the five of us who didn't have his own cell, Jeremy's mother was also the only one of our moms who didn't work.

His mom answered. "Hello?"

"Hi, Mrs. Wilson. This is Patrick Morrison. May I speak to Jeremy?"

"Why, good morning, Patrick, dear. How are you this morning?"

From past experience, I knew I wasn't going to get off the phone and get Jeremy on without telling Mrs. Wilson I was fine; my mother, father, brother and sister were fine; the dog, the cat, the goldfish and the canary—if we had a canary—were all fine. She really was a nice lady, but geesh, it was the same routine every time.

When she finally seemed satisfied that the entire Morrison household was in tip-top shape, I heard her call, "Jeremy, dear, one of your little friends is on the phone."

She never even bothered to put her hand over the phone. She'll probably still be calling us Jeremy's little friends when we graduate from high school, maybe college even.

In the background I heard the pounding sound of feet rushing down stairs.

"Okay, mom," good old Jeremy yelled as he went out the door. "Tell them I'll meet them at the cul . . . uh . . . at the cul-de-sac."

I said, "Thank you, Mrs. Wilson, I heard," and touched the 'Off' button. Not exactly polite, but Mrs. Wilson already knew my whole family was fine. If I went through all that again Jeremy would be at the culvert before I even got off the phone.

I put my phone in my pocket, looked at James and Brendan, and said, "So, I guess you figured out where the rest of the team is."

They nodded.

I picked up my back pack and slung it over my shoulder.

"Okay, guys," I said to them, "let's head out."

It didn't take long for us to get from my house to the dead end. While we waited for Max and Jeremy, we checked our gear—flashlights, extra batteries and bottled water. We could be in the culvert a long time, we had no idea right then. It all depended on what we found. But, we'd want plenty of light to see our way around and we might get thirsty. I'd also thrown in a few Oreos, just in case.

Max and Jeremy both lived in another housing develop-ment not far away, just one major street over. They made it in record time, huffing and puffing from their bike ride.

"You guys need a couple minutes to catch your breath?" I said, not really feeling a lot of sympathy for either of them right at the moment.

"Uh-huh," Max wheezed.

After a few minutes, I asked, "Are you ready?" We were burning daylight and I was ready to get the show on the road.

Max nodded.

"Ready," Jeremy said, moving forward.

I took the lead as we stepped around the concrete barrier that marked the end of the street, and stashed the bikes behind some tall brush. We made our way down to where the culvert emptied out, careful not to step off the narrow path.

At one time, the area was meant to be a small lake with a green belt for the housing developments on either side. But something happened to the original plans. The green belt was all wild brush and weeds, and the lake became a pond of mostly stagnant water that overflowed into the ravine during heavy rains. The pond was surrounded by really smelly, nasty black mud. When we were little, my sister, Taylor, got stuck in the icky goo once and my dad had to come pull her out. Her shoes and socks are still somewhere in that muck.

Once inside the big round mouth of the culvert, my friends and I stood tight together. I figure someday I'll make it to well over six feet tall, like my dad, but at the time I was about a foot shy of that. I made the opening to be around four and a half feet because I had to duck as I went in.

I looked over my shoulder at my friends. James, Max and I were about the same height so they had to scrunch down, too. Jeremy was so short the top of his crazy-wild, curly black hair barely grazed the upper side of the pipe. Brendan topped us all by several inches and he had to really hunch over to make his way through.

"Okay, guys, here we go," I said, my heart beating faster. I clicked on my flashlight and shined it into the darkness. Four light beams joined mine as I took a deep breath and walked into unknown territory.

After a few yards, I stopped. "Hey, isn't this supposed to be a drain? Like for run-off into the pond, or ravine?"

"Yeah, I think so," James said. "Why?"

"Well, you'd think there would be some water or mud," I said, shining my flashlight around on the floor. "But there's not even a puddle in here, not a drop of water anywhere. Even the leaves that blew in are dry."

"It looks like water came through here at one time, though," he said. He pointed the beam of his flashlight a few feet in front of us. "See. There's a pile of leaves and trash that look like they washed through here sometime."

"But it's dry as a bone now," I said.

Things weren't living up to what I'd imagined. I'd pictured us sloshing through water, at least maybe a puddle or two. Maybe come upon the skeleton of a baby crocodile or some exotic pet that had been dumped in the drain and died because it wasn't able to survive in the wild.

"Hey, guys," Max said, "have you noticed how our voices bounce off the walls?" He made a noise that sounded like he was trying to yodel. "Listen!"

The sound echoed through the culvert as he kept up the noise. It got super annoying real quick.

"C'mon, Max," Jeremy said after a while. "That's enough."

"Yeah, let's go on," I said and started walking forward again. Knowing Max, he wouldn't be able to walk and yodel at the same time.

After nudging bits of trash with our toes and poking sticks through piles of junk we came across, and coming up with nothing interesting, we decided to take a break. We sat against the curved walls and pulled water bottles from our backpacks. I passed around the Oreos.

"Wonder where we are?" James said as he shined his light overhead.

We had been walking for about thirty minutes, including breaks to look at stuff. We'd taken a couple turns and back-tracked once for a short distance, then headed off a different way, so it was kind of hard to tell what direction we were going. None of us had a compass. We'd never needed one before when we explored.

We knew the culvert ran under the street that divided one housing development from another, but we had no idea if it actually went beneath homes. I knew where we went in, my goal of this whole exploration was to learn where we might end up.

I stood up and hit my head. Hard. I pitched forward onto my hands and knees. A sharp pain spread through my skull and for a few seconds I saw stars.

"Hey, man, are you okay?" James crawled over and knelt beside me. He started checking out my head, shining his flashlight right in my face.

"Yeah, except I can't see with that thing in my eyes," I said, pushing the flashlight away. I sat up and rubbed the top of my head. I felt a goose egg but nothing sticky, so I figured at least I wasn't bleeding. "I'm fine," I said and shook it off. I stood up, being sure to stay hunched forward, and said, "Let's keep going."

A little further on, the guys started poking at a big pile of junk with their sticks. Max and Jeremy got all excited when they found some glass marbles and started digging deeper. I walked on a few feet and stopped dead in my tracks.

"Crap! Crap!"

My heart hit the roof of my mouth beating at cyber-speed. My breath caught in my throat, I couldn't breathe. I cannot be seeing what I think I'm seeing! No way, I thought. Maybe I got a concussion after all when I bonked my head. I inched forward a step for a closer look. That was all I needed. I was sure. My knees shook and I took a step backward, then another.

When Brendan heard me yelling, he turned his light toward me. When I looked around at them, it was right in my eyes, blinding me. Enough with the light in my eyes, already.

"What's up?" he called. "You hit your head again?"

The others stood up and shined their lights directly at me. This time, I put my hand up to shield my eyes and hurried toward them.

"We need to go, guys," I said.

Their mouths hung open as I pushed them aside and plowed a path straight through them.

Someone said, "What do you mean? We—"

"We have to go. Now!" I said and kept going. I didn't want to leave one of them behind, but I wasn't going to wait to see if they were following me. I just hoped they were. I went as fast as I could, trying not to panic and break into a run.

"Patrick! Slow down," they yelled. "Hey, man, wait up!"

When I heard them hurrying, hustling to catch up with me, I went faster. I made it out of the drain in a lot less time than we'd spent in there. I sucked in fresh air as I cleared the entry. Scrambling up the small incline, I kept on going, and didn't stop until I made it all the way home. I plopped down on the grass when I reached my front yard, and pulled off my backpack.

"What is up with you, dude?" James demanded as he sat down beside me. "What is your problem?"

One by one, and out of breath, the others plunked down on the ground with us.

I looked around at each of them. Slowly, quietly, I said, "Crap."

"Yeah, we heard what you said," Max said, looking around at the others. "Before you tore out of there like you'd been shot out of a cannon." He shook his head.

"Yeah, that was weird, man," Jeremy said. "What's the deal?"

"Right. Weird," Max agreed. "But what happened, Patrick? Crap . . . what?"

"Crap." I said again, very clearly. "A huge pile of it. I'm telling you guys, there was the biggest pile of crap I've ever seen. And I wasn't waiting around to see what dumped it there."

They stared at me, their mouths wide open.

All I could think was there was no way I would be satisfied until I found out where that mess came from.

AVAILABLE AT: